MEMORY HUNTER

AN INVESTIGATION DUO NOVEL

LIANE CARMEN

ISBN: (paperback) 978-0-9984247-8-1

ISBN: (ebook) 978-0-9984247-7-4

Cover design by 100 covers.

Author photo by Bill Ziady. (www.matchframeproductions.com)

For Woody Kamena.
Thanks for always volunteering to read
the early drafts.

CHAPTER ONE

So much blood. His gaze drifted around the room. Elongated drips on the walls told the story of a vicious attack. A river of red flowed past the boundaries of the bedroom comforter and into the cracks of the hardwood floor. It would live there in the crevices—where the old planks of wood weren't perfectly flush—until the floor was torn up. A tell-tale hint of unimagined horror.

He swiped at the sweat on his forehead, then glanced down at his fingers. Her blood. He cursed that he'd forgotten to wear gloves. How could he be so stupid? He backed away carefully from his handiwork. When he made his way into the kitchen, his nose wrinkled as the smell of bleach prickled the tiny hairs in his nostrils.

He lathered his hands under the faucet with a generous amount of soap and rubbed at the blood caked into his cuticles. He held them up. Scrutinized them from all angles. Satisfied, he rinsed away the remnants of what he'd done and watched the evidence disappear down the drain.

He pulled out a can of Ajax from the cabinet and sprinkled it generously around the stainless steel. As the water hit the cleanser, the mixture bubbled on the surface before it then swirled down the drain, leaving a gritty layer behind.

He gripped the paper towel hanging from the roll and ripped the end sheet carefully. He used it first to wipe and shut off the faucet and then to dry his hands. After he wiped his forehead, he noted a bit of blood-tinged staining. A wet pink splotch. More evidence of blood on him.

He stepped into the small bathroom, and after carefully shredding the pieces of damp paper towel, he watched as they circled the bowl of the toilet before disappearing.

He threw the black hooded sweatshirt over his head and gave his hands another once over when they popped out the end of each sleeve. He now slipped his hands into leather gloves, then grabbed the purse she'd left sitting on the kitchen table. He expelled a prolonged breath, then swung open the door off the kitchen that led to the garage.

He pulled the car keys from the pocket of his jeans and slipped into the driver's seat. His shaking hands fumbled as he attempted to insert the key into the ignition. The keychain fell to the floorboard by his feet.

"Crap."

The last thing he wanted to do was turn on the dome light in the vehicle. He slid both hands around the dirty mat, his gloved fingers searching for the keys until he felt them in his grasp. He gripped them tightly as he took in a deep breath, then exhaled.

This time, he managed to insert the key correctly, and the Lexus sprang to life. As he reached up for the button on the garage door opener, he considered the toll tag located on the windshield. An electronic tattletale depending on which route he chose to take.

When the door lifted, the towel he'd already placed over the automatic light left him in the relative darkness he had hoped for. He backed the car out of the garage to the street and then pulled forward a small distance.

His gaze swept around the sleepy neighborhood. Deathly quiet. No middle-of-the-night dog walkers, but any camera within surveillance distance of the house could be recording every moment onto an account in the cloud. It would live silently in that unknown place, just waiting for someone nosy to come looking for it. That short clip of footage would be the answer to whether something suspicious had happened in the middle of the night.

After putting the Lexus in reverse again, he glanced over his left shoulder and aimed the back end at the driveway. He then watched the screen on the vehicle's dashboard as he slowly maneuvered himself toward the garage. When the car was three-quarters of the way inside, he tapped the brakes and killed the engine. He'd left just enough room to exit under cover and access the trunk from the security of the garage.

Pulse racing, he hurried back into the house. He scooped up not only the vial of prescription sleeping pills but also the bottle of iced tea that had served as the method of administering them undetected. On the drive, he'd toss the drink out the window. It would be found on the side of a dark road, not as evidence of a sinister plot, but as the disregard of a lazy litterer.

He slipped the coverings off his shoes, carefully gathered all the plastic bags, and placed them in his backpack. He would discard those appropriately. He knew if the police saw them, the gig would be up.

The heavy bookend sat off to the side of the comforter, a long strand of her hair visible and encased in blood that had started to darken. Carefully, he wiped the smooth surface with a bleach-soaked cloth. He then used the rag to prop up the books lying on the shelf like fallen dominos and set the bookend back in its proper place. He pressed his lips together and chastised himself again silently that he'd forgotten to put on gloves. Being sloppy would land him in a prison cell for the rest of his life. Or worse.

His gaze drifted around the room. After eying the wall, he carefully ran the cloth down the blood spatter until it was all but invisible to the naked eye.

He added the rag to the load of blood-soaked towels already sitting in the washing machine in the laundry room. Then, after adding more bleach and detergent, he spun the dial. When he got back, he'd add the towel from the light in the garage and start the cycle.

He stepped back into the living room and gathered the corners of the blood-soaked comforter. A rusty, metallic smell mingled with the adrenaline-induced odor coming off him. He dry-heaved. Once, and then again before he commanded himself to pull it together. He held his breath, and as he dragged the bedding and its contents toward the garage, a dark, maroon-colored smear trailed along the floor behind him. Damn. He'd need to clean that too.

He deposited the comforter in the trunk, folding the ends toward the middle so the contents were no longer visible. It was the eyes. They seemed to be watching him, which he knew was ridiculous. Still, if he got pulled over, there'd be no easy way to explain himself.

He spun around and reached for the new shovel, the price tag still on the handle. This wasn't the reason it had been purchased, but it would serve his purpose nicely. An unexpected gift. He tossed it in on top and glanced at his watch. Daybreak was a few hours off. Plenty of time to make a quick pitstop and then get to the spot in the woods and back before hell broke loose.

He retrieved a fresh towel from the laundry basket and stepped back inside for one final walk-through. He rubbed the towel against the blood smear on the floor until the dark red color transferred to the white terrycloth fibers.

He tossed it into the washer, slid back into the driver's seat, and closed the car door. After he pulled forward, he hit the button, and the garage door rumbled shut behind him. He rolled past the white Hyundai she'd never drive again and couldn't help but remember how it had all started.

Everything he did was against company policy, no doubt, but he couldn't let her leave without saying something, anything. As he rushed through the parking lot, she began to fade into the distance. He'd picked up his pace to a jog as he watched her slip into the white hatchback.

Out of breath and standing next to her car, he'd waited a moment to see if she would roll down the driver's side window. She did, and without thinking, he'd leaned in and kissed her. A chaste lingering of his lips on her cheek.

At that moment, he could never have imagined where that kiss would lead. The suitcase by the front door. Her blood on him. Fear of getting caught and spending the rest of his life in prison.

He drew in a deep breath to try and calm his racing heart.

Thirty minutes. That's all it would take for the round-trip drive. At that point, there'd be no turning back, no changing his mind. In a few hours, the evening's events would escalate like a torpedo launched through the air. Once that happened, all he could do was pray he'd thought of everything. Covered his tracks.

With any luck, they'd be looking to dig up a body. He just hoped it wasn't this one.

CHAPTER TWO

"So, you don't remember anything about what happened? How you got hurt?" Jules pulled one of the uncomfortable-looking chairs closer to the hospital bed and lowered herself into it.

Her partner, Becky, eyed the other guest chair in the room. She began to drag it toward where Jules was sitting and grimaced when it scraped loudly against the floor. "Sorry about that."

"Seriously?" Jules asked. "That thing weighs more than you do."

She stood to help her best friend, and a moment later, they were both sitting side by side next to the woman's bed.

"Sorry about the seating, but I haven't had any visitors. Other than the detective on my case, that is." The woman shifted uncomfortably and attempted to sit up. The face that winced as she moved was pale, the color of her skin an odd match for her dark hair. "I don't remember what landed me here or anything before that, but the doctors told me I was in pretty bad shape when I showed up. I have no idea how I even got to the hospital." There was something detached in the way she relayed the details of her situation, almost as if she was simply reporting on a television show she'd watched.

Jules and Becky had compiled a short list of successful cases since they'd opened their detective agency. None had involved someone who'd lost their memory. They specialized in using DNA testing to discover someone's biological story—adoptions and long-lost family connections. Jules supposed this really wasn't any different.

Becky spoke up. "Dr. Summers said an older woman found you in the shopping center parking lot." After a car accident, Dr. Summers had been her neurologist, and he'd been the one who'd asked if they could take his patient on as a client. "She called 911, and an ambulance brought you to the hospital."

The woman gave a half-hearted nod. "Oh, right."

Jules covertly studied the woman lying in the hospital bed. The sleeve of her hospital gown didn't entirely cover the bruise on her upper arm, now turning an odd shade of chartreuse. Remnants of a similar injury lingered on her jaw, and it appeared stitches had recently been removed from her temple. If she had additional injuries, they were covered by the blanket pulled up high on her chest.

Jules sat back in her chair and crossed one leg over the other, her sandal dangling from her foot. "If you're told what happened, does it help you to remember any of the details?"

"I already told you. I don't remember that night at all." An edge to the woman's voice suggested annoyance at not having a different answer.

Jules flinched and came forward in her chair. Empathy was usually Becky's strong suit, not hers. She pressed her lips together to keep herself from responding to the woman's tone on auto-pilot. Really, Jules didn't blame her for being frustrated. She understood only too well how it felt to not know who you really were. Still, she wanted to see what the woman would say next.

They sat in uncomfortable silence as the moments ticked by.

"Dr. Summers says you're ready to be released today," Becky said finally. Jules knew it was her attempt to fill the awkward void in the air. Her best friend hated silence, though Jules had figured out she could learn a lot by what someone *didn't* say.

"Yeah, he told me." The woman then shifted her attention to Jules. "Listen, sorry I snapped at you." Her cheeks flushed a rosy red. "It's just—"

Jules held up her hand and dismissed the need for an apology. "Don't give it a second thought. I'm sure this can't be easy."

The woman shook her head and leaned forward in the bed. "No, it isn't. I mean, Dr. Summers is letting me leave the hospital, but he's not thrilled I don't have anyone to take care of me, but, how—who—" Her shoulders sagged, and she slumped back down against her pillows.

She didn't have to state the obvious. Even if a family member or friend might step up, she had no idea who they might be at this point. No one had come looking for her.

"I guess I'm going back to the apartment … my apartment." The woman's anxious gaze bounced between Jules and Becky. "I mean, it has to be mine, right? The detective said I had keys for it when I was attacked." She sat up again and glanced around the room, seemingly searching for something. "Supposedly, the police checked it out, but there wasn't much there that—"

"They gave you back your keys?" Jules asked, her pulse quickening in anticipation.

If they could get into her apartment, she was sure they'd find clues to her background. Sure, the cops had already been there, but Jules knew they wouldn't have scoured the place the way she intended to, just as soon as she had the chance.

"Yeah. The detective returned everything I had on me when I got to the hospital. Well, except my actual purse. He said they needed to keep that as evidence." She offered a shrug. "Not that it's much good anymore. He said the strap was broken, but I guess they were looking for fingerprints or DNA." Her lips pulled tight as she stared down at her hands. "So far, I don't think they've found anything."

The woman then aimed her chin at a white plastic bag on the windowsill. "Everything I had on me when I got to the hospital is in that bag. Not that any of it is useful in answering the question of who I really am. That's why Dr. Summers suggested I work with the two of you."

"You took the DNA tests?" Becky had dropped them off at the doctor's office the week before.

The woman's expression was blank for a moment, her head tilted to the side as she stared off. "The nurses give me so many pills, sometimes I even forget the things happening now." She closed her eyes for a moment, and when she opened them again, she let out an audible breath. "Yeah, I do remember spitting in that little tube." She lifted her arm and held her palm to the non-injured side of her temple. "Am I crazy? Why do I actually feel like I took the test more than once?"

Becky offered her a slight smile. "You're fine. I left him tests for three different companies, so there's a legitimate reason why you feel like you took it more than once."

The woman nodded slowly. "I guess that's it, then. Sometimes, I remember something, and I—I wonder if maybe it's an old memory. I get my hopes up …" Her shoulders lifted slightly and then dropped as she expelled a prolonged sigh. "But you're right. That's probably what it was."

"Do you remember if Dr. Summers took the little boxes to mail them?" Jules asked.

"Yeah, I think so." The woman glanced around the room

again. "I haven't seen them, so he must have taken them when he left."

"Okay, don't worry, I can doublecheck with him." Becky pulled a small notebook from her purse and scribbled herself a note.

Jules stood and propelled herself toward the windowsill. The woman's belongings were calling out to her, and Jules was sure if she could take a look, she'd be able to find something she could use. "Do you mind …"

"If you look in the bag?" The woman shook her head. "Go for it. Maybe you can make more sense of it than the cops."

Jules had already started rooting around in it. "What happened to what you were wearing that night?"

"Not that I'd want my bloody clothes back, but the detective said they kept them." She winced. "Evidence."

"Oh," Jules said with a dip of her chin. "Makes sense."

"Do you need something to wear?" Becky asked. "You know, for when they let you out today? I can't imagine they expect you to leave in your hospital gown."

The woman cleared her throat, and Becky jumped to her feet. She reached for the cup that sat on a small table they'd pushed aside to make room for their chairs.

"Are you thirsty?"

The woman accepted the water with a grateful bob of the head, then took a sip. "One of the nurses said the hospital can provide me with a pair of scrubs if I need them. You know, so I don't have to leave in this gown that doesn't leave much to the imagination. Especially for someone walking behind me." She rolled her eyes and then offered a slight smile. "If you know what I mean."

Jules glanced over from where she stood by the windowsill. "I can bring you something. It might be a little big on you, but that would be better than being too small." She was on the curvy side and not nearly as lean as the woman in the bed appeared to be. She bit back a smile. "I'm sure Becky would make the same offer, but I don't know too many people who could fit into her clothes." Jules's best friend was barely over five foot and a hundred pounds soaking wet.

Becky's shoulders hitched up. "What can I say? Good things come in small packages."

Jules strolled back to the side of the bed and set the plastic bag on the chair she'd been sitting in. "So, they found you with a driver's license, right?" she asked as she rummaged through the remaining items. "But no keys to a car?"

"Right. No car key, and apparently, the license was only issued about a month ago. The police said they tried the keys I had on me and confirmed they worked at the address listed."

Jules pulled out the small wallet and flipped it open. Then she held it up to compare the driver's license photo with the woman lying in the bed. "It's your picture, for sure. This says your name is Brittany Mullins."

"So they tell me." She shifted gingerly and sat up. "You can call me Brittany. I mean, that's who my license says I am, right? Not that the name feels familiar to me in the least." The sigh the woman let out was heavy and loud. "There's nothing in that bag that feels familiar."

"Well, there's actually not much in here." Jules pulled a library card from the wallet and held it up. "Maybe you're a reader?"

The woman held out her hands as if the cops had asked all the same questions and gotten the same answer. "No clue."

"Well, there's no credit cards or ATM card in here." Jules thumbed through the wallet's meager contents and pulled out a receipt. "What's this for?"

"Apparently, I bought a phone. One of those prepaid ones, but the police said it hadn't been activated yet." She gestured at the bag. "It should be in there. Seems I bought it right before

I ended up in the hospital. I guess I was too busy getting pummeled to set it up." Brittany's tone held a sarcastic edge.

Jules pursed her lips as she studied the receipt. Brittany had paid with cash. Within the first bag, she found a second plastic bag bearing the name of the store where Brittany had made the purchase. Inside was the phone, still in the packaging. The receipt indicated she'd also bought pre-paid minutes. Jules took a second look. She'd almost missed the thin card that contained the code.

"You'll probably want to activate this, right?" Jules held up the phone and then skimmed the information on the back of the package. "If you're heading home, you're going to need it."

Brittany's shoulders went up, frozen in place as she opened her mouth but nothing came out. Finally, she said, "But who would be calling me? Nobody would even have the number." Her shoulders lowered as a new realization seemed to hit her. "Oh, I guess maybe you might call me on it, right?" Her gaze bounced between Jules and Becky. "You know, if you find out anything."

Becky nodded. "Definitely. We'll need a way to get in touch with you."

Jules laid the phone aside and pulled a ring of keys from the bag. Four keys total. She separated two of them from the others, held them up between her thumb and index finger, and showed them to Brittany. "These look like the apartment keys."

"Yeah, there's a regular lock and a deadbolt," she said, nodding. "At least that's what I was told. It's not like I remember living there, much less what it takes to unlock the door."

Jules held up a small key. "Any idea what this one's for?"

"The detective said it looked like it was for a safety deposit box. He had no idea about the other one," Brittany added before Jules could ask.

Becky held out her hand, and Jules dropped the ring of keys into her palm.

"I suppose the detective had no idea where the box might be located?" Becky asked as she studied them.

Brittany shook her head. "Nope. Apparently, those keys all look alike. You have to know which bank to go to, or you're screwed."

"What about your apartment?" Becky glanced up. "Was there anything there that might help figure it out?"

"The detective said he spoke to the leasing office. Seems I moved in less than a week before I landed in the hospital. I thought maybe I moved for a job, but he said he didn't find anything that indicated that was the case. No paperwork sitting out. No computer. They said there wasn't much there at all. Apparently, I didn't have much of a life." Brittany leaned her head back against the pillow. "I guess now you see why I need help. The police don't even think the name on the license is mine." She managed a thin laugh. "Not that I'm a secret spy or in the witness protection program—" Brittany cut herself off and rubbed her chin thoughtfully. "Although, I guess I could be."

Jules pulled out her license again and studied it. "Why do they suspect the name on here isn't accurate? Just because it was recently issued doesn't mean—"

"I think it was because they couldn't find a record of me ever having a driver's license before this one."

Jules's eyes narrowed. "Anywhere?"

"I'm pretty sure that's what he told me." Brittany held out her hands with a certain measure of defeat. "It's not like I remember anything different to try and argue about it."

Jules's thoughts swirled. It would be unusual but not impossible that a twenty-five-year-old wouldn't already have their driver's license. But why the urgent need to get one when Brittany didn't even have a car? If it was for ID purposes, what had she been using up until now?

"Do the doctors think you'll ever be able to remember your life before the accident?" Becky's voice was soft, her eyes flooded with compassion.

The question prompted an awkward silence, and Jules held her breath as she waited to see if she'd snap again.

Instead, Brittany just shrugged. "Maybe. The doctors can't really explain why I lost those memories to begin with. I could start to remember a little at a time, or it could all come flooding back." She went quiet, her attention drifting toward the window. "There's also the possibility I might never remember any of it." She pressed her lips together and returned her gaze to Becky. "Dr. Summers told me unexplained memory loss can sometimes be triggered by a traumatic event. You know, something happened other than me being attacked. I guess getting slammed on my head just helped seal the deal." Brittany huffed and crossed her arms across her chest. "Of course, I have no way of *knowing* if something even worse happened before the assault." Her eyes welled up.

Becky laid her hand on Brittany's arm. "It's okay. This has to be difficult."

She stared down at the bed. "It's just so frustrating. Something or someone familiar could trigger me to remember, but that seems unlikely—" When she looked up, her cheeks were wet with tears. "It's unlikely because no one seems to be looking for me." Brittany pressed her lips together and adjusted the thin blanket and sheet. She pulled them up, folded the edges neatly across her chest, and then used her hands to brush away imaginary wrinkles. It seemed she needed a moment to get her emotions under control.

Becky traded a sympathetic look with Jules. "Well, it's not

the *fastest* way, but we should be able to use your DNA results to get the answers you need and help find your family."

Brittany jerked her gaze in Becky's direction. She sniffled and swiped at her tears, hope back in her eyes. "How long will that take?"

Becky's shoulders hitched. "Hard to say exactly. Once your results come in, we'll use your matches to build a family tree until we find our way to you."

Jules set the plastic bag on the bed and reclaimed her seat. "We've had cases where we've found someone in a day or two. Some take longer. It all depends on the matches you have." She held up the phone. "Do you want me to activate this before we go? Then you can call us when you're getting out, and we can pick you up and take you to your apartment."

"That would be—" Brittany's face flushed. "But I'm not sure how I can pay you. There wasn't any money or credit cards in the wallet—at least none they found. One of the nurses suggested I should do something called GoFundMe. She also said I should see if one of the news stations would be willing to interview me. You know, put my story out there. People might want to help if they—"

Jules held up her hand. "I wouldn't do that just yet." She exchanged a glance with Becky. "Don't worry. We'll figure out the bill eventually. For now, let's just work on finding you some answers."

Brittany gave a grateful nod. "Okay. I promise I'll pay you when I can. I must have money somewhere, right?" A rueful smile tugged at the corners of her mouth. "All I have to do is figure out the name on my bank account."

It didn't take long, and Jules had activated the phone, loaded the minutes, and saved both hers and Becky's numbers in Brittany's contacts. She then used her own cell phone to call it to make sure it was working. After it rang, she handed the phone to Brittany.

"You're all set. Call one of us when the hospital releases you, and we'll come back and get you. We'll run to my place now and get you something nice to wear."

"You'll also need to get some groceries before we take you to your apartment," Becky said as she rose from her chair. "Even if you had anything from before, I'm sure you need milk, bread. You know, perishables that probably won't be good anymore since you've been in the hospital."

"That would be great. I don't remember much, but I do know the food here—" Brittany wrinkled her nose. "Let's just say it leaves a lot to be desired."

Jules cringed and gestured at the tray that still contained Brittany's last meal. "No kidding. We'll get you something decent to eat later for sure." She caught Becky's eye, dipped her chin, and began inching toward the door. "Okay, then, we'll see you when you're ready to get out of here."

* * *

"I'm okay working for free for now." Becky had waited until they were a respectable distance from Brittany's room. "Though, I probably won't mention it to Bryan."

"I have a big photography job this weekend." As they headed toward the elevator, the heels of Jules's sandals clicked against the tile in the long sterile hallway. "And I'm sure once Brittany figures everything out, she'll be able to pay us. Who knows, maybe her memory will come back, and she won't even need to wait for her DNA results."

"I can't imagine how it feels—not knowing who you are." Becky shook her head. "Getting out of the hospital after what she's been through and having no one waiting for you. That's gotta be rough."

Jules gave a thoughtful nod. "It's not exactly the same thing, but being adopted, I have an idea how she feels. You know, not knowing who she really is. Finding my birth mother and knowing my story made a huge difference to me. And it wasn't like my whole life was an empty slate like hers." She rubbed her index finger along her chin thoughtfully as they came upon the elevator. "Still, the whole situation makes me wonder."

Becky pressed the button, her eyes narrowed into slits as she studied her friend. "You have that look on your face."

"What look?" Jules blinked with feigned innocence, but she knew precisely what look her partner was referring to. She couldn't deny her wheels were already spinning.

The elevator arrived, and Jules heaved a sigh as she stepped in and hit the button for the lobby. "That whole GoFundMe thing made me nervous. I'm not sure it's a great idea to put Brittany's story out there." She faced Becky. "Think about it. She has a new driver's license with a name that's not hers. She buys a *prepaid* phone, for Pete's sake." She huffed in disbelief. "Do you know I didn't even need her name to activate it? Even the apartment Brittany's living in—she'd *just* moved in. It doesn't take a rocket scientist to figure out she's running from something or *someone*." Jules's eyebrows went up. "The last thing she needs to do is make a public announcement about where she is and share the details about her current situation. She's better off waiting on her DNA results, so at least we can help her figure out what's going on. Privately and out of the spotlight."

Becky took in a deep breath, then eased it out slowly. "Yeah, I was starting to think the same thing. Do you suspect that's how she got hurt?"

"You mean like whoever she was running from found her?" Jules stared off for a moment, then bobbed her head. "Yeah, I think it's possible. The thing is, we know what the hospital said Brittany had on her when she was admitted, but we have no idea what she had *before* she was attacked." She tipped her head as she considered it. "Maybe someone *took* something she had. It could be a huge piece of the puzzle, but how would we even know?"

The elevator dinged, and the doors opened into the lobby.

Jules put out her hand to hold the doors open and shot Becky a pointed stare. "If Brittany *was* running from someone and they were responsible for sending her to the hospital, we need to figure that out quickly."

Becky's forehead wrinkled as she stared at her partner. "Well, obviously."

Jules lowered her voice as she strolled out of the elevator. "What I mean is, was someone trying to teach Brittany a lesson?" She spun around to face Becky. "Or were they trying to kill her?" Jules's head tipped to the side as her eyebrows lifted. "Maybe they just weren't successful. This time."

CHAPTER THREE

BECKY EYED the numbers on the apartment doors as they made their way down the dingy concrete walkway of the second floor. It had been evident from the moment they pulled into the parking lot that upkeep on the property wasn't a priority. Weeds sprouted through cracks in the asphalt, and the terra-cotta-colored paint on the wooden railing peeled in the unforgiving Florida sun.

The area around the apartment building was an odd stretch of older shopping centers in one direction and a large cemetery visible from the road in the other. They weren't far from a decent neighborhood, so Becky couldn't imagine why Brittany chose to live here, though she suspected the rent was low. If this had been all she could afford, it might not bode well for her and Jules getting paid when this was all over.

If Brittany was dismayed at the location of her apartment, she didn't show it. "I'm so happy to be out of the hospital finally, and I love this cute dress you brought me." She twirled on the walkway to make the skirt on the sundress lift in the air. "That silly hospital gown was ridiculous, but I'll get this back to you as soon as I can."

Jules waved her hand dismissively. “Don’t worry about it. It fits you much better than it ever fit me. You can keep the sandals too.” She offered a genuine smile. “No point breaking up a great outfit.”

Brittany’s eyes widened with disbelief as she brought her hand to her chest. “Are you sure? That’s so generous of you, and that place you took me for lunch was amazing. I guess I’m pretty confident I used to like cheeseburgers.”

Becky was relieved their new client’s mood had greatly improved since leaving the hospital and getting something to eat. Even the short time outside had left a hint of pink on her pale cheeks.

“After nothing but that bland hospital food, anything would probably taste delicious. You can’t even imagine how much lime Jell-O they tried—”

“This is it.” Becky stopped in front of the door that matched the apartment number on Brittany’s driver’s license. She nudged the three in the unit number to straighten it, but it immediately tilted off-kilter again. “You should get the maintenance guy to fix that,” she told Brittany, then wished she hadn’t. She needed to stop assuming Brittany couldn’t make her own decisions just because she’d lost her memory. “I mean, if it bothers you.”

She didn’t seem concerned. “It’s not like it matters. I’m pretty sure there won’t be anyone coming to visit me.” Brittany inserted one of her keys into the lock. She turned it, then tugged at the doorknob. She glanced back, a scowl on her face. “It won’t open.”

Jules nudged her arm. “You need to also unlock the deadbolt.”

“Oh, right.” Brittany used the second key and then pulled the door open. Her eyes peered into the dimly lit apartment.

“Hang on.” Becky slid her hand against the inside wall

until her fingers felt a switch. The room was illuminated only slightly by a bulb hanging in the small open kitchen off to the right. She frowned. "Okay. There's *got* to be more light than that." She scanned the wall until she found a second switch. When she flicked it upward, a lamp lit on an end table beside a worn, brown leather couch. "That's a little better."

Becky's gaze flitted around the modestly furnished apartment. The detective had been right. There wasn't much in Brittany's apartment. Not even a television.

The kitchen and living room were essentially one open space, the rooms defined by where the dingy white tile met the worn beige carpet. Becky tried to keep her expression from betraying her disappointment. The inside of Brittany's apartment was on par with the outside.

Brittany's nose wrinkled as she took it all in. "I guess I wasn't exactly living in the lap of luxury."

"It's—it's nice," Becky said, even though it was drab and gloomy and anything but nice. "Maybe we should let a little sunlight in."

Two windows behind the empty television stand faced the parking lot. Becky reached for the cord to the blinds, then considered the view and twisted the wands on each set instead. The slats separated to let in some natural light, which only confirmed Becky's opinion that this apartment had seen better days. Much better days.

As Jules looked around, she wasn't as subtle. "Something smells awful." She dropped the grocery bags onto the small kitchen table, then sniffed at the air as she searched for the source of the offending odor.

Becky moved the bags from the table to the counter, but she couldn't argue with her friend's assessment. Something had clearly spoiled while Brittany had been away.

"Do you mind if I go see if there's someone in the leasing

office?" Jules asked, already making her way back toward the door they'd just come through. "Maybe they can shed some more light on how and when you rented this place."

"And more importantly, *why* I rented it, right?" Brittany ran a hand over her face. "I don't mind at all. Hopefully, you'll find out I don't have a very long lease."

After the door shut behind Jules, Becky pulled on the handle for the refrigerator door. It was old but clean, and the only things inside were coffee creamer and a six-pack of beer with three cans missing.

Brittany peered over her shoulder. "Apparently, I hadn't gotten around to buying much."

"You had your priorities."

Becky set the milk and carton of eggs they'd bought on the top shelf.

Next, she checked the freezer, empty except for a single ice tray. Becky pulled it out and frowned before turning it over to show Brittany it was empty. She filled it at the sink and set it back inside.

In the small pantry beside the refrigerator, she discovered an open bag of Doritos, a small sack of sugar, ground coffee, and a stack of filters. "Yup. You had the essentials."

As Becky began to pull open the cabinets over the counter, she found a modest selection of dishes. A small coffeemaker resided on the counter, and a coffee mug sat in the sink filled with brown-tinted water and what appeared to be green dots of mold floating on top.

Becky grimaced as she emptied the contents down the drain. She knelt down to check under the sink but found no sponge or dish soap. This apartment didn't even have a dishwasher.

Brittany flipped open the top of the trash can and reeled backward, her face screwed up in disgust. "Well, here's where the smell is coming from. Apparently, I ate a lot of take-out."

Becky took a look for herself. What she saw were several fast-food bags, a couple of sizable soda cups from the gas station down the street, and something unidentifiable on top. Maybe the remnants of a burrito. She held her breath and let the top close with a thud.

"I guess I need to get some trash bags." Brittany gave her head an embarrassed shake. "Not to mention, a better diet."

Becky loaded frozen vegetables into the freezer. "I saw a dumpster on the way in," she said over her shoulder. "We can toss everything in there and then leave the garbage can outside to air out."

Brittany pinched her nose shut. "I'll get it out of here now so we can breathe easier."

While Becky finished putting away the groceries, she relocated the can to just outside the front door.

"At least now you have decent food to eat." Becky gathered all the empty grocery bags and stuffed them into one open bag, which she hung by the handle over the knob on the pantry door.

"My cholesterol is grateful. Should we check out the rest of the place?"

There was one bedroom. Small, but it appeared the carpet had been replaced much more recently than what was in the living room. It also seemed like it might have had a fresh coat of paint in the not-too-distant past.

Two windows on either side of the bed let in a fair amount of light, and when Becky looked out, she saw a small canal running behind the building. Her shoulders relaxed. The bedroom wasn't nearly as depressing as the rest of the apartment, though the furniture did seem old. A full-size bed, one dresser, and a nightstand with a lamp. The blanket on the bed was pulled down as if someone had slept under it, but the bedding looked crisp and new. Almost out of place.

Brittany opened the closet and pulled out a large shopping bag. "I guess I bought some stuff." She brought it to Becky.

She peered inside. Inside was the packaging for a new set of sheets, the plastic wrapping from the pair of pillows, and a ribbon and tag that appeared to have been tied around the blanket.

Brittany dug around in the bag and pulled out a receipt. "Looks like I got it from that little store we passed." She held up the bag so Becky could see the logo on the front. "Tuesday Morning."

Becky remembered seeing it. The store was located in the strip mall behind the gas station, where it appeared Brittany had been buying her fountain beverages. It also seemed to confirm she probably didn't have a vehicle. Both locations were within walking distance of the apartment, but at least they were in the opposite direction of the cemetery. She shuddered as she considered Brittany having to walk past it by herself. For Becky, that alone would have been ample reason to rent somewhere else.

Brittany handed her the receipt. As she scrutinized it, Becky noted that once again, she'd paid with cash. Clearly, there had been money at some point.

She laid the receipt on the dresser where it wouldn't get lost. "Was there anything else in the closet?"

Brittany slid open the accordion doors as Becky strolled over. A few items hung on hangers. There were some shelves built into the closet, and clothes laid haphazardly on the top shelf. A suitcase on the floor had been propped open to allow access to the contents, almost as if Brittany hadn't bothered to unpack. A small pile of clothes off to the side appeared to be dirty laundry.

A flush developed on Brittany's cheeks. "I didn't see a washer and dryer, but hopefully, there's one here someplace.

Or maybe there's a laundry room. I guess I need to get some detergent."

"Don't worry. At least now we know what we're up against. We can go back out and get you the things you still need."

The front door slammed, and Brittany flinched. Becky rested a reassuring hand on her arm.

"Just me," Jules called out.

Becky stuck her head out the bedroom door, which was probably unnecessary. "We're in here." The apartment was small. There weren't too many other places they could be.

"Wow, that garbage by the front door reeks," Jules said as she headed toward the bedroom. "At least now we know where that horrible smell was coming from."

Becky exchanged a look with Brittany. "Yeah, we know. So, were you able to find out anything?"

Jules pulled up the blanket to make the bed and then sat down. "I had to play the detective card with the lady in the leasing office. You know, privacy issues and all that, but she folded pretty easily. I'm sure she already told the cops the same thing, but she confirmed the apartment was rented about a month ago." She turned to Brittany and bobbed her head. "The lease agreement does match the name on your drivers' license. It was rented furnished with a few bare essentials, and you paid three months upfront. You mailed them four money orders—one for each month's rent and the security—with the signed contract. She confirmed you picked up the keys five days before you landed in the hospital."

"Was there a return address or a postmark on the envelope?" Becky asked.

"I asked, but the woman basically looked at me like I had three heads for thinking she might still have the envelope hanging around. I guess if the police want to dig into where the money orders came from, they might be able to find out more." She aimed a shrug at Brittany. "But if you haven't done anything wrong, I'm not sure they'd get into all that." She glanced at Becky. "I doubt we'd be able to get that information, but I can ask Jonas."

Brittany gave her a quizzical stare. "Who's Jonas?"

"My brother. He's a cop." Jules turned her gaze to Becky. "What about here inside the apartment? Have you found anything that might tell us where she was before she moved in?"

Becky shook her head. "Nothing. We put away the groceries, but there wasn't much in the kitchen except stuff to make coffee and a six-pack of beer."

The corners of Brittany's mouth tugged upward into an embarrassed smile. "I had priorities."

"Right." Becky dropped onto the bed beside Jules. "But it goes along with Brittany moving in not long before the attack. We also found the remnants of a bunch of fast food in the trash."

"That explains the smell." Jules pressed her lips together and eyed Brittany. "It also makes me think it wasn't a local move where you might have moved the contents of a kitchen. Stuff from the refrigerator. At least basic condiments. I mean, who wants to start all over buying that stuff if you don't have to?"

"She did have dishes and some pots and pans in the cabinets."

"The lady in the office said those came with the place." Jules's gaze drifted around the bedroom until the suitcase caught her attention. "Anything in there?"

"We haven't gotten that far," Becky said.

"May I?" Jules had already lifted herself from the edge of the bed.

Brittany shrugged. "Sure, go ahead." She grimaced. "I'm

pretty sure the clothes next to it are dirty, so you probably don't want to get into all that."

Jules strode toward the closet, then studied the worn carpet before sitting with her legs crossed in front of her. She pulled the large, open suitcase toward her.

Brittany and Becky sat on the bed as Jules began to dig through the contents.

First, she rifled through a stack of folded T-shirts. When she removed them and set the pile off to the side, her eyes narrowed, a deep divot forming between her eyebrows.

Becky gave her a quizzical stare. "What? What did you find?" She stood to see for herself, then knelt on the carpet beside Jules as she removed a doll from Brittany's suitcase. It was about a foot long with blonde pigtails and blue eyes painted on a face that looked slightly worn.

Jules turned and showed it to Brittany, but her shoulders went up. "I have no idea why I would have that."

Becky reached for the doll. It wasn't an expensive toy. Certainly nothing like the fancy ones her parents had showered on her as a little girl. Still, it had to be significant in some way if Brittany had chosen to bring it with her.

Becky blinked hard and tried to fight it, but her eyes welled up with tears. She turned away to study the sweet angelic face and tried to imagine the little girl who'd cherished this doll. Though she couldn't bring herself to talk it about much these days, her struggle with infertility still lurked right below the surface. At this moment, it broke through with a brutal reminder she wasn't any closer to having a child to buy something like this.

As if Jules knew what her best friend was thinking, she continued to unpack to let her have a private moment.

Becky sniffled and cleared her throat. Then, she smoothed the front of the doll's dress down and propped her up on one of the shelves. With a wistful smile, she realized the sweet face appeared to be looking down on them.

Becky swiped the tears from underneath her eye with the knuckle of her index finger and turned her attention back to Jules. On the carpet next to the suitcase, there now also sat a few pairs of shorts and two pair of jeans. Socks and underwear. Black sandals. Jules held up a pair of expensive running shoes.

Brittany's face brightened. "Hey, maybe I jog."

"Very possible, especially with all of this." Jules pulled out several pairs of athletic shorts, a tank top promoting a 5K race, and a sports bra.

Becky managed a laugh. "I hope you aren't expecting to go for a run with either one of us. Although Jules has been to a 5K. But just one."

Jules lifted her eyebrows and grinned. "All I needed was one."

The suitcase was now empty, but Jules carefully slid her hand into the gathered pocket on the left side. Out came a pair of cheap flip-flops. Then, she reached into the pocket on the right side and her forehead creased. When she pulled back her hand, it held a framed photograph.

Brittany showed immediate interest. "Hey," she said, reaching for it. "Let me see that."

The three women studied the picture. Two blonde women were holding cocktails in front of what appeared to be a tiki bar, and they were beaming at whoever was holding the camera. Part of a palm tree swooped down over the left side of the frame, and when Becky squinted, she saw what looked like a pool in the background. A tropical setting, for sure. Maybe a hotel.

"That's definitely me," Brittany said as she stared at the photo. "I wonder who the other girl is."

Becky's gaze went back and forth between the picture and Brittany. "I see a resemblance. Around the eyes."

Jules nodded in agreement. "Yeah, I do too. But I also see something obvious that's pretty interesting."

Brittany scrutinized the photo a moment longer, then turned to Jules, her forehead creased in confusion. "What's that?"

"Your hair." Jules shot a look at Becky. "Not only was it longer, but apparently, it also used to be a different color."

CHAPTER FOUR

"I HAVE to wonder why you'd want to make such a drastic change." Jules's gaze was anchored on Brittany. She now understood why she looked so deathly pale. Her skin was far too fair for the hair color she'd chosen.

When Brittany's face fell, Becky placed her hand on her arm. "It doesn't necessarily mean anything. Lots of women like to change out their look."

"Absolutely. I was simply making an observation." Jules backpedaled and hoped she sounded more matter-of-fact and less accusatory. Her tendency to slip into detective mode would need to be toned down for Brittany. She seemed ultra-sensitive. "While we're waiting on the DNA results to come back, it's a good idea to take note of anything we stumble across that could be a clue to your past."

What she was saying made perfect sense, but it was more than that. To Jules, the fact that Brittany had dyed her blond hair a chestnut brown seemed further proof she was trying to alter her identity.

"And my hair? What could that be a clue about?" Brittany's expression held a look of bewilderment. "Don't you think it's more important to see if we can figure out where the photo was taken or who this other woman in the picture is? If we can locate her, obviously she knows who I am. She could tell me what I need to know."

"Of course," Jules said, giving her a reassuring nod. "Why don't you take the photograph out of the frame and see if anything's written on the back?"

While Brittany and Becky went over to the bed to check it out, Jules knelt on the carpet in front of the suitcase. She flipped the lid closed and zipped it shut. Then, she investigated all four sides. Nothing. She flipped it over, checked the backside, and frowned. She still wasn't convinced her hunch was wrong.

"There's nothing written on the photo," Becky called out.

Jules slid the suitcase back into the closet and stood and let out a groan as she stood. "Well, that's disappointing. Even worse, I hate to say it, especially in this cute outfit I'm wearing, but I'm going to go dig in the trash and see if there's anything unexpected." She specifically wanted to see if there was any evidence Brittany had dyed her hair at the apartment. She gestured at the bed. "What's in there?"

Becky reached for the Tuesday Morning bag. "Trash. The bedding was all new. Bought from that store in the strip mall by the gas station."

"Was there—"

"A receipt?" Becky asked.

Jules laughed. They were getting so good at being partners, they could read each other's minds sometimes. "Exactly."

"It's on the dresser. She paid with cash."

Jules picked it up, her lips pulled tight as she skimmed the list of items purchased. "Looks like that's all you bought." She set the receipt back on the dresser. "Let's keep this. Just in case."

"In case what?" Brittany asked.

Jules shrugged. "At this point, I have no idea, but you never know." She reached for the shopping bag. "At least I can use this for the trash as I go through it."

"Okay, while you do that, we'll see if there's anything interesting in the bathroom. And good luck digging past that burrito on top. I doubt it was any good when it was fresh, but now…" Becky winced. "Better you than me."

When Jules left the bedroom, her eyes drifted around the living room, looking for anything that might have hidden meaning. The coffee table was dusty but bare. Same with the end tables, with the exception of a lamp on each. There was a TV stand but no television.

Jules dropped onto the leather couch to give herself a different vantage point. She considered slipping off her sandals to put her feet up, but when she glanced down, something caught her eye. She bent over and ran her finger around a small ash-rimmed hole between the coffee table and couch. It was old. Someone long before Brittany had been the smoker who didn't see the need to use an ashtray.

Her eyes carefully scanned the rest of the room, but the carpet, though old, looked recently cleaned. In the corners where no one had yet walked, she could still see lines left by a vacuum.

Jules rubbed her temple and cringed at the perspiration now on her fingertips. It was November but still warm in Florida. The air in the small apartment felt thick, as if the air conditioning hadn't been on while Brittany was gone. Jules's head swiveled as she tried to locate the thermostat.

Then, as her gaze drifted across the front windows, she reeled back and sucked in a deep breath of air. Her pulse quickened. She sat frozen in place, her brain requiring the extra time to catch up to what her eyes were seeing. When it all came together, she had no doubt. Through the break in the blinds, a pair of eyes were anchored on her, watching her intently. They resided on the face of a man.

"Hey!" Jules jumped up from the couch and heard a thud.

When she threw open the front door, she found Brittany's garbage can had been knocked to the concrete, the contents strewn in her path as the man took off. She kicked a fast-food bag out of the way, stumbled around the trash, and chased after him.

He made it to the landing at the end of the second floor well ahead of her. After a quick glance over his shoulder, he disappeared into the stairwell.

In her sandals, Jules didn't have a prayer of keeping up with him. By the time she got to the stairs, she was breathing heavy, sweat dripping down her face. She raced down as fast as she could without breaking an ankle. When she reached the bottom, she looked to the right, then the left, but there was no sign of him. The man had disappeared.

Jules bent at the waist and sucked in a deep breath. When she stood up straight, she rubbed at the sweat on her temple and cursed under her breath. She gave one final look out into the sea of cars in the parking lot. Nothing looked amiss. He could have ducked into a vehicle or been hiding in any one of a hundred places out of sight.

Jules didn't like this one bit. Had the person who'd hurt Brittany found out she'd been released from the hospital?

By the time she'd trudged back up the concrete stairs and limped back toward the apartment, Becky and Brittany were waiting. They stood in the doorway, confusion etched on their faces.

"What happened?" Becky asked.

Jules stood on the other side of the trash and winced at the overwhelming smell. "Well, this wasn't exactly what I meant when I said I was going to go through it."

Becky reached for Jules's hand and supported her as she

stepped over the mess. "Why'd you knock it over then? And where'd you go?"

Jules huffed as she made her way into the apartment. "I wasn't the one who knocked it over, and I'm pretty sure we need a change of plans."

Her lips were set in a firm line as she gripped Brittany's shoulders. "I have an extra bedroom at my townhouse. You need to come stay with me."

"Why?" She pulled back and frowned. "What happened?"

"I caught someone—a man—looking through your window."

Brittany's gaze flew between Jules and Becky, her eyebrows furrowed. "I don't understand. You mean like a peeping Tom?" Then, she released a deep breath and gave a half-hearted shrug. "It's not exactly the nicest apartment complex. I'm sure that doesn't bode well for the kind of neighbors I have."

Jules considered the possibility, but it didn't feel random. She shot a dubious look in Becky's direction, sure she felt the same way.

"Or maybe it's someone I know looking for me?" Brittany's face brightened, her expression hopeful as if someone spying through her window might be a good thing.

But Jules couldn't shake the feeling she'd gotten when the man locked eyes with her. His face hadn't seemed casual or friendly. She gave a hesitant shake of her head. "I don't know. You would think he would have just knocked on the front door if he knew you. Not peered in your window like that. And if there was really an innocent explanation, it doesn't make sense he would have taken off running like he had something to hide. Wouldn't he have wanted to stick around to find out where you've been?"

Jules set her jaw, prepared to convince Brittany she had no choice but to accept the offer to stay at her place. If she refused, she could find out the hard way the man was up to no good, and she was his target.

"Becky and I were talking when we left the hospital earlier. We think there's the possibility you were running away from someone. And if they already found you once and hurt you …"

Brittany sucked in a gulp of air. "You think someone hurt me on purpose?" She wheeled around and gestured at the window. "And you suspect it was that guy you saw?"

"We aren't sure about anything yet," Becky said in a gentle voice. "But maybe Jules is right about you staying with her. Just in case." She offered a slight smile. "I mean, you don't even have a television here."

"I know, but—" Brittany pursed her lips and then dropped onto the couch. She gazed out the window thoughtfully before shaking her head. "Jules, I can't impose on you like that."

Jules dismissed her concerns with a wave of her hand. "It's not a big deal. Really. I have a spare bedroom that's just sitting empty." She lowered herself to the couch beside Brittany and looked her in the eye. "I'd feel much better if I knew you weren't here alone. Especially since we don't know exactly what's going on."

"Did you get a look at him?" Becky asked Jules. "The guy in the window?"

"Yeah, sort of. He turned around for a second, right before he disappeared down the stairs." She wrapped her arms around her middle. "We should get out of here in case he decides to come back." Her chest felt tight as she threw a questioning gaze at Brittany. "You're coming with us, right?"

She stared down at her lap as if she was trying to decide what to do. Finally, she gave a slow nod. "Yeah, I'm coming."

Jules's shoulders lowered in relief. She stood and put her hand on Becky's shoulder. "Can you help pack her stuff?" Her lips twisted with dread as she picked up the shopping bag she'd left on the coffee table. "I'll clean up the trash on the walkway." She still thought it was important to see what Brittany had thrown away. "But if either of you hears me screaming, come quick."

Becky nodded, and she and Brittany headed off to the bedroom.

Jules left the door to the apartment wide open and stared at the trash that had been tossed across the concrete. She moved to the railing and leaned against it as she stared out over the parking lot. Several people were going about their business, but none of them was the man she'd seen.

Guilty people ran. Not someone who had nothing to hide. Jules didn't like the situation at the apartment one bit. Brittany hadn't been back for more than thirty minutes when this mystery man appeared in her window. Had he just been waiting for her to return?

They had no other choice. Jules needed to get Brittany out of here until they could figure out who this man was and what he wanted.

With a heavy sigh, she turned away from the railing and set about cleaning up the mess he'd left behind.

CHAPTER FIVE

When Becky strolled through her front door, the smell of garlic hung in the air. Jules was always telling her how lucky she was to have a husband who loved to cook.

Sherlock, Becky's orange tabby cat, wove a figure-eight through her legs as he greeted her.

She stooped down and scratched him behind the ear. "Hey, buddy."

Bryan turned from the stove, and she leaned in for a kiss.

"You're later than I thought you'd be, but dinner's almost ready. Everything go okay with the potential new client?"

Becky related the day they'd had after picking up Brittany from the hospital. "We packed her stuff up, and she went home with Jules. She's going to stay there, at least for the time being, until we can figure out what's going on."

Bryan pulled a block of parmesan cheese from the refrigerator. When he turned back around, his eyebrows were knitted together. "Was that really necessary? Did you really think she wouldn't be safe in her own apartment?"

"Well, Jules was the one who saw the guy looking in the window. And he did take off running." Becky snuck a small piece of garlic bread off the plate on the counter. "Plus, her place isn't in a great neighborhood, and she'd be there by herself. She just moved in, so it's not like she even knows anyone in the building." Her shoulders lifted. "At least she didn't think she did, but it's not like she'd remember."

Bryan pressed his lips together and gave his wife a hard stare. "I get that, but you and Jules shouldn't just be inviting your clients to *move in*. You're running a business, not a shelter." He pulled the cheese grater from the utensil drawer, then ran the cheese over the coarse metal at a furious pace. "Neither of you even knew this woman before today, and now she's living with Jules." He shook his head as if he was trying to understand what they could possibly have been thinking. "I can't *wait* to hear what Tim has to say about it," he said as he sprinkled cheese over her pasta.

Becky took her plate and hesitated before responding. "I'm not sure Jules told him before she extended the offer, but I understand what you're saying." She slid into her usual chair at the kitchen table. "I think she feels bad for Brittany because she doesn't know who she is. You know, kind of the way Jules feels, or felt, about being adopted."

Bryan rolled his eyes as he joined her. "C'mon, babe, this is not the same thing at all."

"Jules thinks it is, and who are we to say she's wrong?" Becky picked up her fork and started eating. "Besides, she's convinced Brittany ran away from someone or something bad in her life. Since she lost her memory, we have no idea if that's the case." She reached for her napkin. "What if we left her there and then something horrible happened to her?"

Becky wiped her mouth, then went to the refrigerator and retrieved a bottle of white wine. She poured two glasses.

"Jules wasn't willing to take that chance." She handed Bryan his glass.

Instead of taking a sip, he set it down on the table,

slightly harder than necessary. The contents sloshed against the sides, and Becky was grateful she had only filled his glass halfway.

"And I'm worried about something horrible happening to the two of you," he said, his voice sharp. "Doesn't it seem like an awfully big coincidence that the minute this woman's home from the hospital, a man's spying in her window?"

"I know, but—"

Bryan drew in a deep breath as if he was attempting to calm himself down. "I don't understand why you both couldn't just sit back and wait for her DNA results to come in. Isn't that what she's paying you for?" His eyes begged her to see his point of view. "It worries me you could be getting yourself involved in another case that might be dangerous."

"C'mon, babe. Her case isn't *dangerous*."

Even as she spoke the words, Becky had no idea if they were true. As much as she hated to admit it, Bryan was right. She and Jules didn't know the first thing about Brittany—where she'd come from or what kind of life she'd had before she was attacked. She decided it was in her best interest not to mention to her husband that they weren't even getting paid. At least not yet.

Bryan held his fork frozen in the air as he eyed her with disbelief. "That's what you said about Donna's case, and that could have ended tragically for you. For us. Have you already forgotten the close call you had?"

Becky's shoulders went up in her half-hearted attempt to try and protest. "That was different."

"Was it?" Bryan asked. He slugged down a long gulp of wine, then tilted his head and gave her a hard stare. "You just told me some guy was spying on your new client. A guy who then took off running the minute Jules spotted him."

Becky gave a reluctant nod. "Right. But we don't know who he was." She lifted her hands in the air defensively. "It could be nothing. Brittany had just moved into that apartment, after all."

They ate in silence for a few moments before Becky felt compelled to say more. "Maybe this guy was actually looking for the person who'd lived there before her. Jules just feels—" She hesitated. "She just feels like it's better to be safe than sorry." Her stomach was in knots that their new case had her husband so upset. She reached across the table for his hand. "I know you're worried about us. I get it, babe."

"People don't run without a reason." Bryan squeezed her hand. "I've come close to losing you, not once but twice." He dipped his head as he met her eyes. "It just doesn't seem necessary to take chances like this. I couldn't bear it if anything happened to you."

Becky drew in a deep breath and bobbed her head. "I understand, but really, you don't need to worry. We plan on being careful. And who knows, Brittany could get her memory back at any time. If that happens, we won't even need to wait for her DNA results."

Bryan pulled his hand back and stood with his empty plate. "Well, that would be—"

The ringing of Becky's cell phone interrupted him. She glanced at the caller ID and looked up at him with an apologetic wince. "It's Jules."

Bryan sighed and reached for her plate.

"Leave the rest, and I'll clean up when I'm done," Becky said insistently, but her husband had already moved to the sink with their plates.

She stared glumly at his back and answered the call. "Hey, everything okay?"

"Yeah, Brittany's all settled in. She's in the shower, so I figured I'd call while I had the chance."

"Why? Did something happen?"

When Bryan spun around, Becky pretended not to see the scowl on his face.

"No. Everything's good here."

"Glad to hear everything's *fine*." Becky's voice was louder than necessary.

"Was that for Bryan's benefit?" Jules asked.

"Yeah." Becky didn't need to go into details. Her best friend knew how much he worried about her after what had happened.

"You know, I didn't say anything at the apartment, but something occurred to me when I saw what was in Brittany's suitcase."

Becky tipped her glass back and drank what was left of her wine. "You mean the doll?"

Jules let out a puff of air. "Yeah, that was odd, huh? There's definitely that to dive into, but I was thinking about something else. In that bag of stuff at the hospital, I found a pair of earphones. I guess they'd been in Brittany's purse."

Becky's forehead wrinkled as she tried to figure out where Jules was going with this. "What does that have to do with her suitcase?"

"Think about it. Brittany didn't have a phone, other than the prepaid one she bought that wasn't even activated yet. No tablet or computer or anything to plug earphones into. So, why did she have them?"

Becky shifted in her seat to face the wall instead of Bryan. She lowered her voice. "Maybe she did have something, but it was stolen when she was attacked."

"That's possible, but we know she didn't have a phone, or she wouldn't have been buying a new one. I guess she could have had a small tablet in her purse, but a computer? Not likely. Besides, I think they were the cheap earphones you get when you fly. You know, the ones the airline sells when you're on the plane. You pay five bucks, and then you can plug them into the armrest to watch a movie or listen to music."

Becky bobbed her head. "Oh. I see where you're going with this."

"Brittany doesn't have a car. Well, we're assuming she doesn't have one, but she didn't have keys for one on her. And did you notice everything in the apartment was purchased from stores within walking distance?"

"Yeah, I realized the same thing. So, you think she flew into town from somewhere else?"

"I know she did," Jules said, her voice firm.

"How?"

Becky felt a tap on her shoulder and turned to find Bryan hovering over her wine glass with the bottle from the refrigerator.

"Need a refill?" he asked.

Her husband was so good to her, and Becky felt awful for making him worry. She gave an enthusiastic nod and held her thumb and index finger about two inches apart.

He poured the wine, then leaned over and kissed her—his way of diluting the tension from earlier. Becky didn't begrudge him for being worried about her. In the past few months, they'd been through more than what most couples face in a lifetime.

She mouthed *I love you,* then realized Jules was already in the middle of her explanation. She'd missed the beginning.

Becky interrupted her mid-sentence. "Wait, how do you know she flew here?"

Jules let out an exasperated sigh that she needed to repeat herself. "Her trash, Beck. I didn't find any evidence she dyed her hair at the apartment, but then I started thinking. That suitcase she had was too big to carry on, so if she'd flown, she would have needed to check it. I didn't see a tag, but maybe she took that off at the airport when she landed and tossed it.

But they also put that little sticker on your luggage when you check it."

Becky tried to protest as Bryan began to clear the table around her.

He held up his hand. "I got this. Go ahead and finish your call."

Becky offered him an appreciative smile and possessively pulled her wine glass toward her so he wouldn't take it with the rest of the dishes.

"I didn't notice anything. Was the sticker there?" she asked Jules. "On Brittany's suitcase?"

"It wasn't. Not on the suitcase anyway. But it *was* in the trash."

"Oh, good work." Becky sipped her wine. "Did you find out where she flew from?"

"Well, it *might* have provided that information," Jules said. "But it seems Brittany didn't want to take any chances someone might see it and figure out where she came from. The sticker was ripped to shreds, and all the pieces were stuck together. It looks like she actually gouged out the flight information before she tore it up."

Becky propped her elbow on the table and rested her head in her hand. "Wow. I guess now we know she's not from around here."

"Or at least she's not local. She could have flown from Miami or Tampa. Even Orlando. It doesn't necessarily mean she's not from Florida."

Becky sighed. "So, it didn't really tell us much."

"Not true," Jules said, singing the words. "It told us Brittany *really* didn't want anyone to know where she came from."

"I guess you're right about that."

When Becky glanced up, Bryan was back.

"Did you ask Jules about this weekend?"

She cringed and held the tips of her fingers to her forehead. "With everything that happened, I completely forgot."

"What's he talking about? What's this weekend?" Jules asked.

"Bryan decided to plan a little party for my birthday."

He gestured for Becky to hand him her phone. She wondered for a moment if it was her husband's way of seizing an opportunity to grill Jules about the guest she had staying in her townhouse. She needn't have worried. Bryan was all business, his focus on the party.

"Hey, Jules," he said. "Tell Tim we need a Pictionary rematch. I'm sure they're busy getting ready for the wedding, but can you also see if Jonas and Erin can come?" Bryan paused, his lips pressed together before he bobbed his head. "Sure, that's fine. The more, the merrier, I suppose." Another pause. "That would be great. I'm thinking around seven." The corners of his mouth tugged upward into a slight smile. "You'll have to ask your best friend if Gene's invited. Here she is."

"It's not like Sherlock's going to hang out with us anyway," Jules said before Becky could use her socially awkward cat as an excuse.

Jules wasn't wrong. He was never around for their parties, preferring instead the safety he found underneath Becky's bed.

"It's fine. Gene's part of the family."

"It's just easier to bring him with us than to have to wonder what I might find when I get home." Jules let out a soft groan.

Becky knew the rambunctious golden retriever was still acclimating to his new situation. Her best friend had vented loudly about losing a few pairs of shoes, her one vice. Her one *expensive* vice.

"I warned Brittany about his shoe fetish," Jules said with a laugh. "By the way, Bryan said it was fine if she came to the party. After what happened today, I wouldn't want to leave her alone anyway."

"Of course." It would be a good chance for Bryan to meet their new client. Maybe then he'd understand Brittany was simply lost and needed someone to help her. "You'll also call Jonas?"

"He's actually coming over tonight. I want to talk to him about all this stuff with Brittany."

"Good idea."

"I also realized something else," Jules said. "When I didn't find any hair dye in her garbage, I figured she might have colored and cut her hair before she left wherever she came from. We know the photo on her driver's license matches."

"What are you thinking?" Becky asked.

"Well, we know her license was issued a few days before she ended up in the hospital."

"Okay. So, Brittany obviously dyed her hair before the photo was taken," Becky said. "Either before she got here, or she could have even gone to a salon when she arrived."

"Right. But if the police are right, and Brittany Mullins *isn't* her real name, then how did she get a license with that name?" Jules asked. "And more importantly, if she didn't have it before she got here, then what name did she fly under?"

"We're assuming the police were right that it's not her real identity. Maybe it is. Tomorrow at the office—"

"Oh, hey, I have to go," Jules said abruptly, and Becky assumed it was because Brittany was now out of the shower. "I'll see you in the morning. Oh, I guess *we'll* see you. Obviously, she's going to have to come with me."

The tone of Jules's voice turned serious. "Until we figure out who that guy was at her apartment today, we can't let Brittany out of our sight."

CHAPTER SIX

BRITTANY KICKED off the sandals Jules had given her and reveled in the plush carpet between her toes. Then, she eyed the queen-sized bed. Plump pillows. A fluffy blanket folded at the bottom. She ran her hand over the soft quilt and released a contented sigh. After her time in the hospital, it all felt positively luxurious.

She hadn't mentioned it to Jules yet, but the detective on her case had stopped by before she'd been released. Brittany wasn't sure why he'd bothered. It wasn't like he had anything new to report on her case.

The words Jules had spoken at her apartment replayed in Brittany's head. *We think there's the possibility you were running from someone. And if they already found you once and hurt you…*

Her stomach lurched at the idea she might have been specifically targeted. She'd never considered her attack wasn't just a robbery or random mugging. Brittany groaned in frustration. Why couldn't she remember anything?

At this point, she needed to focus on getting her memory back so she could go home—wherever that might be. And if it turned out that was the very place she was running from, at least she'd remember *why* she'd left. She needed to know the truth.

If nothing else, at least her DNA results would help Jules and Becky figure out who she was. *Someone* had to be out there looking for her. Brittany's throat grew tight, and her eyes filled with tears. Becky and Jules didn't even know her, and yet, they'd offered to help, even giving her a place to stay. She didn't even have the money to pay them yet.

Jules had carried her suitcase up the two sets of stairs and set it inside the bedroom door. "All yours," she'd said before she left Brittany to unpack and shower.

She pulled her suitcase to an open area between the bed and closet and sat in front of it. At the apartment, Becky had helped her pack what little she had.

Brittany rooted through the contents until she found what she was looking for. The framed photograph. As she held it in her hands, she studied it. Was she imagining there was a similarity in the eyes, the mouth? If she had a sister, why wasn't she looking for Brittany?

When she stared at the picture, she now felt something stir inside her. A feeling of peace. Contentment. Was the emotion real? Or was it because Brittany could see genuine happiness in the faces of the women in the picture. It felt contagious, almost like she could pull their joy from the photo and claim it as her own. And why couldn't she? One of those women *was* her, and aside from her hair being different, it didn't look like it had been taken that long ago.

Brittany uncrossed her legs, stood, and set the photo beside the small alarm clock on the nightstand. She was prepared to stare at it until it triggered her to remember something—anything—about who or what had been responsible for the wide smile she wore the day it was taken.

She slid open the closet doors and assessed the situation. It was mostly empty. Hangers ready for her to use hung evenly on a bar beside what looked like a few winter coats pushed all the way to the far end. A few plastic storage bins were tucked on one side, and shoeboxes were lined up in a row on the long shelf above the clothes bar. Brittany's mouth dropped open when she noted the price tag affixed to one of the boxes. Apparently, Jules was a girl with expensive taste in footwear. And she'd just *given* a pair to Brittany. She hurried to retrieve the shoes she'd left haphazardly strewn on the carpet and set them nicely on the floor in the closet.

She had everything she owned hung up in a few minutes. It wasn't much, but she'd have to make do with what she had. There was no money to buy anything new.

She moved her toiletries to the bathroom, accessible not only from her room but also from the hallway. The hospital shower had left much to be desired, and Brittany was ready to wash the entire experience off her.

She pulled out the running sneakers from her suitcase and set them on the floor of the closet beside the other shoes she'd brought. She'd put her dirty laundry in a grocery bag at the apartment, and all that was left were socks, underwear, and bras.

Brittany felt uncomfortable rummaging around in Jules's dresser to make room, but her shoulders relaxed when she slid open the top drawer. There was nothing in it.

She flipped the lid of her suitcase closed, but as she reached for the zipper, she hesitated. Brittany opened it again and ran her hand into the pouches gathered on the sides like Jules had done at the apartment. Then she slipped her fingers behind them and frowned when they touched something. It felt like a small plastic bag secured out of sight with heavy-duty tape.

Brittany was grateful Jules hadn't found it, but dread pushed down on her as she tugged on it. If it was drugs, they'd go immediately into the toilet. She'd flush whatever she found rather than take the chance Jules might throw her out.

Her pulse sped up at the sight of the small baggie, its contents wrapped in a piece of folded paper towel. Heart pounding, Brittany used two fingers to pull out the tiny bundle. She stole a quick glance at the open door, then unwrapped it on the carpet in front of her. Relief whooshed out of her in a loud puff of air. It wasn't drugs.

With a thoughtful gaze, she held the wedding band and engagement ring between her thumb and index finger. The diamond wasn't quite the rock Jules was sporting, but the set suggested Brittany was married. Or had been married. She dug the fingertips of her other hand into the back of her neck as she stared at them. For all she knew, they could have been someone else's rings. It wasn't like she had any recollection of how she'd gotten them. Or from who.

She slid both of them onto the ring finger of her left hand. They were a perfect fit. As she held out her hand in front of her, the modest diamond on the engagement ring sparkled as it caught the light. It was pretty, but Brittany felt nothing. Who had proposed with this engagement ring? Slipped the wedding band on her finger at an alter? She couldn't ignore the fact that they'd been deliberately hidden in her suitcase. Why was that?

Brittany heard Jules's suspicion echo again in her head that she was running away from someone. Maybe it *was* her husband. Why else would she have hidden her rings?

She slipped them off her finger, rewrapped them in the piece of paper towel, and slid them back inside the tiny plastic bag. Her gaze drifted around the room as she looked for someplace safe to stash them. She finally settled on the pocket of one of Jules's winter coats.

Even though it was November, it hadn't been cold enough in North Florida for a heavy jacket. Brittany hadn't realized it while lying in that hospital bed, but the weather outside was beautiful. It felt odd to consider it was already November. Did that mean Brittany wasn't used to the warm temperatures at this time of year? Maybe she wasn't even from Florida.

Brittany patted the pocket of Jules's jacket, needing reassurance the rings were still there. If she had no choice, she might be able to pawn or sell them if she needed money. It wasn't like she felt an emotional attachment to them or the person who'd given them to her. That might have been true even before she lost her memory. After all, it wasn't like she'd been wearing them when she was found.

Maybe she'd known she was being followed. Was it possible she'd made the conscious decision to take them off and hide them? If they'd been on her finger, they probably would have been stolen by the person who bashed her over the head.

Brittany let out a frustrated moan as she turned on the water in the shower. While she waited for it to warm up, she stared at her reflection in the bathroom mirror over the sink. She tipped her head down and scrutinized her roots. She could see the hair growing in was blond. There wasn't much, so the dye job must have been recent. But again, why? Why would she have changed the color of her hair?

Brittany leaned in and scrutinized her reflection. The date of birth on her driver's license meant she was twenty-five years old, but she couldn't deny she looked older. Faint wrinkles around her eyes, the beginning of a crease between her eyebrows.

She stepped back so she could see her entire body. Despite her apparent diet of fast food, it appeared she'd been in shape when she was hurt. Her legs and arms were still somewhat toned, though she imagined she'd lost some of that lying around in a hospital bed. It still seemed plausible she had the build of a runner, so maybe what she'd packed did offer a slight hint to her past.

And that doll. Did that mean somewhere Brittany had a

child? A little girl who was missing the toy she'd buried under a stack of T-shirts in her suitcase. She didn't feel like a mother, and it horrified her to think she could forget having a child along with everything else. Even if she was running away from her husband, what kind of mother could leave her daughter behind?

Brittany needed to get her memory back—to know why she'd abandoned her life. It appeared it had included a husband. Maybe even a child who had to be wondering why her mommy had left her.

At the very least, she'd been reassured Becky and Jules felt confident they'd be able to use her DNA results to confirm her identity. And if Brittany did have a daughter, seeing her again would certainly trigger memories of the life they'd had together. How could it not?

She pulled back the shower curtain and stepped in. As the hot water washed away the weeks in the hospital, a new feeling swept over Brittany.

She almost didn't recognize it.

It was hope.

CHAPTER SEVEN

JULES HOVERED over the saucepan as she waited for the water to boil.

"Are you a big tea drinker?"

She wheeled around to find Brittany in the robe she'd left for her, her wet hair wrapped in a towel.

She gestured at the counter. "That's a lot of tea bags."

"I'm actually making sweet tea. Have you ever—" Jules caught herself. "Sorry. Well, whether you remember having it or not, you've never tasted tea like mine."

It was a southern thing. Jules had gone to college in Georgia and lived in the sorority house her junior and senior years. She'd begged and begged, and finally, the house mother had relented and shared her secret for making the tea Jules loved.

Brittany adjusted the towel on her head. "If the trash can at my apartment is any indication, my guess is I'm a heavy soda drinker."

The water came to a rolling boil, and Jules turned the knob to shut off the burner.

"Well, there's always Diet Coke in my refrigerator if you'd rather have that."

She moved the saucepan to the other side of the stove. One by one, she dunked each tea bag in the water, then left them submerged and hanging over the edge of the pot by their strings. Jules set the timer on the microwave.

"There's good tea, and then there's this. It's all about how long you steep the tea bags." Jules turned and rolled her eyes. "But if I could tell you how easily I get distracted and how much tea I've ruined." She waved at the timer counting down. "Hence the reminder." She pulled a nearly empty pitcher from her refrigerator and rinsed it in the sink. "How was your shower?"

Brittany stuffed her hands into the pockets of the robe and released a soft moan. "Amazing. The ones at the hospital …" She cringed and gave her head a quick shake. "Just awful."

"I'll bet. You found the basket of stuff I left for you?"

"Yeah, you thought of everything." Brittany ran her hand up the sleeve of the robe she wore and smiled. "This is so soft. Feels like a little slice of heaven." Her expression grew serious. "I really appreciate you offering to let me stay here. Not that I didn't think I was safe at the apartment, but it's nice to have company. I mean, if I didn't have a job to go to, what was I planning to do all day? Maybe I was supposed to start looking for one?"

"You don't need to worry about that for right now. You're still recuperating." Jules reached into the cupboard and pulled out a sack of sugar. "By the way, Becky called Dr. Summers and told him you were staying here." She dumped a healthy amount into the pitcher and then spun around. "To be honest, I think he was a little relieved you weren't going to be alone."

Brittany slid into a chair at the kitchen table. "Did he confirm he sent my DNA tests?"

"Yup. He sent them the day you provided your saliva."

Brittany exhaled loudly and leaned her forearms on the table. "Okay, good. I hope the results come soon."

"It does take a little bit, but at least they're out the door." Jules sank down into the chair across from her. "You have everything you need up there?"

"Almost everything. I looked through my suitcase, but either I didn't have a blow dryer, or I left it in the bathroom at the apartment."

"Oh, no problem." Jules glanced at the time remaining on the microwave timer as she stood. "You can borrow mine. I'll get it for you."

As Brittany followed her up the stairs, Jules groaned. "At least it's a good workout going up and down these, right?"

Her townhouse was three levels. She convinced herself regularly that her endless trips from floor to floor meant she didn't need a gym membership.

"Yeah, I'm starting to realize that," Brittany said as they reached the top. "What's on the bottom level?"

"My office and a little photography studio. Since we opened the detective agency, I don't do quite as much, but I do have a job this weekend, so you can come with me."

Brittany eyed the framed photographs in the hallway. "Are these yours?"

Jules smiled proudly. The walls of her entire townhouse were lined with her favorites. "Yeah, mostly everything you see is mine. Give me a minute, and I'll bring you the blow dryer."

The exceptions in Jules's decorating graced the pristine white walls of her bedroom. This is where her most personal memories resided for her to relish in the life she'd made for herself. Candid shots from Becky's wedding where Jules had been the maid of honor. The oil painting her birth mother, Barb, had given her. Newly framed pictures from the magical night at the beach where Tim had asked her to marry him.

Jules pulled her blow dryer from the cabinet under the sink in the master bathroom.

The bathroom attached to Brittany's bedroom was also accessible from the hallway, but that door was closed. Jules rapped softly on the bedroom door instead.

"Come on in," Brittany called out. She was near the closet pulling on a pair of shorts that complemented her long, lean legs.

Jules tossed the blow dryer on the bed. "You can leave it in the cabinet under your vanity when you're done. We'll have to share it, so maybe leave the door to the hallway open when you're not using the bathroom."

She gave an approving nod when she noticed Brittany had the framed photo they'd found displayed on the nightstand. "I'm glad you brought this with you."

"I figured it can't hurt, right? Maybe if I stare at it long enough, I'll remember who she is. But you were right about my hair. It was so pretty. Why *would* I dye it?" Brittany came around the bed toward Jules and let out a yelp. "Ow." She lifted the hem of her shorts and rubbed at an abrasion on her leg.

Jules winced. "Ouch. That'll leave a mark." She tucked the bottom of the quilt on the bed behind the footboard so that the offending corner was now clearly visible. "I swear I've done that too many times to count in here, and I always end up with a huge bruise. You want some ice for your leg, so it doesn't turn black and blue?"

Brittany gave a slight nod. Then, with her hand poised over the red mark on her leg, she froze and stared off thoughtfully.

"Hey, you okay?" Jules didn't think she'd bumped the bed *that* hard, and the quilt should have buffered it, at least a little bit.

Brittany took in a deep breath and aimed her chin at the bed. "From that, yeah. But something—I don't know. For a second, I felt like I remembered something." Her shoulders lifted almost apologetically. "Maybe I've just always been clumsy."

"That had nothing to do with you being clumsy. It's a design flaw in the bed, and I never remember to tuck the quilt in. Every single time I clean in here, I hit that same corner too." Jules gave Brittany's arm a reassuring pat. "I just always pin the blame on the furniture company. But still, it would be a good thing if you were starting to remember things. Even if it means a little bump, right?"

"Yeah. Maybe it will reverse the one to my head." Brittany rubbed at the mark on her leg as she stared out the window, a deep divot between her eyebrows.

"My brother Jonas is coming over, so when he gets here, we'll order in something for dinner." Jules bit back a smile. "Sweet tea is my specialty, but that's about it. If you wanted a home-cooked meal, you would have been better off staying with Becky. Her husband, Bryan, is a great cook. I guess when I get married, I'll have to figure out something so my new husband doesn't starve."

"I noticed your ring." Brittany reached for Jules's left hand and held it up to study it. "It's gorgeous."

Jules couldn't help but smile. "It is, isn't it?"

"When's the wedding?"

"We haven't picked a date yet. We only got engaged last month." Jules's pulse quickened. She loved Tim and had been thrilled when he proposed. Still, her insecurity hadn't abated entirely in finding the story behind her adoption. She needed more time to work through it. "Actually, Jonas's wedding is first. It's coming up in a few weeks." She forced a smile. "Then, I guess Tim, my fiancé, and I will have to dive in and start planning." Jules strolled toward the bedroom door. "He's a great guy."

"What's he do? Is he a photographer too?"

"Tim?" Jules laughed at the idea. "He barely takes pictures with his cell phone. He's a sales rep for a sporting goods company. He even sells stuff to the NFL teams, but his dream is to open his own store someday."

"A man with a dream," Brittany said with an appreciative nod of her head. "I can't wait to meet him."

"You might get the chance soon enough. He's playing basketball tonight, but he'll probably stop by before his game."

In the doorway, Jules spun back around. "Oh, just a heads up. We share a dog, so he'll probably drop him off. You'll love Gene. He has a thing for shoes, though, so keep your bedroom door closed, and you should be fine." She let out a deep sigh. "I've lost a few of my favorites. That dog's lucky that I absolutely adore him."

"His name is Gene?"

Jules leaned her shoulder against the doorframe. "Yeah, he's our official DNA detective mascot. My new aunt volunteers for the golden retriever rescue, so Tim and I adopted him about a month ago."

Brittany tilted her head and gave Jules a curious stare. "New aunt?"

"That's a *whole* other story." Jules heard the sound of her timer beeping downstairs, and she thumped the palm of her hand against the back of Brittany's door. "I'll fill you in when we have more time. Go ahead and dry your hair, and I'll get you some ice."

Jules finished making her tea and set the pitcher back in the refrigerator so it could chill. She'd just reached into the freezer when she heard the doorbell.

Jonas frowned when she answered the door. "Everything okay?"

Jules followed his concerned gaze to the ice pack in her hand. "Oh, yeah. It's not for me. Brittany banged her leg on the bed in the guest bedroom. She just got out of the hospital, so I'm trying to not make it look like we're abusing her here too —" Jules stopped herself. Jonas had taught them not to make assumptions when they were working on a case. Right now, they didn't have evidence of anything, much less proof she'd been abused. "Anyway, come on in."

As they made it to the second floor, Brittany came down the stairs from her bedroom. She gave a half-hearted wave, and Jules noticed her hair was still damp.

"You must be Jules's brother."

He lifted his hand to greet her. "Yup. I'm Jonas. It's nice to meet you."

"I'm Brittany." She shrugged. "At least that's the name I'm going with for now until I can figure out who I really am."

Jonas put his arm around his sister's shoulder. "Well, with Jules and Becky on your side, you're in good hands."

Jules smiled as she glanced up at him. "We decided on Chinese food, right?"

When Jonas nodded, she headed into the kitchen to dig up the menu that had been stapled to the bag the last time she and Tim ordered from the new place around the corner.

She brought it to Brittany to take a look. "Is there anything specific you like?"

Her face went blank as she stared at all the options. "Um, I have no idea."

Jules brought her hand to her forehead. "Oh, duh. I'll get better at this, I swear. I'll just get a bunch of different dishes. We can all share."

After Jules placed the order, Jonas grabbed a water bottle from the refrigerator and dropped into a chair at the kitchen table.

"So, you're the cop?" Brittany asked as she claimed the seat next to Jules.

"Yeah. I hear you've had a bit of a rough time." Jonas

twisted the top off his bottle and took a swig. "Any movement on your case?"

Brittany shifted in her seat and turned to Jules. "I forgot to tell you. The detective came by the hospital before I left, so I gave him my new cell number." Her gaze drifted around the kitchen, then she pushed back her chair and stood. "But now I have no idea what I did with that phone."

Jules waved her hand dismissively. "We'll find it later. Don't worry, it's here somewhere.

Jonas attempted to reel Brittany back in. "So, what did the detective say?"

With one last fleeting glance into the living room, Brittany sat back down. "I guess they checked some surveillance cameras near the shopping center, but they didn't find anything useful. Apparently, I purchased the phone right before I was attacked."

"And there were no witnesses?" Jonas asked.

"Only the lady who called 911, but she told them she didn't see what actually happened. She just saw me afterward. You know, on the ground."

"Well, at least she found you and called for help." Jules considered Brittany's empty wallet. "Does the detective think it was a robbery?"

Brittany nodded. "He thinks that's the strongest possibility. Especially since I was found with no money, no credit cards, nothing of any real value. He did say they have one more shot at finding some footage, but it's been a few weeks, so I'm not holding out much hope."

Jonas's eyes narrowed. He rolled his water bottle between the palms of his hands as he stared off.

Jules knew that look. His cop's brain was formulating a theory.

"What are you thinking?" she asked.

"I'm wondering how someone would even know she had

something worth stealing." He turned to Brittany. "You said you bought a phone?"

She nodded. "Right. I had it on me when I was found. It was one of those pre-paid ones, but it wasn't even activated yet."

"What about the receipt?"

"It was in the bag with the phone."

"Do you still have it?" he asked.

Jules laughed. "See, this is why I said to save everything because you never know when you might need it."

Brittany was already out of her chair. "I'm pretty sure I brought it with me. Let me go look."

She was back a few minutes later and laid the receipt on the table.

Jonas's head bobbed as he scanned it. "Okay, you paid with cash."

"Right," Jules said with a nod. "We knew that. Maybe Brittany didn't have any credit cards to steal. In fact, we also found a receipt for some bedding she bought for her apartment. She used cash to buy that too."

Jonas slid the receipt toward Jules as Brittany peered over her shoulder. "Look at the amount tendered." He used his index finger to point to the bottom of the paper. "One hundred dollars, which wasn't close to the total of her purchase. That means Brittany must have paid with a hundred-dollar bill. Maybe someone saw her at the register and figured there might be more where that came from." He leaned back in his chair. "The address of that store isn't exactly a great part of town. It wouldn't take much to convince some thug it's worth checking to see how much more she's got."

"Do you think it was a robbery that went too far?" Brittany asked. "Maybe I resisted, and that's how I got knocked to the ground."

"I think it's possible." Jonas looked her straight in the eye.

"But if so, it's a pretty big coincidence you managed to get yourself mugged."

She frowned and traded a nervous glance with Jules. "What do you mean?"

Jonas's shoulders hitched up as he lifted his hands into the air. "There's no evidence you had or used a credit card. You bought a prepaid phone using cash which makes it almost impossible to trace." He gave Brittany a knowing stare. "I'm a cop. For me, I now have to wonder if you've got something you're trying to hide."

Jonas had taught Jules and Becky well. They had both made the same assumption.

"You were making a pretty concerted effort to make sure you didn't leave a trail." He pursed his lips as his gaze volleyed between Jules and Brittany. "I guess what you both need to figure out is *why*."

CHAPTER EIGHT

Becky pushed open their office door and flipped the switch to turn on the lights.

Brittany lifted her eyebrows and smiled. "So, this is where all the detective stuff happens." She followed Jules inside and stopped at the reception desk, empty except for a massive flower arrangement. "Wow, look at those."

"A former client sent them. Her way of saying thank you to both of us for solving her case." It was almost time to toss them. Becky had been so touched when they were delivered, she hated to see them go.

Brittany leaned down to smell the flowers. "If I remembered the floral deliveries of my past, I'm sure this would be the biggest one I've ever seen. Did you find her a rich relative or something?"

"Something like that." Becky had also almost lost her life in the process, but as she walked toward her desk in the back, she kept that to herself.

She gestured at the guest chair as she slid her laptop out of the black leather computer bag she'd brought.

Brittany dropped into the chair in front of Becky's desk.

"Hey, maybe I'm rich too. Wouldn't that be a nice surprise?"

"You never know," Jules said.

"So, where do we start?" Brittany asked, her gaze drifting between the two women. "I mean, obviously, you don't have my DNA results yet. Is there anything you can do while we wait?"

Jules moved to the whiteboard. She picked up a marker and nodded at Becky. "Let's write down what we know and what we think we know."

She then wrote *driver's license information* on the board and underlined it.

"Okay, so the name on your license. Brittany Mullins. We'll do some research and see what we can find out." Jules eyed Brittany. "Did the police tell you why they thought your license was fake?"

"They didn't say it was *fake*. At least I don't think so." Brittany ran her hand over her face. "Sorry, some of my time in the hospital is a blur. Maybe they assumed it was because I didn't have anything else on me with that name when I was found."

Becky spoke up. "Except a library card."

Jules tapped the end of the marker against her lips and nodded. "It's worth adding." She wrote *library card* on the board.

"It's still possible whoever attacked me stole whatever else I had," Brittany said. "Just because I didn't use a credit card to buy the phone and the bedding doesn't mean I didn't have one at some point."

Jules nodded, but it was half-hearted. "Well, we know the license was issued a few days after you moved into the apartment, and that's the address listed on it. You said the police couldn't find a record of you having a license before this one, which seems odd. Maybe they just meant in Florida? Is that possible?"

Brittany pinched her lips together as she stared at the board. "I guess. Like I said, they gave me a lot of medication in the hospital. It made me a little loopy sometimes."

"Well, if you had a license from another state, you would have needed to surrender it to get one here. It's not farfetched to think you'd get a Florida license with your new address if you just moved here. I think you're supposed to do it within thirty days if you plan on driving."

"So, you think I'm from somewhere else?" Brittany asked.

Becky waited to see if Jules would mention the sticker from the suitcase.

Instead, she gave nothing away, merely lifting her shoulders in a noncommittal shrug. "Not sure."

Becky kept the information to herself since Jules didn't bring it up. They had no idea where the flight originated, so it wasn't like it offered much help anyway.

"We just need to consider all the possible reasons why you might have gotten a new license. We like to start all our cases being open-minded, right, Beck?" Jules shot her a familiar look.

When her partner made a comment like that, Becky knew she was expected to pipe in with support. "Right. One of the important things Jules and I have learned since we opened the agency is to never assume. We try to let the evidence *lead* us somewhere rather than use it to back up a theory we might start with."

"Exactly." Jules's enthusiastic nodding told Becky she had hit the nail perfectly on the head. "We want to explore every possible option that exists. Not make any assumptions."

Becky bit back a smile. Her best friend had a way of dissecting their cases with a fine-tooth comb.

"The ID could have been fake. Or stolen." Jules wrote the words *fake* and *stolen* on the board under where she'd written *driver's license*.

Brittany scooted forward in her chair, her lips pushed into a pout.

Becky noted the expression on her face and patted her arm. "It's nothing personal. Like Jules said, we need to explore every possibility."

"It's like using DNA to figure out an answer about someone's relatives. You use the DNA to lead you, but there's almost always more than one possibility of how someone's related. The obvious answer isn't always the right one." Jules nodded at Becky. "Remember Elise?"

Becky remembered her well. Her results had provided a huge learning curve when they first started out. "One of our first adoption cases was for a woman who had a DNA match named Elise," she explained to Brittany. "When you look at how much DNA two people share, there's usually more than one possibility for how they're related. So, you usually want to look at other clues to try and figure out which relationship is the most likely. In that case, when we looked at the age difference, it seemed our client and Elise were most likely first cousins once removed."

Brittany's forehead creased. "What's that?"

"That means one of our client's birthparents and Elise were first cousins. The removed part means our client was one generation removed from Elise, which fell in line with the difference in their ages."

Jules piped in. "So, since our client was adopted and looking for her birth parents, that would be a great match, especially if Elise knew all her first cousins. One of them would be our client's birth mother or father." She rubbed her hands together. "Easy peasy, right? Case solved."

Becky laughed. "We thought so at first, but boy, we were wrong. It turned out the dad who raised Elise wasn't actually her biological father."

Brittany's face screwed up in confusion. "So, what does that mean?"

Becky had also been lost when Jules became obsessed with her own DNA results, but now it seemed so straightforward. She had to remember that not everyone understood all the implications she had learned over the last year.

"Our client was actually related to Elise on her *paternal* side," Becky said. "But since Elise had no idea who her biological dad really was ..."

Brittany bobbed her head. "Oh, I get it. So, she couldn't really help your client the way you thought."

"Right, but luckily, Elise decided she wanted answers too. She shared her results with us so we could help determine who her biological father really was." Becky cringed as she remembered the awkward phone call she and Jules had needed to place. "We discovered he was *twenty-five* years older than Elise's mother. So, even though it didn't appear Elise was old enough to be *two* generations from our client, she turned out to be her half-great aunt and not a cousin."

"She was actually a half-sibling to our client's *grandmother*, even though she was only thirty years older than our client," Jules said when Brittany still looked confused. "Elise's birth father got her mom pregnant right about the time his other kids were making him a grandfather."

"Right," Becky said, studying Brittany's face to see if she understood. "Elise's mother and biological father are both deceased, so she has no idea how it happened. Her mom was married at the time, and Elise said she didn't even drive."

Brittany cracked a smile. "They figured it out somehow."

Becky's face grew serious. "Maybe it wasn't even consensual. We'll never know. DNA doesn't lie, but it can't always tell you the story behind *how* the truth came to be. Hopefully, we'll be able to use your results to figure out your biological identity, but we may also have to find people from your past to help explain the life you had."

Brittany set her elbow on Becky's desk and rested her head in her hand as if all the DNA talk was exhausting her. "Maybe my results will prove the police are wrong. It's not like they found out the real Brittany Mullins is someone else."

Jules nodded. "Okay, you're absolutely right. Until we find out why they're so convinced it can't be your real identity, we'll add that to the list." She wheeled around to face the board again and added *identity is accurate*.

"Is it also possible Mullins is your maiden name or a married name you don't use anymore?" Becky asked. "You know, like maybe you got divorced and went back to your maiden name, but everything else is still in your married name."

"It's a possibility." Jules wrote *maiden/married name* on the board. "Anything else?"

Brittany held her head in both hands now as she studied the board. "The name on my license is either me, or it's not." She groaned. "Sorry, that's pretty obvious. What I mean is the picture next to the name is definitely me. So, if I'm not really Brittany Mullins, there had to be a reason why I used a fake name." She sat straight up as if it was all coming together for her. "Maybe you're right. Maybe I *was* hiding from someone."

Becky thought for a moment back to the driver's license Peyton had. She'd fooled DMV, but there was no way that was a possibility this time. It couldn't be.

As if reading her mind, Jules gave her head a quick shake in Becky's direction. "Let's not assume anything. There's also the possibility your license was up for renewal which could explain the recent date on it." She added *renewal* to the board. "Though I'm not sure it would get you a new photo. Maybe it does if you show up in person and you don't renew through the mail."

"If we're exploring all the options, there could very well be a valid reason why you never had a driver's license before,"

Becky said. "You could have lived in a city where there was mass transit or a subway system where you didn't need to drive. I'm sure there's plenty of people who live in New York City who never bother to get their license."

Brittany wrinkled her brow as she considered it. "I guess that's possible. It's not like I had keys to a car. At least not when I was found."

"It would almost have to be something like that," Jules said thoughtfully. "Otherwise, it would be hard to believe you're a first-time driver at your age." She hesitated. "Your license says your date of birth is January 21st, 1996, which makes you twenty-five."

Brittany pursed her lips. "Maybe that's why the police thought …" An awkward silence followed.

Becky decided to state the obvious. They wouldn't get anywhere by beating around the bush. "I think it's fair to say you don't *look* that young, but hey, anything's possible."

"True, and if you're not really Brittany Mullins, maybe if we can figure out who is, that will also help." Jules wrote the date of birth from the driver's license on the board. "If you were trying to run away from a bad situation, someone could have helped you. They could be the connection to the identity you decided to use."

"I still don't feel like I was running away from someone." Brittney lifted a shoulder helplessly. "I guess my bad memory doesn't count for much." She slumped in her chair. "It's my life, and yet, I'm utterly useless."

"That's why you have us. Don't worry, we'll figure it out." Jules turned to Becky. "Can you pull up the requirements for getting a driver's license for the first time?"

Becky typed into the search bar of her computer and reported back. "An original birth certificate or passport, proof of social security, and two documents verifying residential address."

"Like an apartment lease?" Jules asked.

Becky nodded. "That's one of the options. There's a long list to choose from, but I don't think most of these would apply." Her eyes traveled down her computer screen. "Oh, here's one she could have used. A work order for utilities."

"Well, we know the electricity was on in the apartment because the lights worked. What else is required?" Jules asked.

Becky glanced back down at the website. "Just the written tests which can be taken online and the road course test."

Jules wrote the information on the board and then aimed a shrug in Brittany's direction. "If you had all that, they'd print your new license at the DMV, and you'd be on your way."

Becky's brow furrowed. "But if she's not really Brittany Mullins, how would she have the documentation she needed?"

Jules dipped her chin with a knowing smile. "Exactly." She tapped the end of the marker against her lips as she turned back to the board. "Let's think about your library card."

"What about it?" Brittany asked, looking confused.

"Good call, Jules," Becky said, nodding. "It's possible someone at the library might remember you. Just because we didn't find any books at your apartment doesn't mean you didn't spend time there. You obviously got a card for a reason."

"Right," Jules said. "We'll see if there's one near your apartment and check it out. What other clues do we have to work with?"

Brittany shook her head. "There isn't anything else."

The corners of Jules's mouth tugged upward. "Not true. What about the keys you had? Do you have them on you?"

"Yeah." Brittany reached into her new purse, pulled out the keyring, and dropped it in the palm of Jules's outstretched hand.

Jules held them up by the smallest key. "I think the police were right. This definitely looks like the key to a safety deposit box. Let's make a list of all the potential places you could have gotten it from. We'll make a hit list and start checking. Even if you only go into one or two a day, maybe we'll get lucky."

She handed the keys back to Brittany and returned to the whiteboard. She started a new column that read *safety deposit box key list*.

"What about this other key?" Brittany held up a larger key. "This isn't one of the ones we used at the apartment."

Becky took it from her and studied it. "Looks like it fits some sort of padlock. Maybe you have a storage unit? If you moved from somewhere else, you must have stuff stored somewhere."

"I guess it's possible." Brittany eyed Jules, who was still standing at the whiteboard. "Should we make a list of those places too?"

"It's worth a try." Jules spun around and created a new column with *mystery key – storage unit* at the top. "We can try calling some near your apartment to see if you have an account. If we find one, I would think they'll give you the unit number." She gestured at the key Becky was holding. "And obviously, you have a way to get into it."

Brittany didn't look convinced. "I didn't see any bills for a storage unit."

"Well, maybe you pre-paid, like you did with the apartment rent," Jules said. "I'm not sure how long they give you if you stop paying, but eventually, they'll lock you out and sell your stuff."

Brittany's eyes went wide. "Are you kidding? My whole life could be in there."

"We're not even positive you have a storage unit, so don't panic yet," Becky said. "Besides, how far behind could you be? It hasn't been that long."

Jules made circles in the air with the marker. Becky knew she was trying to keep the conversation moving forward. She didn't want Brittany to get too bogged down worrying about a storage unit that might not exist.

"Okay, so, let's think about the stuff you brought with you. What about your clothes? Any clues there?" Jules asked.

"Everything was pretty generic, right?" Brittany eyed Becky, who'd helped her pack. "Nike sneakers. Old Navy T-shirts. I feel like I did have some stuff that seemed like it was for running, but who knows if that's why I had it."

"Those were expensive Nikes specific for jogging, and you did have that tank top for the 5K," Jules said. "The one with the cut-off sleeves. Both those clues seem to suggest you were a runner. A serious runner."

"Oh, yeah, I forgot about that."

Becky stared off as she tried to visualize the shirt. It had caught her attention when they packed. "It just said Lifesaver 5K. No date, no location. It looked like the bottom had been cut off, so maybe that's where that information was supposed to be. I remember the logo had a pink ribbon as one of the letters. Isn't that for breast cancer awareness?"

Jules nodded. "Usually. I think. We can do some research and see what we can find out about the logo." She fixed her gaze back on Brittany. "Did you bring anything else that might provide a clue?"

She seemed to hesitate before shaking her head. "Nothing that I can think of."

"What about her hair color?" Becky asked.

Jules's head tipped to one side. "What about it?"

"Well, you said you didn't find a box of dye in the trash at the apartment when you cleaned up." Becky's gaze shifted to Brittany. "Maybe you had an appointment somewhere local. It could be worth checking."

Jules pursed her lips as she seemed to be considering it. "I guess, though I'm not sure what it would tell us if we found the place where she had it done."

Brittany's eyebrows lifted. "Unless I paid with a credit card. Then we'd know they were stolen when I was attacked."

"Good point." Jules wrote the word *hairdresser* on the board and underlined it. "Might mean other things were taken from you too that night."

Becky remembered their conversation in the elevator at the hospital. *Maybe someone took something she had. It could be a huge piece of the puzzle, but how would we even know?*

Her thoughts were interrupted when Brittany nudged her arm. "If we find out where I had it done, do you think I could reverse it?" Her expression turned hopeful as she stared at Becky.

"Reverse it? You mean go back to being blond?" She exchanged a nervous glance with Jules.

Brittany's eyes pleaded with her. "It can't help me recover my memory if I look in the mirror and don't look like myself. Or what if I run into someone who might know who I am except I look different?"

Becky pressed her lips together as she considered her response. She didn't want Brittany to panic, but they weren't sure they wanted her to be recognized.

Jules piped in with the same thought before Becky could voice it. "But what if you dyed your hair because you didn't want anyone to think you looked familiar?"

Brittany's face fell with disappointment, but then she regrouped, her jaw set squarely with determination. "I'm staying with you now. No one would even know to look for me at your place."

Jules wasn't easily convinced. "I don't know. The guy at the apartment—"

"Who knows if he was even looking for me?" Brittany cut in without letting her finish. "I'd just moved in." Her gaze darted to Becky as if she hoped she'd lend support to her argument. "Maybe that guy you saw was looking for the person who lived there before me. Or maybe in the short time I lived there, I liked to stroll around naked, and he's just a creep." Brittany's voice escalated, her spine rigid as she perched on the edge of her seat.

Then she released a deep breath and stared down at her hands. "I just feel—when I look at that photograph I have, I feel *something*," she said in a soft voice. "I don't know what exactly, but it feels like an inkling of a memory." She brought her gaze up, a determined look in her eye as she challenged Jules. "I *need* to go back to being the person in that photograph, the woman I was before someone attacked me and stole my memory." Her eyes welled up. "Even if the only thing I have to hold onto is that I look like her again."

Becky's shoulders lifted as she shot a questioning gaze at her partner. "Jules …"

Jules let out a defeated sigh, then dipped her chin in agreement.

"Okay, we get it," she said. "I'm not sure how easy it will be to go back to being as blond as you were in that photo, but I can take you to my girl. If anyone can fix your hair, it's Amanda. She's amazing."

Brittany eked out a smile. "Thank you. I really appreciate it." Then her face fell. "I just realized I don't have any way to pay for it right now …"

Becky reached for her hand. "Don't worry about that. It's important you're happy with the way you look, and I can see where it could help your memory if at least your appearance was familiar." She was starting to hope they had answers sooner rather than later. Otherwise, Bryan was going to start questioning her credit card charges. "When's your follow-up appointment with Dr. Summers?"

"Next Tuesday at eleven."

She nodded. "Okay, with any luck, maybe you'll be able to tell him some of your memory is coming back by then."

CHAPTER NINE

"I FEEL bad getting you up early on a Saturday." Jules handed a cup of coffee to Brittany and gestured at the creamer and sugar she'd set on the table. She'd already been up for more than an hour to ensure she had everything ready for her photography job that day.

Brittany slipped into a kitchen chair and set about fixing her coffee the way she liked it. "It doesn't matter to me. Every day feels the same."

"I guess that's true." Jules refilled her own mug and chose the chair across from her. "You'll love the art fair. They close down the main road in this little town on the St. John's River. Rows and rows of white tents with all different kinds of art. People spend the day milling around, just checking everything out." Jules spooned sugar into her cup and poured a small shot of creamer. "There's lots of food, and the artists come from all over the country. Some of the same ones come back year after year."

"I like the eating part, but I don't know much about art." Brittany brought her mug to her lips and sipped her coffee. "I mean, I don't think I do."

"It's actually more fun than you'd think. Yes, there are some fancy pieces, but there's some inexpensive stuff too."

"So, you have to take pictures of the art?" Brittany asked.

Jules wrapped both hands around her UGA coffee cup and leaned back in her chair. "Before the festival, the artists submitted an entry within their specific category. You know, watercolors, oil paintings, sculptures. The committee chose the winners." Jules grinned. "That's where I come in. Today at the show, I'll photograph each of them with their winning piece. Plus, the festival also produces a catalog that's available afterward, which includes all the vendors. You know, in case anyone wants to refer back to an artist they saw that they liked. I need to take those photos too."

"Well, I'm up for wherever you're taking me." The corners of Brittany's mouth lifted into a wistful smile. "My social calendar's pretty open these days."

Jules glanced out the window above her kitchen sink. "Looks like perfect weather. Can you be ready to head out by nine?"

An hour later, Brittany reappeared in the kitchen, showered, dressed, and ready to go. She was right on time.

They made small talk as they drove, and Jules tried not to delve into anything too deep. They had a long day ahead of them, and she wanted Brittany to enjoy it.

"So, you never did explain what you meant about adopting Gene from your *new* aunt," Brittany said after their conversation hit a lull.

"Oh, right. Well, I was adopted when I was a few days old. It's always been a big part of me, not knowing where I came from or why I was given up." She glanced over at Brittany. "It almost cost me my relationship with Tim."

Her eyebrows shot up in surprise. "But he seems amazing."

"Oh, he absolutely is. It had nothing to do with him and everything to do with me." Jules shrugged and kept her eyes focused on the road. "I've always put on a good show that nothing bothers me, but it was always hanging over me—the not knowing where I came from. I think that's a big part of why I want to help you figure out your answers."

Brittany was silent for a moment. "Well, I appreciate it. Not that you had to go through feeling like that, but you and Tim are engaged now, so I guess it all turned out okay."

Jules's heartbeat quickened like it always did when she imagined everything working out for her. A little piece of her refused to believe she'd get the happy ending other people took for granted.

She didn't share that some of her insecurities were still unresolved. "Well, I did a DNA test and found my birth mother. Her name is Barb. Finding out the story behind my adoption went a long way toward lifting that burden I felt." She glanced over at Brittany. "When you meet her, you'll be shocked how much we look alike. And Jonas is Barb's son—so he's my half-brother—but don't let him hear you call him that." Jules laughed. "He always says he's just my brother because he doesn't do anything halfway. Which I have found to be absolutely true. Anyway, my Aunt Bonnie had a barbecue not too long ago to welcome me to the family. She volunteers for the golden retriever rescue."

Brittany bobbed her head. "Ah, so this is where Gene makes his way into the story."

"Yup." She smiled. "Tim and I are sharing him until we get married."

Just then, long rows of white tents came into view. Jules nodded at Brittany. "Can you reach into my purse by your feet? There should be a parking pass there so we can park up close."

She swung into a parking lot marked VIP and flashed the hangtag at the parking attendant. He looked too bored to do much more than glance in her direction before he waved her on. Jules hung the tag from her rearview mirror and pulled into a spot.

"Okay, ready?" she asked when she had her camera bag and the lenses she wanted to use. She clicked the button on her key fob to ensure the car was locked.

"Okay, so all the booths are numbered," Jules said as she handed Brittany a diagram of the festival. "I've highlighted the winning booths, so maybe you can help me make sure I don't miss any. For those, I need to make sure I have photos of the actual artists and their ribbons. The other booths are for the catalog, so I need a shot of the booth and their signage, which hopefully includes their contact information." Jules waved her hand in the direction of people milling around. "I also like to take some pictures of the crowd and people browsing. The festival will use them to promote next year's event."

Brittany nodded and glanced down at the paper in her hand. "Okay, so the first booth highlighted is number seven. It says first place watercolors."

Jules took quick shots of the first six booths but then stopped to introduce herself when they got to the winner. "Congratulations. I'm the photographer for the festival. Could I get a few shots of you with the piece you entered into the contest and your ribbon?"

"Sure. We come all the way from North Carolina for this festival." The artist pulled down the framed piece of art bearing the blue ribbon. She held it in her hands and posed, a proud smile on her face.

"That's beautiful," Brittany said as she stared at it. "I love the lighthouse."

"It's the Cape Hatteras lighthouse on the Outer Banks. You ever been there?" the woman asked.

A flush grew on Brittany's face. She stole a glance at Jules and then shook her head. "I don't think so. I'm sure I'd remember a place this pretty."

As they strolled to the next booth, Jules heard someone calling her name, and she spun around to find Amy Ostrau, the woman who'd hired her. She ran the Children's Art Museum, which benefited from the festival. Jules had photographed her events more times than she could count.

Their paths usually crossed at some sort of gala, so it caught Jules off guard to see the older woman dressed casually in shorts. A white visor shielded her eyes from the sun.

"I'm so glad to see you made it," Amy said as she caught up with them.

Jules laughed. "Of course I did." She gestured at Brittany and made an introduction.

"Well, I know you're doing that detective thing now, so I was so relieved you agreed to do this for me."

"I still do some photography jobs." Jules laid her hand on Amy's arm. "Especially for you. I'm not planning to ever give it up completely. I love it too much."

"That's a relief. Are you finding all the winners' booths okay?"

"Yup. No problems. We're working our way through the layout you sent me, and I'm also taking shots of people shopping so you can use them online for the website."

As Jules shifted her camera bag strap on her shoulder, Amy's mouth dropped open. "Good gracious. Is that what I think it is?" Her eyebrows shot up as she reached for Jules's left hand.

"Yup. Tim popped the question. A couple of weeks ago at the beach. It was all quite romantic." She moved her hand so the diamonds sparkled in the sunlight.

"Oh, my stars, it's gorgeous." When Amy looked up, a genuine smile filled her face. "I'm glad that man finally realized he'll never find anyone more fabulous than you."

Jules laughed. "That's what I kept telling him."

"So, have you set a date?"

At the mention of an actual wedding date, Jules's chest tightened. "We haven't gotten that far yet. I guess we'll have to start looking at places soon and figure that all out."

Amy's face lit up. "Oh, I have the most wonderful suggestion. The Colby Museum. I'm on the board, and the gardens there are spectacular. It's also on the river, and oh, it's such a magical place to have a wedding."

Jules cocked her head. She knew the place well, and Amy was right. It was incredible. "They do that? Rent it out?"

"Oh, yes," she said, her voice lifting with enthusiasm. "Let me place a call and see what I can find out for you. I know they book up pretty far in advance, so I'm not sure how much of a hurry you're in."

"Well, we're not looking to get married immediately, but, you know ..." Jules rolled her eyes. "I'm not getting any younger, and Tim wants to start a family sooner rather than later." Even as she said the words, Jules worried what would happen if she got pregnant before her best friend.

Tim was already clamoring for kids, while Jules was still trying to accept she was getting married. She couldn't also wrap her brain around thinking about starting a family. Not yet, anyway.

"Of course," Amy said with an understanding nod. "You girls start much later than we did in my time, but—"

She was interrupted when the walkie-talkie attached to her hip crackled, followed by a man's voice. "Amy, you there?"

"Dadgummit," she said as she reached for it. "Not a minute's peace, I tell you, with this dang thing glued to me. I'll call you next week and let you know what I find out about the museum." She dipped her head at Brittany. "It was lovely to meet you."

She gave Jules a quick hug, then pressed the button on the side and held it up to her mouth. "I'm here, just saying goodbye to the photographer." Then, Amy held up her hand, waved, and scurried off in the other direction.

Jules got the shots she needed and made it to several of the other winning artists.

When they got to the next booth, it contained inexpensive job-oriented sculptures. "I'm pretty sure there aren't any for a DNA detective," Brittany said. "Teacher, fireman, nope, no—" She stopped short, picked up one, and stared at it.

"What's it say?" Jules asked.

Brittany turned it around so she could see. "Nurses call the shots."

"Cute. Does that mean anything to you?"

"I'm not sure," she said eventually. "Something about it just made me want to pick it up."

"You think maybe you were a nurse?"

Brittany pressed her lips together, then shook her head. "I don't think so. There was a glimmer of something, but it's gone now." She smiled and wrapped one arm around her middle. "Probably just hunger pains," she said as she pointed toward the area where the food vendors had started cooking on grills located behind their tents. "Everything smells delicious."

Jules lifted her nose into the air and inhaled deeply. "I'm getting hungry too, but this next booth should be the first-place winner in the acrylics category. Let me get a few pictures here, and then we'll break to find something to eat."

Jules introduced herself to the artist, an older man with long gray hair and a matching beard. His hands were shaking as he pulled down his winning canvas, and she wondered how he could paint if that was a regular occurrence.

"Oh, wow. The colors are so vivid." Jules turned to Brittany. "Do you like it?"

"Where is that?" A deep divot formed between Brittany's brows as she fixed her gaze on the painting.

The artist stood a bit taller, the smile on his face wide as he answered her question. "This here's the beautiful Great Smoky Mountains of Tennessee. Nothing prettier than when the leaves are all changin'. Like Mother Nature done flung her paint cans all over everything."

Jules snapped a photo as he spoke, his pride shining through as she looked through her lens. She then reached for Brittany's arm. "Gorgeous, right?"

She gave a slow nod, her attention still anchored on the painting. "Very. I also think it looks familiar."

Jules's head tilted to the side. "Really?"

"Maybe it's the mountains. Or it could be the leaves changing colors. I'm not sure."

"I got a great shot of it," Jules said when they walked away. "I'll print you a copy. Maybe looking at it will trigger you to remember why it seems familiar."

"Okay. Oh, look at these," Brittany said as they neared the next booth, teeming with shoppers.

It was one of the more popular vendors. "Yeah, I've seen these before. They always do really well." The booth offered photographs of architecture or elements of nature that resembled letters of the alphabet. "It's not even that expensive. I have an idea. Do you want to put one together for Becky? I haven't gotten her a gift yet for the party tonight. I'm sure she'd love it."

Brittany's eyes lit up. "Sure." She looked happy to have a purpose as she strode off toward the booth.

Jules snapped some shots of her, but then her stomach grumbled, and she was reminded she hadn't eaten breakfast. She gave Brittany one last look, then went on ahead to take care of the next few booths so they could get to lunch quicker.

She paused when she reached the second-place winner in the sculpture category. The artist couldn't have been more pleasant, but Jules didn't dare admit she had no idea what the pieces of metal and used car parts welded together were supposed to represent.

When she turned to head back to where she'd left Brittany, she was no longer by the photographs. Jules frowned, her eyes scanning the surrounding area. There was no sign of her. As her pulse raced, a couple blocking her view walked off, and Jules exhaled loudly. Brittany was at a small table off to the side of the booth having Becky's gift assembled.

Jules held up her camera and peered through the lens. The man assembling the photos Brittany had chosen to spell Becky's name glanced up and said something to her. Just as she leaned her head back and laughed, Jules hit the shutter button. She pulled the camera back to see the shot and smiled at the moment she'd captured. It was one of the reasons she loved being a photographer.

As Jules strolled over, she rubbed her stomach, already anticipating what they'd find to eat for lunch. As she watched the man finish, she picked up her pace, worried Brittany would panic at not having the money to pay for her purchase. Jules lifted her arm and tried to catch her eye, but her attention was focused on Becky's gift.

That's when Jules saw him.

He stood just outside a nearby tent, his gaze fixed on Brittany. Then, as if he knew the hunter was also the hunted, he shifted his attention to Jules. His eyes locked on hers. As she stared in disbelief, he turned and ran.

"Hey, wait!" She took off after him. "Stop him!"

This time Jules wasn't wearing a useless pair of sandals. She ran in the direction he'd gone, her camera bag banging against her hip. She passed Brittany, who looked up wearing a bewildered expression. There was no time to stop and explain, and Jules tried to weave her way through the crowd.

"Excuse me," she said over and over as she attempted to

dodge the people who stood between her and the man stalking Brittany.

She grimaced when she bumped the arm of a woman who didn't move out of the way fast enough. Her water bottle went flying into the air. "I'm so sorry," Jules called out over her shoulder.

She ran past the tent where she'd first seen the man until she found herself at the northern perimeter of the festival. It was fenced off. She panted and spun in every possible direction looking for any sign of where he'd gone. There was nothing. She cursed under her breath and rubbed the hip that had been battered by her camera bag.

As she wiped the sweat from her forehead, she wore a deep-seated frown.

"Who are you, and what the hell do you want with Brittany?"

CHAPTER TEN

When her phone buzzed, Becky glanced at the screen to see a text from Jules.

We're pulling in now.

The car headlights shone through the front window, and when the doorbell chimed, Sherlock hopped off the couch and scampered to the safety of her bedroom. He had no idea Gene could be bounding in at any time, but it didn't matter. Becky's cat didn't hang around for guests.

Jules laughed as she caught the flash of orange fur darting from the room. "See, I told you he wouldn't stay for the party. But you know Gene. He's always up for a good time."

Tim let go of the leash, and the dog greeted Becky, his tail wagging furiously.

"Jonas and Erin here yet?" Jules asked.

"In the kitchen with Bryan."

Jules waved her hand at Brittany. "C'mon, I'll introduce you to my brother's fiancée."

Becky followed them, but when the doorbell rang again,

she gave her husband a curious stare. "Who else did you invite?"

Bryan offered a shrug, but the gleam in his eye told Becky he knew exactly who it was. "Maybe it's a surprise."

When she pulled open the front door, her former partner, Tonya, and her husband, Scott, were standing on the porch.

"Hey, this *is* a surprise." She leaned in for a hug. Becky had only seen Tonya once since she'd left the boutique, and that was to sign the papers to sell her share.

Tonya held up a gift bag and smiled. "Hey, birthday girl. I come bearing gifts from the store."

"Aw. It's good to see you. Come on in." Becky and Tonya had known each other since college. She realized with a start that if Bryan hadn't invited her, it would have been the first birthday in years they hadn't celebrated together.

They'd drifted apart since she'd left the boutique, but Becky had needed time to come to terms with what had happened. Still, it was good to see her.

When Jules introduced Tonya to Jonas and Erin, her cheeks reddened as she shook Jonas's hand. "Yeah, we met briefly once before … you know, *that* day."

Recognition crossed his face. "Oh right. Now I remember. Well, it's good to see you again." He gave an exaggerated wince. "And under better circumstances."

"Jonas and Erin are getting married in a few weeks. They're actually going to Hawaii on their honeymoon." Becky nodded at Jonas's fiancée, Erin. "Tonya and Scott spent two weeks there a couple of years ago."

"Oh, we loved Hawaii." Tonya glanced over at her husband. "Depending on which islands you're going to, we can definitely give you some pointers on places to check out."

Erin ran her hand through her short blond hair. "That would be amazing. After all the craziness of getting ready for the wedding and then deciding to buy a house, I'm thinking the honeymoon is going to be much needed." She reached for Jonas's hand and looked up at him, her green eyes shining with the love of a bride about to walk down the aisle.

He leaned down and kissed her. "Two weeks of bliss with the new wife. No work. No responsibility." He waved his index finger in the air between Jules and Becky. "No crazy calls from these two."

Jules playfully swatted him. "Come on. You love our calls."

Jonas winced and reeled back with mock exaggeration. "Most of them hit me right between the eyes." He tipped his head. "And some have me wondering what I was thinking helping you two open a detective business."

Jules grinned at him. "Well, you're in too deep now to get out."

Jonas claimed to be a silent partner, but Becky and Jules had needed his help more than they'd expected. Especially when things unexpectedly went downhill.

"And this is Brittany," Becky said, introducing her to Tonya. "We've been, uh, working together." She didn't feel the need to go into any more detail than that.

Tonya lifted her hand in acknowledgment. "Becky and I used to work together too. We owned a boutique, but she sold her share to go into business with Jules."

"Speaking of Michelle, how's it going?" Becky asked as she began to pour wine into the glasses Bryan had set out.

"It's working out great," Tonya said as she reached for a glass of cabernet. "She loves the store, and she's working on a website for us. We even have an Instagram account now. Can you believe it?"

"I'm actually not surprised." Michelle had been younger and much more in tune with social media than Becky had been. When she realized most people used it to gush about their kids, she'd jumped ship.

When everyone had a drink in their hand, Tonya engaged

Erin in a conversation about a must-see volcano on Hawaii's Big Island. With Brittany listening in, Jules gestured for Becky to follow her back to the living room.

Becky held up her index finger and then pulled out a plate of cheese and crackers from the refrigerator.

"I'm starving." She set the snack on the coffee table and plopped down on the couch with her wine. "So, how was the photography job today?"

Jules sat beside her, then helped herself to a cracker and laid a slice of cheddar cheese on top. "There were new developments, I think."

Becky's brow furrowed. "What do you mean? What kind of developments?"

Jules kicked off her sandal and tucked her foot underneath her as she turned toward Becky. "I think Brittany's memory might be starting to come back."

"What?" Becky threw a glance toward the kitchen to confirm Brittany was still where they'd left her. "Something triggered it? Did she see something she recognized?"

"Not sure. She got this odd look on her face with this thing she saw about nurses. Then she seemed almost mesmerized by a picture of the Great Smoky Mountains.."

Becky's eyebrows knitted together. "The smoky mountains?"

"Yeah. The painting was gorgeous. All the colors of the leaves changing. She said she wasn't sure if it was the mountains or the colors in the trees. She just said it felt *familiar*."

"If she's starting to have flashes of memory, that could be a good sign. Maybe it's starting to come back." If that was the case, maybe they wouldn't even need to wait for her DNA results. Bryan would be happy if her case could be resolved sooner rather than later.

"Let's hope, but that wasn't actually the big news of the day." Jules tipped her head mysteriously and sipped her wine.

"There's more?" Becky asked on cue.

"I saw that guy again," Jules said in a loud whisper. She set her glass on the coffee table, her expression intense as she leaned closer. "He was watching Brittany from behind one of the tents."

Becky's mouth fell open. "The man from the apartment?" Once might have been a coincidence, but if Jules had seen him again, there had to be something more to it. "You're positive it was the same guy?"

"I'm pretty sure." She hesitated and held her head in her hands. "I mean, it all happened so fast. But, Beck, he ran when he realized I saw him. Just like last time."

"No better luck catching him this time?" Becky sipped her wine thoughtfully. "Sounds like we should be looking for a track star."

"I had on my tennis shoes, so I was better prepared this time." Jules shook her head. "He was lucky the fair was so crowded. I kept yelling at people to get out of the way, but somehow he managed to escape." She huffed and gave an aggravated nod. "Yeah, again." She picked up her wine glass and took a long sip. "But it *had* to be him. Why would someone run if they were just innocently browsing art?"

Becky lifted an eyebrow and fixed herself a cracker. "Uh, maybe because you were screaming and chasing him. What about Brittany? Did she see him too?"

"I don't think he had the chance to get close enough to talk to her. She said she didn't notice anything, but she was busy picking out your birthday present."

Becky cocked her head. "Oh, really? That sounds artsy."

"Just something cute we thought you'd like, and I know she enjoyed doing something that felt a little normal." Jules stood and caught Brittany's eye as she stood in the kitchen. She waved her over. "Do you want to give Becky the present you picked out?"

Brittany gave an enthusiastic nod and retrieved the gift from the end table where she'd deposited it when they arrived.

When Becky held it up, she smiled. "Pretty cool, huh? The B is one of those swirly poles at the playground, and the E is from a barn fence. The C looks like …"

"Are we doing presents now?" Tonya said as she wandered into the living room. She lifted her gift bag from the coffee table and placed it on the couch.

"How cool is this?" Becky turned her present around so Tonya could see. "Brittany picked out all the photos for the letters." She turned to her with an appreciative smile. "I absolutely love it. Thank you." She nudged Jules with her elbow and lowered her voice. "Maybe I should get one for Jonas and Erin. You know, for the new house. I haven't even had a chance to look at their registry, and I still have to get something for Erin's bridal shower."

"Oh, that's a great idea," Jules scrunched her lips into a pout. "Why didn't I think of that?"

Becky reached for her wine glass and held it up in her direction. "Ha, beat you to it."

"The art festival in Riverside is being held tomorrow too," Jules said. "You might need to go and get it done in person before they leave because the vendor is based in Georgia. Who knows how long it would take to get it shipped. Erin's shower is in two weeks."

"Works for me." Becky glanced into the kitchen at her husband. "It will give Bryan and me something fun to do tomorrow for my birthday."

Tonya tapped her arm. "Open mine now."

"Okay, if you *insist*." As Becky laughed, she realized this party had been exactly what she needed. She dug into the tissue paper and uncovered a small box. She opened it to find it contained a bracelet from one of the jewelry designers at the boutique. "Oh, it's beautiful. You know Kara's one of my favorites."

Becky held out her wrist, and Tonya opened the clasp and put it on her.

"There's more," she said. "I know it's a little early, but we already have all the Christmas stuff in the stockroom. Can you believe it?"

"I can. I saw trees up at Target this week. Weren't we just handing out Halloween candy?"

"Michelle and I have discussed it. I refuse to put any of the holiday merchandise out until after Thanksgiving, but I nabbed something for you."

Becky pulled out a fitted white button-down shirt. It had silver tinsel embroidered on the collar and buttons that looked like Christmas lights.

"How cute is this?" she asked, holding it up so Jules and Brittany could see.

"Okay, that's just darling," Jules said before turning to Tonya. "Do you have one that will fit a regular person?"

Tonya laughed. "We do. I'm just so used to checking to see what's available in Becky's size. It's a tough habit to break."

Becky felt a slight twinge that she no longer owned part of the boutique. She loved working with Jules, but not being at the store for the holiday season would feel strange. She dipped her head and offered Tonya a bittersweet smile. "I love it, and I'll absolutely wear it." She held up her hand. "But not until after Thanksgiving, I promise. Thank you." The gift bag felt empty, so she moved it to the coffee table. "What about Madeline? Did you order—"

"Ornaments? Of course." Tonya reached for the bag and handed it back to Becky. "There's something else in here. I asked Maddie to make something special for you."

Becky lifted her eyebrows. "Wow. I feel honored." She

reached in and pulled out a lightweight bundle of tissue paper. When she unwrapped it, she drew in a sharp breath.

Tonya set her hand on Becky's arm. "I know you didn't officially lose the baby last year, but still … I thought you might like it. Not to remember the bad part—"

Becky held up the handcrafted cherub by the looped string at the top and studied the detail in the face and wings. "It's incredible." Her eyes welled up.

Tonya's face fell. "I'm sorry. I wasn't trying to make you sad."

Becky shook her head. "No, I know." She hugged her. "I appreciate this more than you know. Maybe more than I realize myself right this second."

Tonya shrugged, her lips pressed together. "Just my way of saying I'm sorry—"

Becky waved off her apology. "There's nothing to be sorry about."

Jules put her arm around her best friend. "It's almost too pretty to only hang on the tree once a year."

Becky sniffled. "I was actually thinking the same thing."

Just then, Bryan called out from the kitchen. "Ladies, you all coming to eat?"

Becky carefully wrapped the ornament back in tissue paper and put it back in the bag with the shirt on top of it. She stood, placed the gift bag on the mantel over the fireplace, and gave Jules a pointed look. "Not that I don't trust Gene, but I'm not taking any chances."

She shrugged. "I get it, but lately, I think he only has a taste for shoes. The more expensive, the tastier he finds them." She groaned as she pushed herself up from the couch.

"C'mon," Becky said. "Wait until you see all the food Bryan made. He's been cooking since last night."

After they'd all eaten, Bryan talked the group into a rousing game of Pictionary.

He and Becky were just claiming victory when Gene bolted toward the front door. As he stood there with his hackles up, someone knocked.

"Who needs a doorbell when he's around?" Becky gave her husband a questioning stare as she headed to see who it was. "Another surprise, babe?"

"It's okay, Gene." She patted the dog to reassure him and then opened the door. Mrs. Ritter, their neighbor from across the street, stood there holding a covered cake plate.

"Happy birthday, dear," the older woman said with a smile.

"Well, it's officially tomorrow, but I'll celebrate any day there's cake," Becky said with a grin. She stepped out of the doorway and gestured with her hand. "Come on in."

Her neighbor hesitated. "Oh, I don't want to disturb your party, honey. Bryan told me you were going to be celebrating tonight, and I insisted on baking the birthday cake."

"You're not disturbing anything. Really." Mrs. Ritter was always welcome at their house. "We're all finished with dinner, and Bryan and I just claimed our Pictionary victory. Your timing is perfect."

"Well, okay then." Mrs. Ritter trotted off into the kitchen and set the cake on the counter.

Becky carefully lifted the cover as Jules hovered over her shoulder. "It looks delicious. I've said it once. I'll say it again. If you opened a bakery, I'd be your best customer."

She introduced her neighbor to Brittany, then added behind a cupped hand. "Mrs. Ritter's muffins are *legendary* around here."

A few minutes later, they gathered the group in the kitchen. Bryan lit the multitude of candles and flipped the switch for the kitchen lights. As they all sang to her, he rubbed his wife's shoulder. He leaned down to whisper in her ear, "Don't forget to make a wish."

Becky closed her eyes and thought of the ornament Tonya

had given her. There was only one thing she wanted, and she prayed this would be the year. She wasn't sure how much longer she could wait to be a mom. The ache she felt without a baby was painful.

She took a deep breath and then blew out every candle with one drawn-out puff. Amid applause for her efforts, Jules turned the lights back on.

A low growl rumbled in Gene's throat, and the dog raced from the kitchen into the living room.

"What's the matter? You didn't like our singing, buddy?" Bryan called out.

Jules glanced into the other room. "Gene, watcha doing?" When the dog didn't respond, she turned to her fiancé. "Tim, call your dog."

Becky couldn't help but laugh. "I love how Gene's ownership flip flops based on his behavior."

Bryan handed his wife a cake knife and a stack of plates. "You get the honors, birthday girl, but make sure to cut me a big hunk of that." He nodded appreciatively in Mrs. Ritter's direction. "It looks delicious."

Becky had just made the first cut when the knife in her hand faltered with the shock of a deafening crash.

Bryan frowned. "What the hell was that?"

"Gene!" Jules leaped from her seat, but as the group followed her to the other room, it was clear what had caused the horrific noise. The front window was shattered, shards of glass littering the living room floor where they had just been playing Pictionary.

"Be careful." Jules held out her hand to keep them from coming any closer.

"Oh, heavens." Mrs. Ritter's hand flew to cover her mouth as she took in the scene.

Becky's mouth dropped as she stared at the gaping hole in their big window. "How did that even happen?"

The dog cowered next to Tim's leg. When he reached down to comfort him, Jules called out a warning. "Don't pet him yet. He has glass in his fur."

Then she bent down and retrieved something from the floor. "This isn't Gene's fault." Jules shot Becky a nervous glance. "I guess the guy at the festival wasn't my imagination."

"What do you mean?"

Becky gingerly stepped around pieces of glass, then caught her breath when she realized Jules held a brick in her hand. She flipped it around so Becky could see the note attached to it. As she read what it said, a sinking feeling hit the pit of her stomach. Bryan was right. She and Jules didn't know enough about Brittany. This brick now made it impossible to ignore the possibility her case could be more dangerous than they thought.

Brittany nudged her way in between Tonya and Scott. "What's it say?"

Becky exchanged a glance with Jules, then read what was written on the piece of paper aloud.

"Stay away from her. You've been warned."

CHAPTER ELEVEN

"Did he see who did it?" Jules asked Tim as Jonas took off out the front door.

Erin stood huddled beside Mrs. Ritter. "I guess I'm going to have to get used to his instincts telling him to run off after the bad guy. The price of marrying a cop." Her worried gaze landed on Becky. "But who would do something like this?"

Brittany stared at the brick in Jules's hands, her eyebrows knitted together. She searched Jules's face looking for clarification. "You—you think whoever wrote that note was referring to me?"

Jules shrugged. "I don't know who else they'd be referring to."

Tonya stepped forward. She took the brick from Jules to see what it said for herself, then cocked her head as she eyed Brittany. "You have a bad ex after you or something?"

When her face turned crimson, Jules stepped in and put her arm protectively around Brittany's shoulders. "We're not sure. She was attacked a couple of weeks ago, and it caused her to lose her memory."

Erin's mouth gaped. "You mean like amnesia?"

"Exactly," Jules said. "And it appears some guy's been following her around since she got out of the hospital. Since Brittany doesn't remember anything, we have no idea if it's the same person who assaulted her."

"Oh, wow. That's terrible." Erin's face filled with compassion as her gaze drifted to Brittany. "I'm so sorry."

"And I'm pretty sure I saw the guy stalking her today at the art festival in Riverside." Jules turned to Brittany, whose face had paled, worry now residing between her eyebrows. "I'm sorry, but it seems like too big of a coincidence that this brick came flying through the window tonight with a note like this."

"But we're not *positive* it was the same guy," Becky said, casting a reassuring gaze in Brittany's direction. "Or that he's really stalking her."

Was she kidding? Jules gave her friend a hard stare. "Do people *usually* throw bricks through your front window?" She winced at Tonya, still holding the brick. "There could be fingerprints or DNA on the note. Jonas will hate that everyone's handling it."

"Sounds like a jealous ex-boyfriend or husband to me." Tonya shrugged and set the brick on the coffee table. "He probably thought you were here with another guy."

"We're considering all the possibilities," Becky said. "One theory is that she might have tried to leave a bad relationship before she was attacked."

Tonya pursed her lips and dipped her head in Brittany's direction. "That gets my vote, but it looks like he found you. You need to be careful." She jabbed her index finger in the air toward Becky. "You too. If that guy followed her here tonight, you and Jules need to watch your backs. I'm surprised Tim and Bryan—" She glanced around and scowled. "Where'd all the guys go? And the dog?"

Jules stepped outside to find them on the front lawn. Tim

had Gene on the leash, and Jonas was slightly out of breath as he made his way up the driveway.

She rushed toward him. "Did you see who did it?"

He shook his head. "I couldn't catch the guy. I'm not positive, but I think he drove off in a dark-colored sedan. Too dark to figure out the make and model."

Tim patted Bryan on the shoulder. "I'll take a ride with you to get some plywood. You're going to need to board that up until you can get someone here to fix it."

"I can go too," Tonya's husband said.

Becky wrinkled her nose and sighed. "So much for my birthday date at the art fair."

Brittany stared at the ground before lifting her eyes to meet Becky's. "I'm so sorry."

Jonas frowned. "What are you sorry about?"

"Well, Jules thinks—"

"It's gotta be the guy who's been following her around," Jules said, her voice insistent. "He was at the art festival in Riverside today too. I saw him."

Jonas ran both hands over his face and let out a deep breath. "Maybe. I guess it's possible."

Jules could usually see where her brother was coming from, but what did he mean by *maybe*? "Who else could it have been? People don't randomly throw bricks through windows. Especially with a warning like that attached to them."

Jonas glanced back toward the street, then moved to Erin's side and reached for her hand. "C'mon, let's go back inside."

Becky moved toward the door. "Hang on. Let me at least get a broom and brush a path through the glass."

A few minutes later, she waved them all inside.

Jonas eyed the broken window. "So, I've never had this happen before, but my first thought was it might be about a guy we arrested last night."

Erin's eyes grew large as she looked up at him. "What?" The word came out as a high-pitched squeak.

Jules stared at Jonas, trying to make sense of what he was implying. "So, who's the 'her' in the note? It says to stay away from *her*."

"I know," he said with a bob of his head. He pulled Erin close to him. "Last night, I arrested this guy for selling drugs, but he's apparently part of a much bigger operation. When I brought him in, they tried to get him to implicate the guy he's buying from, but he wouldn't give them anything. Then I heard they brought his girlfriend in for questioning and kept her there all night. I guess they wanted to see what she knew."

"Oh. So, you think maybe …?"

He tipped his head. "I have to admit, it was my first thought. Though I don't know why I'd be targeted unless someone knew I was the one who made the arrest." Jonas glanced around the room. "What did you do with the—"

"On the coffee table." Jules cringed. "I touched it, and so did Tonya." She held up her hand. "But just the brick and not the note on it."

Jonas shook his head. "At least there's that, although neither is ideal for fingerprints." He turned to Becky. "Do you have—"

"A plastic bag? Sure." She headed off to the kitchen and returned with a clean dishrag and a large Ziploc bag.

Jonas carefully moved the brick into the bag and sealed it. "Hopefully, there's something we can use to figure out if this was your guy or ours."

Jules turned to Tim. "How's Gene?"

"He gave himself a good shake outside, but I don't want him to step on any of this glass."

Becky put her arm around Mrs. Ritter. "Why don't we all have some of your delicious cake before we officially end the party? Then, I can finish sweeping up this mess while the guys go get some wood."

The festive atmosphere had faded, but the group trudged behind Becky back into the kitchen.

She cut slices of cake and slid them onto plates which Jules handed out.

"This is delicious." Tonya eyed Becky with a slight smile. "So, let me guess. When you blew out your candles, you didn't use your wish to hope a brick wouldn't come flying through your front window."

Becky rolled her eyes. "Yeah, that wasn't exactly on my radar."

As Jonas ate his cake, he stared vacantly toward the living room.

Jules gave his arm a gentle nudge. "What?"

He responded instead by turning to Mrs. Ritter. "When you brought the cake over, did you see anyone outside? Any vehicles you didn't recognize?"

The older woman gave a helpless shrug. "I knew the kids were having a little party, so I didn't even think about whose cars were out front. But when I walked over from across the street, I didn't see anyone lurking outside." Her face fell. "But I wasn't necessarily looking." She reached for Becky's arm. "I'm sorry, dear."

"Well, obviously Gene heard someone," Jules said. "The guy who did it couldn't have been out there long because he ran to the front window right before it happened." Her lips lifted into a satisfied smirk as she turned to Tim. "*My* dog is such a good watch dog."

Becky shook her head and groaned.

Jules lifted her shoulders with an innocent smile. "What? He is."

Bryan shoveled in his last bite of cake, then set his plate in the sink. "Jonas, you mind staying with them while we run to get the wood?"

"Of course. Take my truck. It'll be easier." Jonas dug into the front pocket of his jeans and tossed the keys to him. "I'll help Becky call it in. You need to get a police report," he said in a firm voice as his gaze traveled between her and Bryan. "Just in case this isn't the end of it."

Jules felt a shiver go through her as Tim handed her Gene's leash.

He leaned down and kissed her. "Don't go outside looking for trouble," he said when he pulled back. "You or Gene. Both of you need to stay in the house and away from the other windows. We'll be back as soon as we can." He gave her a stern stare. "But we're going to need to talk about all of this later." The look he shot Brittany wasn't at all subtle. "I won't have you putting yourself in danger for a case. I don't like what happened tonight. I don't like it at all."

CHAPTER TWELVE

Becky pulled into the office parking lot right behind Jules and Brittany. When she got out of her car, she popped the trunk and grinned.

"Want to see the present I got for Erin's shower?"

"I still can't believe you managed to pull off the art fair. How did Bryan get a glass company out first thing on a Sunday morning?" Jules asked.

"Apparently, a big gaping hole in your front window is considered an emergency. Not to mention Bryan didn't want us to spend the day waiting for them on my birthday. But it's all fixed. It's like it never happened."

Brittany lowered her eyes. "I hope what happened wasn't about me. If it was, I'm really sorry."

"It's not your fault. No matter who did it." Becky reached for her arm. "You weren't the one who hurled that brick, so don't give it a second thought. I mean it."

Brittany gave a helpless shrug. "Still, maybe I should go back to my apartment." Her eyes drifted between Jules and Becky. "I don't want to put either one of you in danger."

"You heard her." Jules flicked her wrist dismissively. "Everything's fine now." She eyed the open car trunk. "So, Beck, show us what you got."

Becky reached for the gift she'd had made at the art festival the day before. "Isn't it great?" She'd laid out the photographs to spell Mr. & Mrs. Kirkland.

Jules's eyes lit up. "Oh, it's incredible. Erin and Jonas are going to love it."

Becky set it back in her trunk and slammed it shut. She told them the art festival had been followed by a romantic dinner where Bryan had managed to book a window table overlooking the water. "And afterward, we worked on that wish I made," she said, lifting her eyebrows as she smiled. "It turned out to be the perfect birthday."

"I had a feeling that might be what you used it on." Jules turned to Brittany to explain. "Becky's been trying to get pregnant." She hesitated and rubbed her friend's arm. "It hasn't been easy."

"I kind of thought so with the gift Tonya gave you."

"Oh, right." Becky was relieved when Jules headed toward the stairs to the office without saying more. There was no way she wanted to tell the story of what had happened with the IVF. She almost never talked about it. Not with her best friend. Not even with Bryan.

"So, how'd it go with Tim when you left my house?"

Jules gave a slight shake of her head. "Not great. I'll tell you later," she said in a soft voice.

Becky could only imagine. Bryan hadn't needed to say I told you so, but it had lingered in the air when they went to bed that night. She was relieved he'd let it go so she could enjoy her birthday, but Jules had Brittany living with her. She was sure Tim had quite a lot to say about it. Her best friend wasn't used to having someone tell her what to do, and Becky hoped it hadn't caused a rift between them.

Jules inserted her key into the office door and pushed it open. "So, I printed some of the pictures from the art festival."

"What about the guy you were chasing? Did you manage to get a shot of him?" Becky asked as she and Brittany followed Jules in.

"Nothing great." Jules slid her bag off her shoulder and onto her desk. She pulled out the stack of photos, sifted through them, and handed one to Becky.

The picture was of Brittany at the same booth she'd visited the day before to have Erin's gift made. In the photograph, she stood off to the side where the letters were assembled onto the frame. She was laughing.

Becky's gaze traveled to Brittany. "This is a great picture, but what am I—"

"The guy in the gray baseball hat." Jules tapped her index finger on the upper right-hand corner of the photo. "Of course, he looked down at the exact moment I snapped the picture."

Becky squinted at where she'd pointed. "What's it say on his hat?"

Jules blew out a deep breath. "I don't know. Some sort of logo, I think. I tried to blow it up, but I couldn't make it out either."

Becky turned to Brittany, but before she could ask, she shook her head. "The picture didn't trigger me to remember anything, and I didn't see him at the festival. The only thing I saw was Jules running past me yelling."

Becky lifted her eyebrows and gave her partner a knowing stare. "Again, maybe that's why the man ran. Just sayin'."

Jules shot her a look but ignored the comment as she pulled a stack of papers from her computer bag. "Which list should we tackle today? Storage units, banks, or hair salons?"

"Let's go out after lunch and hit a few of each." Becky slid into the seat at her desk facing Brittany. "Maybe we start near your apartment. If you didn't have a car, it would make sense it would have to be someplace within walking distance."

Jules waved Brittany over. "Why don't you move your chair here. We can dive back into the information on your driver's license until then. See what we can find."

"Okay, I'll research that T-shirt she brought with her," Becky said as Brittany dragged her chair over to Jules's desk. "If we can figure out when and where that 5K was, maybe that will help too. But first, I need some caffeine. Anyone else?"

When they all had fresh cups of coffee in front of them, they settled in and got to work.

Becky pursed her lips as she studied the logos on her screen. One in particular resonated with her, so she leaned in and clicked to read more. As she stared intently at her screen, Jules glanced over.

"Did you find something?"

"Not sure," Becky said. "I found a group in New Jersey that's organized by the police for caretakers of people with Alzheimer's or dementia. It's called Project Lifesaver."

"Oh," Jules said in a soft voice. "What is it exactly?"

Becky read from her screen. "It's a radio tracking system for people with diagnoses that involve risks of wandering, such as people with dementia or autism. They wear a transmitter on their wrist or ankle with a unique radio frequency. It emits a signal every second, 24/7/365, so if they wander, their caregiver contacts the police, and they can track them."

Becky leaned back in her chair, an ache in her chest. "That would have been helpful with my mom. You know, before …" She met Brittany's inquisitive gaze. "My mom is in a memory care facility with dementia now, but there was one time before I realized what was happening. She ended up at the supermarket and had no idea how she got there or how to get home." Becky remembered how scared she had been that day. Now there were days her mom didn't even know who she was. "Luckily, a neighbor saw her and was able to call me."

Brittany's face filled with compassion. "Oh, I'm so sorry. That must be hard to see her like that."

Ironically, Brittany's situation wasn't that different than Becky's mom's, except hopefully, Brittany would regain her memories. Her mother would only get progressively worse.

"It's not easy, that's for sure." Becky took a deep breath and focused on her screen. "The article says it could also be used by families who have someone suffering from autism. Or really any condition that might cause someone to wander off." She looked hopefully at Brittany. "Does that trigger anything?"

Brittany shook her head, almost apologetically. "No. Nothing."

"Was there anything else that might be relevant?" Jules asked.

"There's a bunch of Lifesaver events around aquatics safety," Becky said, clicking her mouse. "Those 5Ks were held in Ohio, Louisiana, Indiana, and Virginia. There's also an annual Lifesaver 5K race in Texas organized around learning CPR. But there's no pink ribbon in any of their logos."

Jules leaned back in her chair and frowned. "It seems like it should support a cause related to breast cancer, no?"

Becky scrolled down the items on her screen. "Well, here's a 5K in Pennsylvania promoting awareness of getting a mammogram. That seems like it could be related." She reached into her drawer and pulled out a pad of yellow-lined paper. "I'll start a list of the possibilities."

"Does that mean anything to you?" Jules asked Brittany. "Maybe your mom or a family member had breast cancer."

Brittany gazed off as she considered it before finally shrugging again. "I don't think so."

"That's all I've found so far. What about you two?" Becky asked. "Having any better luck?"

"We're scrolling through Instagram accounts now. When we did a general US search, we found ninety-nine people named Brittany Mullins. Only one was the right age, but the date of birth didn't match. Still, we managed to find the woman on social media. Just to make sure."

Brittany scowled. "It was a bust."

"Right. But we're still looking."

An hour later, Becky stretched in her seat. She had made a list of potential organizations that could have held the 5K, but it was like looking for a needle in a haystack. She hadn't found any that had a logo that matched the one on Brittany's shirt. She'd obviously cut the bottom to crop out crucial information about where and when it had been held. Maybe there was even something on the sleeve. But then why keep the shirt at all? What meaning did it have that she'd been so determined to bring it with her?

Becky rubbed her eyes, and when her stomach grumbled, she glanced at the time on her phone. It was later than she thought. "You guys getting hungry?"

Jules nodded. "Yeah, let's grab lunch and check out some of these places on the list. We can research some more when we get back." She stood and stretched. As she reached for her purse, her cell phone rang. She checked the caller ID and held up a finger for them to wait.

"Hey, Amy," Jules said when she answered. "Looks like the art festival had a perfect weekend. Becky even went yesterday and said there was a nice crowd." She was silent and nodded while she listened. "Right. I sent you a link to most of the pictures and pulled out the ones I thought you might want to use on the website." She dipped her chin at Brittany and smiled. "You know, people enjoying the fair and buying from the vendors."

Becky closed her computer and grabbed her purse.

"Wait, what?" Jules asked into the phone. There was a

pause, and Becky couldn't tell if it was good news or bad. Her best friend's expression was blank.

"No, no, that sounds incredible," Jules said finally. "It's just so … soon." A pause. "Right. I get that. Okay, I'll talk to Tim about it. I really appreciate it."

Jules dropped back into her chair, the phone frozen in her hand.

"What is it?" Becky asked. "Was that Amy Ostrau?" She wondered what the woman could have said that had her best friend looking so rattled.

"Yeah. When I saw her at the fair, Amy mentioned she was on the board for the Colby Museum. Apparently, they rent it out for weddings, so she offered to call them for me. Sounds like they just had a cancellation." She met Becky's eyes with a nervous shrug. "The date's mine if I want it, but I have to make a decision right away. If not, they're booked for the next eighteen months."

Becky leaned against her desk. "That's great that Amy was able to help you, isn't it? It's beautiful, and the gardens there are incredible. Is that where you'd have the ceremony?"

"We can. And it wouldn't even be that hot yet."

Becky tipped her head to the side and stared at her best friend. "Yet? What's the date of the cancellation?"

Jules planted her elbows on the desk and wrapped her hands around her head. She drew in a deep breath, then let it escape in a long hiss. "April twenty-second." She enunciated each part of the date slowly before she glanced up at Becky. "What do you think? Can I pull this off in five months? That's no time at all to plan a wedding, right?"

Becky slipped into the chair in front of Jules's desk and scooted closer. "Don't you mean, can *we* pull this off?" She folded her arms on the desk in front of her and leaned toward her best friend.

Jules bit her bottom lip. "Really?"

"Of course. If that's where you want to have your wedding, then I'll help you figure out how to make it happen. That's what best friends are for."

"Well, I should snap it up, then," Jules said in a firm voice. "The museum would be an incredible place to get married, and I certainly don't want to wait eighteen months." She rummaged around in her purse, then her gaze skipped across her desk.

"Looking for this?" Becky slid Jules's cell phone across the desk toward her.

"Thanks, I couldn't figure out what I did with it." She tossed it in her purse, stood, and turned to Brittany. "You ready to get something to eat? I'm starving."

Becky followed them out of the office, but she couldn't stop thinking about what had transpired. Jules had said all the right things, but she knew her best friend almost better than she knew herself. Something was off. Becky couldn't help but wonder if Jules was as ready to get married as she said she was.

CHAPTER THIRTEEN

"I APPRECIATE you offering to take Brittany to the hair salon," Jules said when she answered the door.

Gene bolted forward, so excited to see Becky she could barely get in the front door.

Jules nudged him backward with her knee. "You have to actually let her come in, bud."

Becky stooped to give the dog a proper greeting. "It's not a problem, and since I was going out, Bryan decided he'd go play racquetball after work."

"Okay, good, because if I had to cancel her appointment for tonight, it would have taken weeks to get her penciled back in," Jules said as they plodded up the stairs.

They'd spent the morning shuttling Brittany to her doctors' appointments and then gone their separate ways.

With the call from Amy weighing on her mind, Jules had then called the event coordinator at the museum only to learn she had an opening later in the day. Before she could second guess herself, she'd gushed appropriately and said, of course, she and Tim would love to come see the venue.

"When she said she had an appointment available today to

show us what the museum could offer for the wedding, I figured I should grab it," Jules said when they got upstairs. "Plus, Tim and I really need some alone time to talk about it all. There's a ton to figure out."

"You sound excited to get started." Becky pulled a Diet Coke from Jules's refrigerator and slid into a chair at the kitchen table.

"Of course I'm excited. I get to marry the most wonderful man in the world."

When she'd gotten the call from Amy and learned about the possibility of an earlier wedding date, Jules couldn't deny she'd had a sick feeling in the pit of her stomach. It was all about to move so quickly. She'd thought she'd have more time to enjoy being engaged, to adjust to the idea of a new normal.

Then she'd gone home, poured a stiff drink, and given herself a stern talking to. For so long, she'd dreamed of Tim proposing. She'd imagined their wedding day. Jules just needed to push that old doubt aside because her heart knew she and Tim were meant to be together. Another cocktail and the alcohol leaned in to convince the portion of her brain that had difficulty accepting change. Jules just hoped her newfound conviction wouldn't waver.

"He'll love the museum. How could he not?" Becky asked. "And he's a guy. We'll be the ones doing all the planning. If I know Tim, he'll go with whatever you want."

Jules leaned against the counter, too nervous to sit. "He's already said he wants me to have the wedding I've dreamed about. Still, so long as we both like the place, I want to get the reservation on the books before we miss out on the opportunity." She glanced at the time and wondered what was taking Brittany so long. "She went upstairs to change, but she'd better hurry up. Amanda will hate me if she's late for her appointment."

Becky dismissed her concern with a wave of her hand. "We

have plenty of time, don't worry. She and I can grab dinner afterward and then hang out at my house. Either stop by on your way home, or call me when you're done, and I can run her back over." She raised her eyebrows suggestively. "Unless you want Brittany to stay at my place tonight. Are you and Tim looking to have a sleepover?"

"Maybe." Jules glanced toward the stairs and lowered her voice. "It's been a little odd between us. We're not used to … someone being here all the time." Especially Brittany, but she didn't say that out loud.

After the brick incident, Tim had expressed his concerns about her living with Jules. "I can't even imagine what I'd do if anything happened to you," he'd said that night when they were finally able to grab a moment of privacy. "Pretty soon, it won't be about just you anymore, Jules. Once we're married, we're going to need to start making decisions together."

Tim's words had paralyzed her. A long time ago, Jules had decided the only person she could count on was herself. She knew Tim was just worried and not trying to control her. Still, his comments had caught her off guard. Jules couldn't help but wonder if their conversation had contributed to her hesitation about pushing up the wedding.

"I'm sure it hasn't been easy for the two of you, especially being newly engaged and all." Becky took in a sharp breath. "I can give you a break tonight if you need one. You've taken so much of this on yourself, and it's a lot to contend with."

Jules stole a glance at the stairs, then slipped into the seat across from Becky. "I just—I don't know. I feel for Brittany, not knowing who she is." Her palm moved to her chest. "I can relate to what she's going through in some way. Not that being adopted is the same thing, but I know how desperate I was to figure out who I was and where I came from. Obviously, I know all about Barb now, but I'll never forget the way that felt."

Becky reached for her friend's hand. "It's all going to work out for Brittany, just like it did for you."

A wry smile lifted Jules's lips. "Well, I've worked half of it out anyway."

It had been difficult for Jules to learn she had three additional half-siblings, especially since she treasured her relationship with Jonas. She just hadn't been able to resolve the conflicted feelings she had for her birth father. Until recently, Lee Cantrell had never wanted anything to do with his long-lost daughter. Her half-cousin, Lucy, had told Jules he'd expressed interest in speaking to her. She wasn't ready.

Becky hadn't brought up the subject since Jules said she needed time to decide what she wanted to do. That was the best part about being friends for so many years. She always knew when Jules needed time to stew on something before she could make a decision. Then, Becky was usually the first to know when she'd finally made up her mind. Once she was married, would Jules have to reserve that premier spot for Tim?

"It's like the changing of the guard." There was a trace of sarcasm in Brittany's voice as she strolled into the kitchen.

Becky glanced up. "But hey, you'll be blond again soon."

"That's true, and for that, I'm grateful. I hope it's true that blonds have more fun because, I have to say, being brunette has been a drag."

Gene sat up, tail wagging, and Brittany bent at the knees to wrap her arms around him. "See you later, handsome."

"He'll be here alone while Tim and I are out." Jules eyed Brittany with a suspicious tilt of the head. "You closed your bedroom door, right?" She seldom remembered, and while she'd been lucky enough not to lose anything to Gene's chewing obsession, her streak was due to end at any time.

After a guilty shake of her head, Brittany trotted back up the stairs.

"She obviously didn't have a dog before, or at least she

doesn't remember having a dog like Gene." Jules rolled her eyes. "I can only do so much to protect the little she has."

Moments later, Brittany was back downstairs. She grabbed her purse off the kitchen counter. "Have fun, and don't do anything I wouldn't do." She scrunched up her face. "Not that I remember if I used to do that or not." She offered an amused smile and hitched up her shoulders. "Just a little amnesia humor."

Becky shook her head and offered a reluctant chuckle. "C'mon, let's go."

Jules followed them down the stairs to the front door so she could lock it after they left. The idea of that brick sailing through Becky's window still had her on edge. Better safe than sorry. She had promised Tim she'd at least take extra measures to be careful.

But as Becky opened the front door to leave, he stood on the other side.

"You're leaving already?" he asked.

"We're off to the salon, but you'll love the museum." She smiled at Tim, then gave him an exaggerated wink. "It's a perfect spot for a wedding."

"I already told Jules that if she's willing to marry me there, then that's good enough for me." His eyes locked on hers. "The only place I'll be looking is at my gorgeous bride-to-be."

At the sound of Tim's voice, Gene came racing down the stairs, his tail beating everyone in his path as he tried to get to him.

"I know, buddy, but he's not staying long," Jules said before turning to Tim. "Give our boy some love while I run up to grab my purse. I told the woman at the museum we'd be there by four-thirty, so I'm glad you managed to finish work early today."

"You said wedding emergency, so I came running." He shot a smile at Becky. "Probably not the last one, right?"

Jules pressed her lips together. Tim didn't understand what this abbreviated timeline would entail. "We need to lock this down because April's going to come way too fast. At least the venue's the hardest part."

His eyebrows lifted. "Harder than the dress?"

Jules shot a glance at her best friend. "Oh, no. Wedding dress shopping is going to be the fun part."

"I'm thinking … a gown worthy of Scarlet, maybe." Tim turned to Becky. "Do I know my fiancée or what?"

Jules waved her index finger in the air at him. "Don't start picturing what my dress will look like. You're not supposed to see me in it before the big day." She tried to look stern. "Even in your imagination."

Becky laughed. "On that note, we've got to go."

"Sure, leave me to fend for myself," Tim said, but he was laughing too.

He understood this was the wedding Jules had been sure she'd never get. For so long, she'd pushed away the possibility. She'd photographed other people's big days, never daring to dream about her own. But now, her turn had arrived.

Tim slipped his hand into hers as they walked to his car. "Everything fixed now at Becky's house?"

"Yeah, they got a glass guy to come and replace the window first thing Sunday morning."

"Do you still think it could have been the guy who's been following Brittany?" Tim asked as they got into the car. He shifted in the driver's seat to face her, and his hesitant expression told her he wasn't sure how she'd react after their brief conversation the other night. Jules knew he hadn't finished what he wanted to say before Brittany walked in, but the last thing she wanted was to rehash it and ruin the night ahead.

She reached for his hand and met his concerned gaze with a non-committal shrug. "I don't know. Maybe."

Tim's eyes narrowed. "If it is—"

"Listen, I know you're nervous about Brittany staying with me, but we're being careful. Yes, a guy was peering in her window, but he could have been looking for the person who lived there before her."

Tim didn't look convinced. "And he just happened to also be at the fair?"

Jules pulled back her hand and rubbed her temple. "I know. That would be a pretty big coincidence." She inhaled deeply, then let it escape in one long breath. "It all happened so fast. Am I *positive* it was the same guy?" She faced him and shook her head. "I'm not. I thought it was, but I could just as easily be wrong about it. About everything." She leaned forward and kissed him. "Besides, even Jonas said the brick could have been related to the arrest he made."

Tim shook his head as if he wasn't sure what to believe. "I hate that you and Becky are involved in another case that could be dangerous. You know, when we went to pick up the plywood, Bryan and I were talking—"

"We're not in danger." She let out an exasperated sigh. "Everything's fine, and hopefully, Brittany's DNA test results will come in soon. If we haven't already figured out her story, I'm sure we'll find the answers we need when we have her matches to work with." Jules leaned back in her seat and pulled her seatbelt across her chest. "Her case isn't really that different than helping someone who's adopted. I get it, Tim. I understand how Brittany feels. You know, what it's like to not really know who you are."

"I understand you want to help her, hon, but she's living with you. What if—"

Jules didn't let him finish. "Right now, I don't think I could handle knowing Brittany was living in that apartment by herself." She fixed her gaze on him. "And not because I'm afraid the boogeyman will get her. Can you imagine being alone, not knowing the first thing about why you came here or what your life was like before you moved into that dreary, depressing place? Spending every day wondering why your family doesn't seem to be looking for you?" She shook her head firmly. "I can't do that to her. I won't."

Tim studied her, and then the corners of his mouth lifted reluctantly. "You have a heart the size of Texas. You know that?"

Jules smiled back at him. "If I do, I know it's filled with love for you." She waved her hand in the direction of the gearshift. "C'mon, let's go book ourselves a place to get hitched."

He started the car, then leaned over and kissed her again. "I can't wait for you to be Mrs. Hendricks."

Jules drew in a sharp breath. They hadn't really talked about whether she'd change her name. She'd built up her photography business as Jules Dalton. That's who she was. She swallowed hard, the pit of her stomach burning again. She met his eyes, and this time, she had to force the smile she gave him. "Me either."

Still, her nerves were forgotten as they wandered the property of the museum and gardens. Jules got caught up in planning the wedding and couldn't help but envision how it would all look. Chairs on either side of a long white runner which would lead to the gazebo where Tim would wait for her. A harp player off to the right. The glorious blooms of the garden surrounding them as they took their vows.

The balcony on the building overlooked the gardens. Their guests would mingle outside during the cocktail hour before retreating inside for the main event.

"It's set up for a small charity function we have scheduled for tomorrow night," the event coordinator said before pulling open a set of doors to reveal a ballroom that was exquisite. "But at least you'll get a feel for the space."

Jules's mouth fell open as her eyes scanned the room.

Crystal chandeliers. The rose-colored walls. Crisp white linens on the tables. "It's gorgeous."

"I'm not sure how many people you're thinking, but the room can hold up to two hundred comfortably," the woman said. "Though the dance floor does get a little tight if you have that many guests who all like to …" She put her hands in the air and moved her feet. "You know, get out there and bust a move."

Jules's gaze drifted to the dance floor and then to Tim. "We haven't even thought about putting together the guest list yet. But I think it will be fine. I have a small family."

Tim shook his head. "You *used* to have a small family. It's gotten noticeably bigger recently, and I assume you're planning to invite them all?"

Jules cringed when she realized she'd almost forgotten the newly found relatives on her birth mother's side. "Oh, you're right. I definitely want to invite them." She nodded at the woman. "I still think we won't be anywhere near two hundred guests."

The coordinator gave her a knowing smile that said it wasn't the first time a bride had underestimated how many guests she thought she'd have. "You'd be surprised how fast the numbers can go up. But take a minute to look around."

Jules turned to Tim expectantly, but he waved her on. "Go ahead. Make sure this has everything you want."

Tim and the coordinator parked themselves at one of the round tables while Jules wandered silently through the room.

She imagined tables filled with the important people in their lives—laughing and eating. As Jules's gaze drifted around the room, she envisioned the band and the spot where she and Tim would cut the cake.

Jules could see their first dance as husband and wife and the father/daughter dance. Without a doubt, the honor of that moment belonged to the dad who'd loved her unconditionally.

He'd never had any doubt he wanted Jules as his daughter. He wasn't anything like Lee Cantrell, who'd asked Barb to terminate the problem that could get him in trouble with his wife.

As Jules's thoughts threatened to turn bitter, they were interrupted when Tim and the coordinator approached her.

"So, I know Amy told you we had a cancellation for April." The woman threw her hands up in the air. "I guess they're lucky they called it off now, right? Much easier to get out of a bad relationship than a marriage," she said with a knowing chuckle.

Jules dipped her chin in agreement and reminded herself she *wasn't* a nervous bride. Tim was the man she was meant to be with. She wanted to be his wife, and the museum was everything she'd dreamed of having for their wedding. It was perfect.

She reached for his hand. "So, what do you think?"

Tim gazed into her eyes. "You haven't stopped smiling since we got here. If this is where you want to tie the knot and celebrate, I'm all for it. We'll figure it all out in time."

Jules took in a deep breath, then nodded at the woman. "Okay, we're in. Let's draw up the papers." She squeezed Tim's hands and tried to ignore the nerves gnawing at her stomach. She loved Tim, and he loved her. "April twenty-second. Big day for us, and it will be here before we know it."

"After we sign the contract, let's go have a romantic dinner to celebrate." Tim leaned over and kissed her. "I've missed having time for just the two of us."

"Becky offered to let Brittany stay at her place tonight. You know, if you want to—"

The ringing of Jules's cell phone interrupted her. She stared at her phone and hesitated, a guilty flush on her face.

"Go ahead and answer it," Tim said. "I'm well aware my new wife comes with a best friend she's crazy about. You should make sure everything's okay."

He really was the most wonderful man in the world.

"Hey," Jules said when she answered Becky's call. "We're just finishing up at the museum and getting ready to make it official. April twenty-second. Save the date. If you need a more ceremonious invite, let me know, but naturally, you have to be my matron of honor."

"Well, I'd better be."

"So, how's it going at the salon?" Jules asked. "Is Brittany finished?"

"She's almost done. Amanda said she can't get her quite back to her original color in one appointment, but it's definitely lighter. She also just got a call from the detective handling her case."

"Really? Did they find out who attacked her?"

"He said they found some surveillance footage, and he thought seeing it might jog her memory. We're going to head to the police station as soon as she's finished."

"Tonight?" Jules glanced at the time on her phone as her pulse quickened. "When will you be there?"

"In about thirty minutes."

"Okay, I'll—" Jules's gaze flew to Tim, who was chatting with the wedding coordinator while he waited patiently.

He tipped his head to one side as he studied her. "Everything okay?"

Tim would understand if Jules asked to change their plans. That's who he was. Still, her cheeks burned with shame for even considering it. As much as Jules wanted to go, this was their night. Hers and Tim's.

She smiled and gave him a reassuring nod.

"Tim and I are getting ready to head to dinner to celebrate. Can you handle it?"

Becky didn't hesitate. "Yup. Go enjoy your night. I still have that picture of the guy from the fair. It's not great, but I should be able to see if there's a possibility it's the same guy."

Jules held up her index finger in Tim's direction.

"I definitely got a better look at him at the apartment," she said into the phone. "He's about five-ten, dark brown hair, cut pretty short, I think. Brown eyes. He seemed fairly thin."

"How old do you think he is?" Becky asked.

Jules pressed her lips together as she thought about it. "Maybe mid to late thirties?" She realized with a sinking sensation she probably couldn't even pick him out of a lineup. So, how had she been so sure it was the same man at the art festival?

"Do you want me to call the detective back and tell him we'll all come tomorrow?"

"No. You two need to go tonight," Jules said in a firm voice. "The sooner we can figure out who hurt Brittany, the better we'll all feel."

CHAPTER FOURTEEN

"Nervous?" Becky reached for the handle of the heavy glass door.

Brittany shrugged. "A little, I guess."

At the front desk of the police station, Becky spoke up on her behalf. "We're looking for a Detective Torok."

The woman waved them toward a set of uncomfortable stiff-backed chairs. "He'll be out in a minute."

A few minutes later, a man stuck his head through the door, his loosely knotted tie swinging as he craned his neck to look around the lobby. His gaze slowed and drifted past them. His brow furrowed, and then his eyes landed back on Brittany.

"It is you," he said as he came out to greet them. "You look different."

"Yeah, maybe it's because I'm out of the hospital bed." Her hand flew to her hair as if she'd just remembered it was now a different color. "Oh, and I just had my hair highlighted. Apparently, I was a blond in a former life."

He gave her an approving nod. "It suits you." He waved his hand in the air and leaned his back against the door to hold it open for them. "Come on back."

"So, there's a frozen yogurt place in that plaza where you were attacked," he said over his shoulder as they followed him down a long hallway. "It went out of business a few weeks ago, but they hadn't gotten around to shutting off their cameras. We finally got in touch with the owner—I guess he went out of town to deal with going belly up." He scratched the side of his head as if the man hadn't really thought through his business plan. "I'm not surprised he didn't make it. It's not really a frozen yogurt kind of neighborhood."

Becky nodded and tried to prod him toward the reason they'd come. "You said the yogurt place had footage?"

"Yeah, hang on, let me show you what we found."

Detective Torok gestured for Becky and Brittany to sit in the two chairs in front of his desk. His leather chair creaked in protest when he dropped into it and leaned forward. He fiddled with the mouse for his computer before finally reaching behind him to turn on a large television that sat on a metal stand with wheels.

"The yogurt shop was a standalone building on the outskirts of the parking lot." He gestured at the TV. "Their camera caught you traveling toward the exit as you headed for the sidewalk." He stood and tapped the screen. "You can see you already had the bag with the prepaid phone in it, so it looks like you were probably heading back to your apartment."

Brittany bobbed her head, her eyes glued to the video.

"Watch the two guys in the hoodies at the top right-hand corner of the screen," the detective said.

They weren't too far behind Brittany, but then they both broke into a run. In an instant, they had caught up and were confronting her.

"There's no sound?" Becky asked without taking her eyes off the television. "Is there any way to hear what they're saying to her?"

Detective Torok shook his head. "'Fraid not."

Even without sound, it was clear this was a robbery. As they watched, one of the guys yanked Brittany's purse strap from her shoulder and pulled something from inside.

"I know the footage is a little grainy, but it looks like Brittany had a significant amount of cash on her," the detective said. "We know she paid cash for the phone and the card with the minutes on it. My guess is they saw what she had when she made the purchase. They went right for her purse."

"The motive was money?" Becky's forehead wrinkled as she glanced over for confirmation. "Why didn't they just take it and run? Why hurt her?"

The detective held up his index finger. "There's more."

Becky squinted at the screen, wishing it was easier to see. "What are they doing now?"

Detective Torok glanced at Brittany. "Looks like you were wearing a ring." He huffed in disgust. "These two decided they wanted it."

Becky watched the struggle on the small screen as Brittany yanked her hand away and attempted to run. She didn't get far before the taller guy grabbed her by the shoulder and dragged her backward. The other guy reached down and picked up something. He then raised whatever he had in his hand and brought it down on Brittany's head.

Becky grimaced and reeled back in her seat. This was clearly the blow that had left her crumpled on the pavement.

"See there." The detective pointed at the screen where the smaller guy hunched over Brittany as she lay there.

"After she went down, he took the ring right off her finger." The detective paused the video, leaving it frozen on the man lifting her lifeless hand.

Becky shook her head in disbelief and rubbed Brittany's arm. "You okay?" she asked in a soft voice.

Brittany looked dazed but gave a slow nod. "It's odd. I feel like I'm watching something that happened to someone else."

The detective hit the play button again. "Right here, it looks like something spooked them. See them look up? Maybe it was a car, or someone could have yelled something at them." They watched as the smaller guy made an attempt to run for Brittany's purse lying on the ground about twenty feet from where she lay bleeding. But he didn't get the chance to grab it. The other guy pointed at something off-screen, then yanked him in the direction of the wooded area bordering the parking lot. As he did so, the shorter guy's hood slipped and revealed a head of curly brown hair. But that was all it showed. The men took off running and disappeared from the camera's view.

Becky let out a deep breath, feeling drained. Watching the footage had put her through the wringer. She could only imagine how Brittany felt.

"That's not much to go on," she said to the detective. "What are the odds you'll be able to find these two guys?"

"Hang on." Detective Torok held up his index finger and returned to his computer. After a few clicks, he pointed at the television. "We were able to find another camera that gave us a better view of Brittany leaving the location where she bought the phone." He pulled up a still shot that showed her from behind as she walked away from the store. "Wait," he said. "That's not the one."

He fiddled with his mouse, and another image appeared on the screen. Brittany had her hand raised as she rubbed her forehead, the ring she'd been wearing clearly visible.

Brittany got up and moved closer to the television, her eyes narrowed into slits.

"Do you recognize it?" Becky asked.

Brittany stood frozen, her mouth hanging open as she stared intently at the screen. "I'm not sure. Maybe. I definitely feel *something* when I look at it, but it's hard to tell what the ring really looks like."

The detective pulled a large photograph out of a file on his desk. He passed it to Brittany, and Becky could see it was a close-up shot of what appeared to be the actual ring.

"You'll be able to see it in person if you're interested," he said. "They sold it to Rocco's Pawn Shop on Washington Street." He sighed and rested his hand on his forehead as if dealing with these kinds of criminals was child's play. "Not exactly the sharpest tools in the shed. They had to show their IDs, and the pawnshop recorded their entire transaction."

He pulled up a still shot from the store. There on the television were the two guys from the parking lot, still wearing the hoodies they'd worn during the robbery. Only this time, their faces were clearly visible.

"How's your memory now?" he asked Brittany. "Do you recognize them at all as the guys who assaulted you?"

She stared at the screen and then shrugged helplessly. "Maybe. I don't know."

Becky shook her head in disbelief. "They're so young." Neither looked anything like the man Jules had described.

The detective rolled his eyes as if nothing surprised him anymore. "Both just turned eighteen. Dropped out of school, and it seems they've been robbing houses in their free time. Which they seem to have way too much of, if you ask me. Brittany's ring wasn't the only thing they were trying to sell that day."

Becky rubbed her chin thoughtfully. "Did they hurt anyone else? During those other robberies?"

"Nah, they went in during the day when people were at work. I told you, these two are amateurs. Just looking for anything they can lift to make a quick buck." The detective shrugged in Brittany's direction. "To be honest, I'm surprised they took it so far with you."

Becky couldn't believe two teenagers were responsible for the robbery and assault that robbed Brittany of her memory.

"Are you saying the attack was random? A matter of just being in the wrong place at the wrong time?"

"I think they saw a wad of cash and couldn't resist. They must have panicked when Brittany tried to run because it's not even like the ring was worth that much. Luckily, the pawnshop still had it."

The detective stood and switched off the television. "But don't worry, we actually picked them both up this morning, and we've already matched the smaller guy's prints to one we lifted from Brittany's purse. They haven't confessed yet, but don't worry, they'll crack. In addition to this surveillance, they were caught on a couple of the homeowners' cameras. Much better quality than the footage you saw." He offered a reassuring nod. "It won't leave much room for them to try and deny any of it."

Brittany held her head in her hands. "But if I can't remember, how can I help? I can't identify them."

"Even without your testimony, they'll have a slew of other charges against them. At least three counts of burglary and dealing in stolen property. Obviously, we want to nail them on your assault, and the footage we found will go a long way. Not to mention the guy's fingerprint is on the purse he ripped off your shoulder."

The detective pushed up from his chair. "Hopefully, this provides some comfort that at least the guys who put you in the hospital will be behind bars."

"We're definitely grateful for that." Becky shook his hand, but she still didn't feel at ease. None of what they'd seen answered the question about the man outside Brittany's apartment. She sucked in a sharp breath as she remembered something that had caught her by surprise. "Sorry to ask, but can you pull up the shot of Brittany outside the store again?"

He sat back down at his desk. "The one that showed the ring?"

"No, the other one."

The detective looked up, confused. "The one behind her as she's walking away?"

"Yeah."

He gave Becky a quizzical stare. "But you can't even see the ring in that photo."

"I know. I want to see something else."

The detective pressed a few keys on his computer and then stood and hit the power button on the television. When it came to life again, the image Becky asked about was on the screen.

Brittany was wearing a top with spaghetti straps, and there was something on her right shoulder blade. Becky got up from her seat, touched the screen, then shifted her gaze to the detective. "What's that?"

"You mean the tattoo?"

Becky studied the screen again. "Is that what that is?" She eyed Brittany curiously. "Did you know you have a tattoo on your back?"

The shocked expression on her face told Becky what she needed to know, even before Brittany shook her head. "I had no idea. I know that sounds crazy, but I can't really see back there."

"Do you mind if I …"

"No, I'd like to see it too," Brittany said. "Can you take a picture?"

Becky reached for her phone. She stood behind Brittany and used her other hand to pull down the neck of her T-shirt until it revealed what was inked on her back. She pressed the button, a click confirming the photo had been taken. Becky checked to make sure it was clear before stepping back.

"What is it?" Brittany pinned a hopeful gaze on Becky. "A butterfly, a cartoon character? Hopefully, it's not anything dark or goth."

It wasn't any of those things.

Becky handed her the phone, the picture of the tattoo still on the screen.

"Any idea who you would have gotten that for?"

Brittany didn't respond. Instead, she covered her mouth with her hand as she stared at the image. Then, she began to cry.

CHAPTER FIFTEEN

"How was last night?" Jules asked as they waited for Brittany to come out of the first bank on their list for the day. She let out an audible yawn. "I appreciate you driving. It was nice to have Tim spend the night, but I didn't get much sleep."

Becky grinned as her eyebrows shot up. "I'll bet."

"Well, from that, but it was mostly the snoring." She let out a moan. "What am I going to do when we're together every single night?"

Her friend offered a sympathetic chuckle. "You'll be fine. Bryan snores too, but somehow, I've gotten used to it. Brittany didn't complain last night, so I guess she didn't hear him. I offered to put the inflatable mattress in the—" Becky stopped herself and stared down at the steering wheel. "In the other bedroom. Anyway, she wanted to watch TV, so she said she was fine sleeping on the couch."

Jules knew Becky used her spare bedroom primarily for storage. She kept the door shut, so it wasn't a constant reminder about what that room was supposed to be. Ever since she and Bryan bought the house, her best friend had known it was meant to be a nursery. That time just hadn't come yet.

"I pulled the curtains closed on the big window," Becky said. "Not that Brittany seemed to give it a thought, but you know, just in case. I figured it was better if no one could see in."

Jules remembered what Tim had said in the car the day before. He and Bryan seemed aligned that the women in their lives courted danger whenever Brittany was around.

"And Bryan? He was okay with her staying over?"

Becky took in a sharp breath of hesitation. "Well, he wasn't *thrilled*, but he agreed you needed a break."

Jules hung her head and dug her fingertips into her temples. Lack of sleep had given her a headache. Or maybe it was the conversation from the night before.

"Tim wants me to ask her to move out." Jules lifted her head and met Becky's eyes. "Is that what Bryan thinks I should do too?"

Becky took a moment before she responded. "He didn't say that. They're just worried about us. About something bad happening." Her expression turned apologetic as if she knew she was about to say something Jules wouldn't want to hear. "But I can understand where they're coming from. We don't know a single thing about Brittany's past, so someone dangerous *could* be after her." Her lips pursed. "And by association, *us*."

Jules leaned her head back against the headrest and took in a deep breath. "So, the detective really thinks it was just a random robbery that went too far?"

"He does, and it seems highly unlikely either suspect was the guy you saw at Brittany's apartment or the fair. Pretty sure they were just your average street thugs."

"Unless someone *hired* them to attack Brittany." Jules's eyebrows lifted, but deep down, she knew she was grasping at straws.

Becky dismissed the idea with a firm shake of her head.

"Doubtful. Robbing houses while people are at work doesn't seem like they have a side business doing ordered hits. The detective was actually shocked they'd been violent with Brittany, especially after they were stupid enough to hand over their IDs at the pawnshop." Becky leaned back in the driver's seat. "He said they were amateurs."

"I was hoping it was all related. You know, if we figured out who put Brittany in the hospital, we'd have our answer to who's been following her around. Not to mention throwing bricks." Jules gazed out the passenger side window. "I guess it's possible I could have been wrong about that too," she said in a soft voice. Had she blown the entire thing out of proportion? Made a big deal when it was all just a series of coincidences?

When Jules glanced back at Becky, her shoulders lifted slightly. "If the guy from the apartment wasn't responsible for Brittany's assault, it's possible we don't have a reason to be worried about her after all."

"Maybe he's an ex-boyfriend. They broke up, which is why she got the new place. Then, of course, she disappeared while she was in the hospital. Maybe he wanted to try and get back together, but then he had no idea what happened to her." Becky's eyebrows shot up. "Hey, what if he's the reason she got the tattoo?"

Jules pulled up the photo Becky had texted her—a broken heart with the initial L inside. "I still can't believe we never realized she had this. I guess it's possible she could have gotten it because of a bad breakup."

"She told me she didn't know what it meant, but she had an immediate reaction when she saw it." Becky glanced toward the bank entrance and then back at Jules. "She started crying."

"She might have had a boyfriend or a husband that died." Jules didn't want to mention it could have also been a baby or a child. That would explain the doll. A treasured toy of a daughter whose name started with an L.

Becky didn't bring up the possibility of a child either. Not a complete surprise.

"Well, in the footage, she was wearing the ruby ring on her right hand," Becky said, gesturing at her own finger. "She didn't have anything on her left hand. Though I guess if she was married and her husband died, she might not wear her rings anymore."

"Or we could be right that she's married and hiding out from her husband," Jules said, gazing out the window again before letting out a soft groan. "Which puts us back to square one, wondering who this mysterious L could be."

"Well, now that she's wearing the ring again, we can only hope it triggers her to remember who gave it to her." Becky's nose wrinkled. "That pawnshop did make me a little nervous last night. The whole time we were there, I kept thinking we'd run into the guys who mugged her. You know, like somehow the police let them go." She rolled her eyes as if she knew her best friend would have hoped for the opportunity to run into them.

Jules huffed in disgust. "I still can't believe you had to pay to get her ring back. Something that was hers to begin with."

Becky held up her hand. "Don't get me started. Luckily, it wasn't that much money." She squirmed in the driver's seat. "You didn't see the video, Jules. She *fought* to keep the guy from taking that ring. I figured it had to have more than just monetary value to her. I felt like she should have it."

"No, I absolutely agree." Jules stretched and stifled a yawn. "Add it to her tab, I guess. Let's hope those guys didn't get every penny she had."

"At least now we know they didn't steal anything other than the cash she had." Becky ran her hands mindlessly around the steering wheel. "Well, that and the ring."

"So, what we saw at the hospital and in her apartment was all she had, which wasn't much." Jules shook her head, trying to make sense of it. "There has to be more. Somewhere. It's not like those thugs got her keys and then robbed her place while she was laid up in the hospital. But who doesn't have at least one credit card?" she asked, pinching her lips. "Or an ATM card?"

"Apparently, Brittany Mullins doesn't." Becky nudged Jules's arm and aimed her chin at the bank.

She was coming out of the bank, and she was scowling.

"Any luck?" Jules asked, even though the expression on her face made the answer seem obvious.

Brittany slid into the back seat and slammed the door. "Nope. It's crazy how they won't tell you anything except yes, you have a box there, or no, you don't. The lady just handed me back my license with a big fat '*you don't have a safety deposit box in this bank, so I can't help you.*'" Brittany wagged her finger in the air as she mimicked the woman. "It's exhausting. They all look at me like I'm crazy for not knowing where my own box is located."

"Did you ask about the other branches?" Becky asked.

Brittany blew out a puff of air, then shook her head. "I didn't. If that uppity bank lady saw something on her computer screen, it wasn't anything she was going to share with me."

"Did you tell her you were in an accident and lost your memory?" Becky shifted in her seat. "You should have made her feel guilty for being so mean."

"I tried. Trust me, she wasn't interested, and she didn't feel bad." Brittany mimicked the woman again. "*Sorry, bank policy.*" She expelled a frustrated sigh. "Let's write this one off as a possibility."

Jules drew a line through it on their master list. "We still haven't checked out the library, so let's go there next. There's only one that seems feasible based on you not having a car." She glanced over her shoulder. "It would have still been a hike if you were walking from your apartment, but I think it's worth a try." She plugged the address into the car's navigation system.

Becky gave a nod and pulled out of the bank parking lot.

When they passed a local park, Brittany stared longingly out the back window at the joggers on the outside trail. "I used to be one of them. I'm sure of it."

Jules shifted so she could see into the back seat. "Tim says if you're a real runner, it's in your blood." She bit back a smile. "Tim and I actually met at a 5K race. That's the one Becky was referring to the other day."

Brittany leaned forward, her face brightening. "You used to run?"

When Becky let out a snort, Jules glared dramatically in her direction.

"Tim was one of the runners, and I was there to take pictures," she said, directing her story at Brittany. "It was a 5K to support the St. John's County Animal Shelter, and we met after the race was over. They had pens of puppies and dogs available for adoption." She crossed her arms over her chest and smiled wistfully. "Tim and I both fell in love with the same dog."

"Gene?" Brittany asked. "I thought you said you got him from your aunt?"

"We did, but this was over two years ago." Jules let out a soft moan as she remembered being taken by the dog's sweet face, whitened with age. "Her name was Abby. She was an older cocker spaniel, and she looked at me with these eyes that just melted me."

At the time, Jules knew she wasn't home enough to have a dog, but she couldn't stand the idea Abby might not get adopted because she wasn't a puppy. She also wasn't willing to let the tall, handsome man playing with her get away either.

"It was how Tim and I met. We agreed to put Abby in between us to see who she'd choose. Luckily, before we could finish fighting over who she wanted to be with, the lady from the shelter told us someone else was smitten with her too. They'd already paid the adoption fee and were coming back to pick her up."

"So, Abby found a home, and you found a fiancé?"

It hadn't been that simple, but Jules dipped her head and smiled. "Yup. Pretty much. I may not run, but I'm definitely a fan of people who do."

"Maybe I met someone while I was out running," Brittany said as she sat back and pressed her nose against the window. "Maybe it was even at the Lifesaver 5K. That might explain why I brought that T-shirt with me."

Her voice got soft, and Jules barely caught what she said next.

"Why isn't he looking for me?"

CHAPTER SIXTEEN

Brittany clicked a button on the remote, and the television came to life. She leaned back and let out a soft moan. "This might be the most comfortable couch I've ever had the pleasure of sitting on. Not that I remember all the furniture of my past, but I'm pretty sure this one is hard to beat."

"I take it the couch at Becky's wasn't comfortable?" Jules asked.

"It was fine. Maybe not great for sleeping, but for one night, I survived." It had been a luxury to watch television as she fell asleep, even if it meant sleeping on the couch. Brittany laid down and rested her head on one of the small pillows. "I should try sleeping down here one night."

"You say that now, but just wait until you try to get out of it." Jules fought a smile. "My mom always gets sucked in, and I have to pull her out."

Brittany sat back up. "Your adopted mother or your birth mother?"

Jules flinched. "Even though Barb gave birth to me, and I'm thrilled we have a relationship now, I—Well, I always consider my adopted mother to be my *mom*."

Brittany's cheeks burned. She hadn't meant to offend Jules. "Oh, I'm sorry. I didn't mean to—"

Jules dismissed her apology with the wave of her hand. "No, it's okay," she said as she dropped into the armchair.

"You're lucky you got adopted into such a wonderful family."

Jules bobbed her head in agreement. "I know. It didn't change my need to know where I came from because that wasn't about *them*. It was about me and who I was. So, finding Barb and knowing my story took this enormous weight off my shoulders."

"I wonder if I have good parents." At this point, Brittany would settle for even the smallest nugget of information about her family.

"I'm sure you do. Want to try some of my sweet tea?"

Brittany shrugged. "Will I like it?"

Jules grinned. "The way I make it? You'll love it."

Brittany didn't want to hurt Jules's feelings that she wasn't even willing to try it. "Okay, then."

"I know we didn't find out anything useful at the library, but there are books on the bookshelf. Help yourself to anything that looks interesting."

Brittany nodded, but when Jules left the room, she picked up the television remote and started flipping through channels.

She was already engrossed in a movie by the time Jules came back with her tea. She'd watched as a young couple who'd been celebrating the husband's award for his work as a child psychologist realized someone had broken into their house. A former patient. Brittany couldn't lift her eyes from the screen, and as she watched, the intruder whipped out a gun. She shrank back on the couch, her hand flying to her mouth when he used it to shoot the husband.

She heaved out a deep breath and glanced up at Jules. "Wow. I didn't see that coming."

"Oh, an oldie but goodie. I loved this movie." Jules set Brittany's tea on one of the coasters on the coffee table. "You've never seen it?"

Brittany cocked her head and shot her a look of disbelief. She didn't remember her past, but she'd recall the plot of a movie?

"Oh, sorry. Right. I guess that's one benefit of losing your memory. You can watch movies all over again and have no idea what happens." She aimed her chin at the glass. "Try it."

Brittany picked up the glass and took a sip. It was surprisingly good. "Mmm. I like it."

Then her attention was drawn back to the television as the child psychologist spoke to a young boy in a church. Brittany scratched the side of her head. "Wow, he's alive? I thought he was a goner for sure."

Jules lifted her shoulders, a knowing smile on her face as she shrugged. "You're only about ten minutes in. I have to go to the fitting for my bridesmaid dress in a few minutes, but I can record it if you want. We can finish watching it later." She laughed. "I promised I won't spoil the ending, but trust me, it's a doozy."

Brittany dropped her head. She enjoyed spending time with Jules, but the feeling she was being babysat was getting old. "Do I really have to go with you?" She tried to keep the annoyance from her voice but was sure she hadn't pulled it off.

Hurt flickered across Jules's face, but she managed to recover quickly. "I'm just trying to keep you safe."

"I know, but nothing's happened," Brittany said, her voice firm as she set her glass back on the table. "We don't know for sure that anyone's after me and the guys who attacked me are in jail."

Jules looked hesitant. "But the brick—"

"Even Jonas said it could have been related to that drug case. And if it was somehow because of me ..." Brittany lifted her shoulders but wasn't ready to give up. "Then I feel terrible about the damage at Becky's, and I'll reimburse her for the new window when I can. But not a single thing has happened since then."

"And what if it was the same guy at the art show?" Jules clearly wasn't willing to give up so easily either.

"Even if it was, it's not like he tried to hurt me or even talk to me." Brittany waved her arms in the air to make her point. "There could be a perfectly innocent explanation. Maybe I had a boyfriend I ghosted, or—or—or a job I never showed up at."

Jules took in a deep breath and eased it out slowly. "I guess that's possible."

"You go to your fitting, but I'm going to stay here and finish watching the movie." Brittany hoped the determined tone of her voice conveyed the discussion was over. This need to be joined at the hip was getting ridiculous. "Maybe if I've seen it before, it will even trigger my memory."

Jules pressed her lips together but didn't respond. Brittany held her breath as she waited to learn whether she'd won the battle.

Then Jules crossed her arms across her chest and pinned her with a stern stare. "You'll stay put?"

Brittany bit back a smile. "You said I wouldn't be able to get myself out of the couch."

"Okay, fine." Jules's head bobbed in defeat. "When I get back, we can order a pizza or something. Tim's bringing Gene back tonight."

When Brittany heard the front door slam shut announcing Jules's departure, she propped her feet up on the coffee table. She let out a prolonged sigh, almost delirious at the sense of freedom enveloping her.

Since leaving the hospital, she hadn't been alone for more than the time it took to take a shower or dry her hair. It felt good to have a break from the constant surveillance as if she was a child that needed to be monitored. Brittany knew Jules and Becky were worried about her, but still. Even if she couldn't remember who she was, she was an adult. That had to count for something.

Brittany ran her hand over her thigh and flexed her foot. If her legs used to be toned, those muscles were fading. She remembered the joggers at the park the day before, and her gaze flew to the window. It was late afternoon and still glorious outside. Perfect for a quick run.

Brittany hit the pause button on the movie, and with newfound excitement, she raced up the stairs. At the top, she felt a sense of satisfaction. She was barely out of breath. Hopefully that meant she was still in shape.

She threw on running clothes and her sneakers and hurried down the two flights of stairs to the front door. She hesitated and glanced around for a spare key to lock up behind her. There wasn't one.

Brittany groaned. Could she risk leaving Jules's place unlocked? This might be her only opportunity to get out for a bit by herself, and she wouldn't be gone long. Jules's townhouse sat on a lake, and Brittany told herself she'd just run where she could keep an eye on it.

The door shut behind her with a satisfying thud. She stretched for a few minutes and then took off.

It didn't take long before Brittany had no doubt this was a regular indulgence. As her sneakers hit the path, she felt a familiarity all the way into her bones, into her soul. It was a freedom she hadn't felt since she'd left the hospital. Though she was aching to open it up, she kept an easy pace. If she hurt herself, she'd have no way to explain how it had happened.

As she ran, the breeze blew through her hair, the late afternoon sun warming her face. She gave a brief nod as she passed other people on the path. It wasn't like they'd tell Jules. For all they knew, Brittany was an ordinary woman out for an afternoon jog. She began to relax and found a comfortable pace. She could get used to this.

Though she wasn't ready to quit, Brittany couldn't risk Jules returning to find her gone and the house unlocked. Reluctantly, she turned around to head back. She'd shower off, change, and be back on the couch before Jules got back from her fitting. Brittany felt vindicated that she'd been right. Nothing terrible had happened. She'd gotten to go for a run, and Jules hadn't needed to worry about her. It was a win, win.

Brittany crossed from the running path to the sidewalk that would take her back to the townhouse, then slowed to a walk to cool down. There had to be a way to convince Jules to let her go running again by herself. Maybe she could go with Tim. He ran almost every day, but Brittany wasn't sure he liked her much. She attributed it to the fact that he wanted his fiancée all to himself.

But what if she could get Tim to agree to let her join him? There was no way Jules could argue about it then. The whole thing was silly anyway. Here, she'd gone for a run and been perfectly safe. Nothing had happened.

Brittany wanted to skip down the sidewalk, positively giddy she'd pulled it off. Finally, she felt like an adult capable of making her own decisions. How long had it been since she could do what she wanted without Becky or Jules telling her it was too dangerous?

All their worrying had been for nothing. There was no crazy stalker following her, no mystery man ready to nab Brittany the minute she was left alone.

As the townhouse came into view, Brittany checked Jules's parking spot and allowed herself a satisfied smile. It was still empty. She chuckled to herself about how easy her escape had been. And much needed. Just that brief amount of time on her own had left her feeling like everything was going to work out.

For the first time since she'd left the hospital, Brittany was happy. Content.

That's when she spotted him.

It took only a moment, and the smile slipped from her lips. A million things ran through her mind as she stood frozen on the sidewalk, eyes wide, her legs paralyzed. Her chest visibly rose and fell as she took in rapid gulps of air. The run had barely winded her, but now she felt like there was a vice squeezing her chest.

When he stepped out from behind the parked car, she felt herself sway on her feet. This wasn't her imagination. The memory was real.

She could tell by the way he stared at her.

CHAPTER SEVENTEEN

WHEN JULES GOT BACK from her fitting, Brittany was on the couch exactly where she'd left her. Her glass of sweet tea was still full, the ice now melted as condensation dripped down the sides. Brittany hadn't had more than the obligatory sip, but at least it was on the coaster and hadn't left a water stain on her wooden coffee table.

"How was the movie?" Jules asked. "Did you love it?"

Brittany didn't have time to respond before the doorbell rang.

Jules glanced at the clock. "I didn't expect to be gone so long. That must be Tim and Gene."

She took advantage of a rare moment of privacy to greet her fiancé at the front door. The dog bounded upstairs without them.

As they headed up, Jules heard Brittany's enthusiastic greeting. "Hey, buddy. I'm so glad you're back." Then she glanced up with a wide smile. "Hey, Tim. It's good to see you too."

Jules nudged his arm. "Hey, hon, be right back. I'm going to go up and change into something that doesn't involve Spanx."

As she passed Brittany's bedroom on the way to her own, Jules let out an exasperated sigh. She reached for the doorknob to prevent Gene from wandering inside, but she couldn't help but notice the trail of clothes on the floor leading to her bathroom. Her forehead wrinkled as she tried to make sense of it. They hadn't been there earlier. She was sure because she'd been in Brittany's closet to get the heels she needed for her dress fitting.

She'd gone through the hallway entrance into Brittany's bathroom and then into the bedroom. Not only was the door to the hall closed now, but when Jules tried the knob, it was locked.

Jules tiptoed to the top of the stairs and stood rigid and quiet as she listened to ensure no one was coming. Her shoulders lowered when she heard Brittany and Tim downstairs, engaged in what sounded like a casual conversation.

With the coast clear, she stepped into Brittany's bedroom and headed to the adjoining bathroom. The shower curtain was pulled back, the tile on the shower walls and floor wet. She ran her hand over the towel hanging on the hook on the back of the door. Damp.

Brittany's running shoes looked like they'd been kicked off in a hurry. One was on its side in front of the shower, and the other sat cockeyed on the bed. Jules frowned when she realized the trail of clothes included what Brittany would wear to go jogging. After the conversation in the car the day before, had she decided to go for a run after Jules left? Was that why she was so adamant about not going to the fitting?

Jules's mind was spinning as she backed up and left everything as she'd found it. She wasn't sure yet how she wanted to handle her suspicion.

She changed her clothes quickly, and as she headed back down the stairs, Jules overhead Tim discussing dinner with Brittany.

"What do you like on your pizza?" he asked. "Jules isn't that adventurous, so I'm always happy if someone will veer off with me."

Her response was immediate. "I'm good for anything. I usually like peppers, onions, mushrooms. I'll even do ham and pineapple if that's your jam."

Jules stepped into the kitchen and eyed Brittany. "Hey, you remembered what you like on your pizza."

She glanced up, confused. "What?"

"You just told Tim what kind of pizza you like, almost like you remembered."

"Oh, yeah, you're right." Brittany shrugged. "I guess it just came to me when I wasn't thinking too hard about it."

Tim waved the pizzeria menu dramatically and took a bow. "Glad to help."

Jules swatted at his arm. "I'm sure it was all you, hon." Then her eyes were back on Brittany. "Something must have triggered you to remember. Has there been other stuff?"

A pink flush grew on Brittany's cheeks. It was almost as if she was embarrassed her memory might come back about something as insignificant as her pizza preferences. "Little flashes here and there. I just never know if they're real or not."

Jules could still picture Brittany on the couch when she'd walked in after her dress fitting. Sitting in the exact spot she'd been in when Jules left. Wearing the same clothes. Clearly, she was trying to hide the fact she'd left to go for a run. Had she simply forgotten to clean up her clothes? Or had Jules come home earlier than expected? Maybe she had needed to make a mad dash to get back to her designated spot on the couch.

"So, you never did tell me, did you like the movie? Especially the ending." Jules wrinkled her nose. "Wasn't that crazy?" There would be no faking it now. It wasn't a twist most people guessed, so if Brittany tried, she'd be caught.

Brittany looked down, and Jules wondered if she was

trying to buy herself time. When she brought her gaze up to meet Jules's inquisitive stare, the yawn she let out seemed forced. "I'm embarrassed to admit I fell asleep. But I blame my nap on that comfortable couch of yours. I couldn't help myself."

Jules pressed her lips together to keep from blurting out that she knew Brittany was lying. She still wasn't sure what to make of it. "You must have been really tired."

"Yeah, I was. And now I'm starving."

When the doorbell rang with the pizza delivery, Gene barked, then bolted down the stairs. "Hey, buddy, don't forget to tip the driver," Tim called out. "If only he could retrieve food deliveries, we'd be set, right, hon?" He stood and then headed for the stairs. "I'll go get it."

"I'll help," Jules said, jumping to her feet. When Brittany shot her a curious look, she gave a non-committal shrug. "I have to sign the credit card receipt."

After Tim closed the front door, two hot pizzas resting on his palm, Jules sidled up close to him.

"Can you do me a favor?" she asked in a low voice.

He looked amused. "You want to carry the pizza up?"

When Jules's face turned serious, he nodded. "Sure. What do you need?"

"Tomorrow, while Brittany and I are out, can you install a camera over the front door?"

Tim tipped his head and stared at her through narrowed eyes. "Sure, but why?" he asked, the words clipped.

"I'm pretty sure Brittany went out while I was at my bridesmaid fitting."

"Went out where?" he asked. "She doesn't have a car."

Jules crossed her arms and pulled them close against her chest. "I think she went for a run. Probably here around the lake."

Tim let out a relieved sigh. "Okay, but that's not a crime,

Jules. Trust me, sometimes you just *need* to get out and go for a run. I get that you don't understand—"

Jules glanced at the stairs and put a finger to her lips. "Shh. I get that you runners need your endorphins or whatever those things are you claim to find when you go jogging. But, Tim, she deliberately *lied* about it. You heard her. She said she fell asleep on the couch."

"Well, yeah, but that's probably because she knew you'd freak out if she told you she went out," he said in a loud whisper. "Did you make her swear up and down she'd stay in the house?"

Jules lifted a shoulder. "Well, yeah, pretty much."

He let out an amused snort. "Well, there you go. Obviously, Brittany's fine, and nothing happened while you were gone. She probably just didn't count on the fact that my eagle-eyed fiancée doesn't miss a thing."

Jules scowled at his words, his indifference frustrating her. He was the one who had said she needed to be careful. "I'm not being nosy. I'm being cautious. You were there when that brick came flying through the window." She set her jaw as she gave him a pointed stare. "You were the one who wanted me to tell her to move out."

He tapped Jules gently on the nose with his finger. "And you, my big-hearted girl, were the one who basically told me to mind my own business."

Jules pursed her lips. "That isn't exactly what I said." But she knew his recollection wasn't entirely off-base. "So, will you install the camera for me?"

Tim leaned over and kissed her. "Of course, I will."

"Thank you." She leaned in close and lowered her voice. "I don't want Brittany to know it's there, so can you try to get something that won't be obvious?"

"Yes, dear," Tim said robotically, but then he smiled and kissed her again.

As they came up the stairs, Brittany glanced over from the couch. "I was starting to get worried you'd both been kidnapped by the delivery guy. Then what would I do?" Her face broke into a grin as she leaned on the arm of the sofa and pushed herself up. "There'd be no pizza, and I'm starving."

Jules pulled three plates from the cupboard and set them on the table beside the two open pizza boxes. She reached for the plain pie and slid a piece onto her plate.

Brittany took a large bite of her slice, overflowing with toppings, and let out a satisfied moan. "So good." When she reached for a second slice, she rolled her eyes. "If I'm going to keep eating like this, I really need to start exercising."

Her tone was casual, but Jules knew precisely where she was going with this conversation. In her head, she'd already begun to formulate her response. She was still uncomfortable with Brittany going out by herself, to go running or otherwise.

As Jules ate her pizza and waited for Brittany's inevitable request, her eyebrows shot up when instead she turned to Tim.

"I know you go running all the time. Would you mind if I went with you sometimes?" Her voice was saccharine sweet.

Tim's eyes flew instantly to his fiancée, a panicked expression on his face as if he'd done something wrong. As he sputtered to respond to the unusual request, Jules took a bite of her pizza and stared at Brittany from across the table.

Just what was she up to?

CHAPTER EIGHTEEN

Becky reached across the table and gave her best friend's arm a gentle pinch. "Cut it out. I'm pretty sure Brittany can handle going to the restroom by herself."

Jules had her neck craned so she could keep an eye on the door to the ladies' room. She let out an aggravated groan and settled into her seat. "I know. I just can't shake the feeling there's more going on than we're aware of, but I get it. It's not like I can follow her everywhere."

Becky was sure Jules would cuff Brittany to her wrist if she could.

"I still can't believe she asked Tim if she could go running with him. Your fiancé." Becky had gotten a text from Jules the night it happened, but then she hadn't mentioned it again. Not that Becky thought she had anything to worry about with Tim, but the request was still odd. "Do you think there's anything to it?"

Jules flicked her hand in the air dismissively. "I think Brittany really just wants out of the house. A bit of freedom. She probably got a taste of running and knows the only way I wouldn't have something to say about her going again is if she went with Tim."

"You're probably right. But do you think maybe you're making more of her leaving than it was? You said she was fine when you got back." Becky glanced up toward the bathroom door and leaned across the table. "Has there been anything suspicious on the camera Tim installed?"

Jules shook her head. "Not that I've seen, but I can't really check it when she's around. Every little thing sets it off, so I had to change the settings so she wouldn't ask what kept dinging on my phone. Last night it was a black cat strolling by my front door." She smiled at her best friend, a gleam of mischief in her eye. "You're the cat lady here. Is it bad luck if it crosses my path, but it's only on camera?"

Becky rolled her eyes and snatched a menu from the pile at the end of the table. "I am *not* a cat lady. I have one cat, and you barely know he's there."

Brittany slid into the booth next to Jules just as Becky shot her an aggravated look. It didn't go unnoticed.

"What?" Brittany asked, her gaze drifting between the two women. "What did I miss?"

"Nothing. Becky's just worried she might be turning into a cat lady." Jules smirked and handed her a menu. "You hungry?"

After a momentary flicker of confusion, Brittany flipped open the menu and nodded. "I'm starving. Do you think they have something here like that sandwich Bryan made last week?"

"The steak sandwich?" Becky asked.

"Right," Brittany said with an enthusiastic nod. "That was amazing."

Becky glanced around the little luncheonette. "Not sure it will be up to Bryan's standards here, but you can try."

They placed their orders, and the waitress had just delivered their sodas when a woman strolled by with a take-out order. She gave their table a passing glance, then backtracked with a puzzled expression on her face.

Her head tipped to the side as she stared at them. "Britt?"

Brittany glanced around, then pointed at her chest. "Me?"

The woman's lips lifted into an enthusiastic smile. "Oh, it is you! I haven't seen you in years. How have you been?"

The color drained from Brittany's face. "You know me? Really?"

The woman's smile faded. "Of course I do." She stared at Brittany with a look of bewilderment. "Britt, what's wrong?"

Becky slid over and patted the space on the booth beside her. "Do you have a second to sit?"

The woman hesitated, then pulled her phone from her purse and glanced at the time. "Um, sure, I guess I have a few minutes." She held up her take-out order. "I can't take too long, or my boss will be screaming for his lunch."

Brittany drew in a stuttered breath. "So, I had a little … accident. I sort of lost my memory."

"Really?" The woman's mouth went slack as her eyes searched Becky and Jules's faces for confirmation. "Oh, that's awful." Her shoulders lifted. "You don't—"

"Remember?" Brittany cut in. "Not much from before it happened, no. But the doctors said if I had someone that could help me, you know, trigger some familiar memories. It might help."

The woman let out a breath. "Oh." Then she managed a nervous smile. "It's so weird you don't remember me." She placed her hand on her chest. "I'm Cami. We went to high school together. In Tampa. Man, we had some good times."

Brittany squinted at her. "Were you a—"

"A cheerleader? I was. You were too." Her smile was back. "See, you *do* remember."

Brittany tilted her head as she stared at Cami, her nod slow in coming. "I think I might."

Jules wore a dubious expression as she observed their exchange. "Do you remember if she had siblings?"

Cami pressed a finger to her lips. "A brother, I think. No, a sister." She shrugged. "Honestly, I never spent any time at her house. We used to just go out to eat after practice and the football games."

The woman glanced down at her phone and then at Brittany. "I'm sorry, but I've got to run. Britt, let me give you my number." She reached into her purse and dug out a pen. "I'm happy to get together and help in any way I can. I even have some photo albums from high school somewhere I can probably dig up. I'm sure I can help jog your memory."

"You must know her last name too," Becky said.

Cami hesitated for a moment, then wrote her phone number on a napkin. "Well, it used to be Schroeder, but of course, that was her maiden name. I never heard if she got married, but it's been a while." She handed her number to Brittany. "I've really got to run, but call me, and we'll catch up. Don't worry. I'll help you figure it all out."

As the woman rushed out the front door of the restaurant, Brittany stared at the napkin, a deep divot between her eyebrows. "So, my name really is Brittany."

"I guess it is." Becky offered her a small smile. "How do you feel?"

"Numb." She set her elbow on the table and rested her chin in the palm of her hand. She stared off as if she was trying to connect the dots in her brain. "Maybe I do remember being a cheerleader. Football games. Parties. I'm starting to get these little flashes of memories. I think I remember kissing a boy on someone's living room couch. I feel like he was kind of cute." The corners of Brittany's mouth lifted into a smile.

"Remembering a cute boy is a good thing," Becky said in a soft voice.

Brittany bobbed her head in agreement. "Definitely. So, I'm from Tampa."

"Sounds like it. Or at least you lived there during high school." Becky traded a glance with Jules. She could still have come from out of state, but this new information was like striking gold.

"How far is Tampa from here?" Brittany asked.

Becky looked to Jules for confirmation. "It's about a three-and-a-half-hour drive, I think?"

"Sounds about right," Jules said before rubbing her chin thoughtfully. "If Cami's from Tampa, I wonder what she was doing here."

Brittany sipped her soda. "Didn't she say she had food for her boss? She must work here. I guess I'll find out when I call her."

"Maybe we can do that tonight," Jules said.

Becky noticed she'd used the word we, a clear indication Jules wanted to be part of any reunion Brittany might have. She still had questions, and she'd expect Cami to have answers.

"If your maiden name was Schroeder, then Mullins must be your married name. And now we know you lived in Tampa." Becky shot Brittany a hopeful smile. "This should be easy to figure out now."

Jules didn't look so convinced. "I wonder why the police were so convinced you weren't using your real name." Her eyes narrowed. "And if you're married, why are you in a different city in a new apartment?"

"Maybe I'm divorced but never changed my name back." Brittany lifted her shoulders as if none of it really mattered anymore. "I have no idea, but it sounds like I won't need to waste any more of your time. If Cami can give me more information, I'm sure I can find my family. Then I can pay you for the time and money you've spent so far. Wouldn't it be amazing if I didn't even need to wait for the results of the DNA tests?"

Just then, the waitress arrived with an armful of plates.

"Imagine that," Brittany said as her lunch was placed in front of her. "I thought I was just going out to have a bite to eat, and now there's a chance Cami can help me remember who I went to prom with or where I went to college." She looked genuinely happy as she picked up her sandwich. "Maybe I'll even be able to figure out who the girl is from the picture. Wouldn't that be something?"

CHAPTER NINETEEN

"I APPRECIATE you hanging out here with me." Jules handed Becky a Diet Coke, then leaned against the kitchen counter and rubbed the back of her neck. She'd been a bundle of nerves all day. "I have no idea what time Brittany will be back. I mean, she has to come back, right? All her stuff is here."

"Of course she'll be back." Becky popped the top on her can of soda and took a sip. "What time did Cami pick her up?"

Jules glanced at the clock on the wall. It was almost four. "Ten o'clock this morning." She had a bad feeling festering in the pit of her stomach. "What could they be doing for so long?"

Just then, the doorbell sounded up the stairs. As Gene barked, Jules's shoulders dropped in relief. "That has to be her."

"Can't you check the new camera?"

"Oh, I guess I could." Jules's gaze drifted along the counter until she spotted her phone. She pressed the button for the app and gave a nod. "It's her. It looks like she's alone."

Jules hurried down the stairs, with Gene following eagerly behind her.

She inhaled deeply and took a moment to collect herself before she pulled open the door. "Oh, hey, you're back." Jules wanted to sound casual, like she hadn't been anxiously waiting for Brittany's return. Despite having already seen the camera footage, she made a show of stepping through the opened door to look outside. "Did Cami leave? You could have invited her to come in."

"She had to get to work," Brittany said as she stooped down to pet Gene.

Cami hadn't wanted to come in that morning either. She'd called from her car to announce her arrival, and Brittany had just grabbed her purse and left. Jules couldn't fight her feeling that Cami didn't want to be grilled by anyone but Brittany.

Jules peered over her shoulder as they plodded up the stairs. "Was she able to help you remember anything?" She couldn't help but notice the plastic bag in Brittany's hand.

"We had a great day."

Jules bristled at the simplicity of her statement. She was going to need more than that. Much more.

When they got to the kitchen, Brittany lifted her hand to acknowledge Becky. "Hey, you're here too. Perfect. I can tell you both everything at the same time. Let me just run upstairs quick to drop off my stuff and change."

She returned a few minutes later in a T-shirt and shorts and claimed a chair at the table. Jules pursed her lips when she noticed the bag hadn't come back downstairs with her.

Brittany drew in a deep breath. "So, it turns out I did move here from Tampa. Before that, I was an ultrasound tech at Tampa General." She turned to Jules and gave a half-shrug. "It's not exactly the same, but maybe that's why that nurse thing at the fair seemed familiar."

Jules gave her an obligatory nod. It wasn't the same at all, but she let it go. "You quit that job?"

"Yeah, I guess I did. Cami helped me find a phone number

for my parents. When I spoke to them, they told me I met a guy on Bumble who lives here. His name is Derek."

"Bumble?" Becky asked, confused. "Is that one of those online dating things?"

"Yeah." The corners of Brittany's mouth tugged upward into an embarrassed smile. "Not sure why I couldn't meet a guy in a bar like most people. Anyway, my parents told me I quit my job and planned to look for a new one here. Derek was the reason I moved, so I'm sure he's the guy who's been looking for me." She stood, as if that was the entirety of the story, then pulled open the refrigerator and grabbed a Diet Coke.

"Your parents? They've met this *Derek*?" Jules was aware she'd said his name as if she didn't believe he was a real person. She couldn't help it.

"Oh, yeah, he's been to Tampa, and my parents and sister have met him. Of course, he probably thought I was ghosting him once I got here and disappeared." Brittany leaned against the counter as she popped the top on her soda can and took a sip. "But at least he's not some crazy guy stalking me, so nobody has to worry anymore."

"Well, that's a relief," Becky said, glancing over at Jules. "Maybe the brick actually *was* related to Jonas's suspect."

Jules pursed her lips, her eyes narrowed into suspicious slits. "It still doesn't make sense why Derek ran at the apartment. Wouldn't he have just knocked on your door and asked for you?"

Becky answered for Brittany. "Maybe he was embarrassed to be caught peeping through the window. It's possible he never saw her. Just you, Jules. Maybe he thought he had the wrong apartment."

"And the art fair?"

Becky cocked her head. "Are you *positive* it was the same guy?"

At the time, the look in his eyes had been so familiar that Jules had been convinced. But now, she couldn't say for sure. "I thought it was …"

Brittany dropped back into her chair. "I'm sure it had to be Derek at the apartment looking for me. Maybe the festival was someone else. You know, just a coincidence. I'm sure he wondered why he couldn't get in touch with me, and so he came to the apartment to see if I was there." She shrugged. "Probably more than once, which is why he was shocked to finally see someone inside."

Jules nodded almost begrudgingly. She supposed the scenario Brittany proposed wasn't outside the realm of possibility.

"I'm not sure what happened to my phone, but I must have lost it, which is why I bought a new one." Brittany rolled her eyes as she leaned back in her chair. "My parents were going crazy when they didn't hear from me. You know, new city, new guy, and then their daughter stops answering her phone." She took a long swallow of her soda.

Becky waited for her to finish. "What about your last name, Mullins? You were married?"

Brittany wiped her lips with the back of her hand. "Oh, yeah. Very briefly, but apparently, it didn't work out. I guess I was too lazy to change my name back."

Jules stared at her thoughtfully, but her stomach still felt unsettled. What if she was being fed misinformation for some reason?

"You remember all of that now?" she asked, running her finger across her chin. "Being married. Getting divorced."

Brittany hesitated, then lifted a shoulder. "Well, not all of it, but, yeah, some of it's starting to come back. When I talked to my parents, they helped fill in some of the missing pieces, and I left a voicemail for my sister. I'm waiting for her to call me back."

"Just the one sibling?" Becky asked.

She bobbed her head. "Yup. Just the one."

"Was that her in—"

"In the picture I had? Yeah. I guess you were right that we looked alike."

Just then, they heard the faint ringing of Brittany's phone upstairs.

"Oh, maybe that's her calling me back. Excuse me."

As she hurried up the stairs, Jules pinched the bridge of her nose, a deep-set crease between her brows. "I don't know what to think about any of this."

"Why?" Confusion flickered across Becky's face as she sipped her soda.

"She moves to a new city to be with a guy she met on an online dating site and then suddenly stops returning phone calls to her family." Jules shook her head firmly. "No way. My parents would have been here so fast to figure out what was going on with me." She leaned across the table. "It doesn't sound like her parents even came down. I mean, Beck, don't you find that odd? Tampa's *not* that far. Especially when your daughter stops communicating and you're worried something could have happened to her. I don't care how old she is."

"Maybe they didn't have the address for her new apartment, so they had no idea where to look." Becky set her can down hard on the table and huffed. "Or maybe they're just crappy parents."

"No, it's more than that." Jules rubbed the side of her head as she tried to make sense of it all. It didn't add up. "Her sister didn't come looking for her either?" She threw her hands up in the air. "C'mon, *really*?"

Becky glanced over at the stairs and then gave her friend a stern stare. "Shhh. She'll hear you." She leaned across the table, her voice low. "Don't you think you're jumping to conclusions? Just because we didn't see Brittany's sister doesn't mean she didn't try to look for her. We were at her apartment for what thirty minutes? It's a miracle we even saw Derek."

Jules's mind reeled. She knew Becky was trying to be the voice of reason in an attempt to get her to calm down. She couldn't deny the whole thing had her agitated, but she took a deep, cleansing breath and met her friend's worried gaze with a dip of her chin.

"Okay, you're right. Maybe her sister *did* come looking for her." Jules leaned back in her chair and pressed her hand to her forehead. "But the story still doesn't sit right with me. Brittany rented a *furnished* apartment. Was she living with her parents when she moved? Where's all her stuff? From what we can tell, she appeared in town with a single suitcase, and that's it."

"Maybe she put it all in storage where she used to live. That way, if it didn't work out with this guy, Derek, she could just go back." Becky gave Jules a pointed stare. "She does have that key we never figured out. Most likely we didn't find a unit here in her name because she's got it in Tampa."

Jules stared off thoughtfully. "Maybe," she said after a moment. "But Brittany didn't even have a car here. Is that why she didn't bring more of her stuff? Because she flew here? She was only three and a half hours away. Why wouldn't she drive?"

Jules heard footsteps on the stairs and put her finger to her lips.

A moment later, Brittany strolled into the kitchen, a wide smile on her face. She tossed a thick white envelope onto the kitchen table between Jules and Becky.

They exchanged a glance, then Jules's forehead creased as she stared up at Brittany. "What's that?"

"My parents knew about the safety deposit box because they drove me down when I moved in. My mom actually went with me to the bank." She reclaimed her seat at the table next to Becky. "Apparently, my car in Tampa was on its last legs, so I was planning to buy a new one. I guess once I did that, I was going to drive back up. You know, to get some of my stuff out of storage."

Becky raised her eyebrows and shot Jules a look as if to say, *there you go*.

Jules pursed her lips as she eyed Brittany with suspicion. It was too perfect. It was almost as if she'd been listening to their conversation.

Brittany made a weak attempt to smile. "But you know, then I got viciously attacked and forgot who I was before I could do any of that." She pushed the envelope toward Jules. "Anyway, my mom told me the box was at the Wells Fargo on Madison. Cami took me there today, so I was able to pull everything out of it."

"Oh." So that's what she'd had with her when she got back. "Anything interesting?" Jules attempted to sound casual, but she was desperate to know what had been in the damn bag.

"Well, turns out I do have credit cards, and I opened a bank account there." Brittany waved her hand ceremoniously over the thick envelope on the table. "I was able to make a withdrawal, so I could pay you back what I owe."

Jules reached for the envelope, and her mouth fell open when she saw how much cash was inside. She handed it to Becky. "You could have just written us a check."

Brittany lifted and dropped her shoulders matter-of-factly. "I hadn't gotten around to ordering any yet."

"So, you really were starting over." Becky set the envelope back on the table.

"Seems so. I guess I need to get started looking for a job. The money in my account isn't going to last forever."

"You don't think you'll go back to Tampa?" Becky asked.

Brittany hesitated, then shook her head. "I don't think so. If I can find a job, I might try to make a go of it here."

"And what about the guy from Bumble?" Jules asked. "Derek."

Brittany crossed her arms on the table in front of her. "I'm not sure how I feel about him." Her shoulders lifted as if it didn't really matter one way or the other if she ever saw him again. "I guess I won't know unless I see him in person. I mean, who knows if we can start over at this point? Hopefully, he'll come around again now that I'm going back to my apartment. I feel like I should at least explain to him what happened."

Jules shifted forward in her seat, a scowl on her face. "You're going back there?" She wasn't sure how she felt about that. This didn't feel settled. Not at all.

Brittany flinched. "Well, yeah," she said as if it was the most logical decision. "You've both been very nice to me, but you've gone above and beyond. Especially you, Jules." She gestured at the envelope. "Hopefully, that covers your time and the money you laid out."

Jules let out an aggravated snort that Brittany would think this had anything to do with money. "It seems more than fair, but—"

She held up her hand, determined not to let Jules finish. "I hired you both to figure out who I was, but now I have the answers I was looking for." The corners of her mouth tugged upward into a smile. "You've both got Jules's wedding to plan, so this will free up your time to let you get going on that. April will be here before you know it."

Brittany pushed herself up from the table. "Don't take this personally, but you're both officially fired."

CHAPTER TWENTY

After Becky left to go home, Jules pulled the pitcher of sweet tea from the refrigerator. As the door swung shut, the magnet holding Erin's bridal shower invitation slipped. She set it back in place, even though she didn't need the information. It was being held at Barb's house, and as part of the bridal party, Jules had helped plan and fund it.

"I suppose I'm not invited to the wedding anymore?" Brittany asked.

Jules was trying to come to terms with the announcement that she was moving out but wasn't prepared to cut ties completely. In her gut, she knew there was more to this story. She was determined to keep tabs on Brittany until she figured out what it was.

"Don't be silly." Jules poured herself a glass of tea and then turned to face her. "We already RSVP'd for you, so there's a chicken dinner with your name on it." As she laughed, she caught a flicker of emotion that moved across Brittany's face. Was it sadness?

"Hey, you okay?" Jules tried to coax a smile from her. "I'm

sure it's not *rubber* chicken. Erin promised the food was going to be really good."

Her approach worked for a moment, but then Brittany's face grew serious again. "You and Becky. Your families. Everyone has been so nice to me. I just can't tell you—" She choked up and couldn't finish.

Jules moved to hug her. "Come on. You're not just a client. We all became friends, and that doesn't have to change. I'm thrilled you have the answers you were looking for." She pulled back. "Trust me, no one understands more than me what that feels like." Jules took in a sharp breath and hesitated, afraid to say too much. She didn't want to scare her, so she simply said, "But if going back to your old life doesn't turn out to be all you thought it would be, we're still here for you."

Tears now streamed down Brittany's face. She reached up to wipe them from her cheeks. "I'm not sure I remember everything about my past yet, but I'm pretty sure I didn't have friends like you and Becky."

Jules reached for a napkin and handed it to her. "It's not like you need to rush right back to your apartment, right? Why don't we order something nice for dinner? Then, tomorrow is Erin's bridal shower. She'll be disappointed if you aren't there, and I'd love to introduce you to Barb."

"I would like to meet your birth mother." Brittany folded the napkin and dabbed under her eyes, then stood silent for a moment. "Can I ask you something?"

Jules gave her a reassuring nod. "Sure. Ask me anything."

"Were you angry she gave you up?"

"Angry?" Jules pressed her lips together and stared off as she considered her response. "No, I wasn't angry. I love my parents, and I had a wonderful childhood. I think it was more that being adopted made me *insecure*. I couldn't understand how she could give me up and never look back." At that moment, Jules realized that even though she now knew Barb had wanted to keep her, all those years of feeling unworthy had left wounds that still hadn't healed. "It really made it hard for me to trust that other people wouldn't disappoint me too."

Brittany was watching Jules intently. "I can see that," she said with a nod.

Jules leaned against the kitchen counter, grateful for the support as she continued. "My parents raised me to be secure and confident. And I am, on the outside. But deep down, I've always felt like that little girl who couldn't understand why her mother didn't want to keep her. If the person who's supposed to love you more than anything could just walk away …" She twisted the engagement ring on her finger. "I almost let it sabotage my relationship with Tim."

Brittany's mouth fell open. "But now you two are good. You're engaged."

Jules gave a slow nod. "We are, but I'm still a work in progress. Some days it's hard to accept Tim loves me, that he's not going to leave me."

Brittany rolled her eyes, then placed her hands squarely on Jules's shoulders. "The way that man looks at you. Trust me, he's not going anywhere."

"He is pretty wonderful. I've very lucky he hung in there with me."

Gene nudged Brittany's leg with his nose, and she stooped to pet the top of his head. "And besides, it's not like Tim can go anywhere. You two have a dog together."

Jules laughed. "That we do. And neither of us would give him up."

Brittany pulled Gene close. "I'm not ready to leave you yet either, sweet boy." She glanced back up at Jules. "How about if I go back to my apartment after the shower tomorrow?"

"Sure." Jules still hoped Brittany would change her mind, but at least she'd bought a little more time to keep an eye on her.

After they'd perused a stack of menus, they decided on dinner, and Jules called in their delivery.

"You want to help me wrap Erin's shower gifts while we wait for the food?" she asked. "I can get everything and bring it down here."

As Jules headed to the stairs, Gene trotted up ahead of her.

When she passed Brittany's bedroom, she let out a sigh. No matter how often she was reminded to close her door, she never remembered. Gene had already wandered inside to investigate sandals strewn on the floor by the side of her bed. Jules scowled. They were the expensive ones she'd given Brittany.

"Hey." She called the dog with a commanding whisper. "Get out of there."

When Gene found the shoes far more interesting than the command she'd given him, Jules stepped into the bedroom and reached for his collar. As she tried to aim him toward the door, she couldn't help but notice the plastic bag Brittany had come back with earlier had been tossed on her bed. A folder had partially slid out.

Jules hesitated, glanced over her shoulder toward the door, then slid it from the bag. She flipped it open and stared at the paper on top—a photocopy of an obituary. Jules had just started skimming it when she heard footsteps on the stairs. Her heart raced as she hurried to slide the folder back into the bag. Then she bent over and scooped up one of the sandals from the floor.

"Jules?" Brittany was now standing in the doorway, her lips set in a hard line. "What are you doing in here?"

She held up the shoe. "Just saving these. I keep telling you this dog has a taste for the expensive ones." Jules's cheeks were hot, and she hoped the guilty flush she wore didn't betray she was lying. "Your door was open, and it didn't take Gene but a minute to figure out he had a golden opportunity to destroy these." She laughed, but it sounded forced even to her own ears. "*Golden* opportunity. That's pretty funny, but really, one more minute, and he would have destroyed at least one of these. Not that the other would be any good without—"

"Okay, thanks." Brittany strode into the room, took the shoe from Jules, and stooped to pick up its mate. "Sorry for leaving them out. I do love these, so I'd hate for anything to happen to them." She set them on the floor inside the closet and shut the door.

Brittany's gaze then landed on the bed as if she wanted to reach for the bag too. Instead, she side-stepped toward the doorway and patted the side of her leg. "C'mon, Gene, there's nothing in here for you."

When she turned, the dog followed her out. Jules resisted the urge to give the folder a lingering look of her own.

"The gifts are in my closet," she said as she continued down the hall to her own bedroom. "I'll get them."

When she emerged with several large shopping bags, Brittany was waiting for her in the hallway.

"Here, let me help you with all of this." Brittany reached for one of the bags loaded with gifts, and the aggravation on her face from only moments earlier was gone. "Geez, Jules. Did you buy everything on the registry?"

She tipped her head as she considered it. "I just might have." Erin was going to be her sister-in-law, and she'd never had siblings to spoil.

They had just finished wrapping all the gifts when the doorbell announced their food had arrived. Jules ran down to get the door, and when she returned, the table was set. She drew in a stuttered breath as it hit her how much she'd miss Brittany's company. Some nights she had dinner with Tim, but most nights, Jules ate alone.

"This looks amazing," Brittany said, pulling her food from the bag. "I just realized how hungry I was."

"Did you get anything to eat with Cami for lunch?"

"What?" Brittany asked as she sat down and reached for her fork.

"Did you eat lunch?" Jules asked again.

"Oh, yeah. There was a deli over by the bank. We grabbed sandwiches."

There was no more talk of Brittany leaving, and when they finished with dinner, Jules began to clear the table.

"Did Cami say anything about you being a runner?" She tried to sound casual as she reached for Brittany's plate. "You know, back in high school."

She tilted her head and gave Jules a curious stare. "She didn't say. Why?"

Jules opened the dishwasher and began to rinse off their dishes. "I was just thinking. Tomorrow you'll go back to your apartment, and I guess you'll be able to start running if you want." She shut off the faucet, then made a point of glancing out the window, even though it had been dark for hours. "Although, it's probably nicer and a bit safer to run here around the lake. At least it's lit at night. If you decide to get back into it, you're welcome to come here." She turned and gave Brittany a non-committal shrug. "You know, if you want. You don't need to go with Tim, although maybe you could take Gene with you. He loves to go outside for a run. Even a walk works for him."

The buzzwords Jules had deliberately thrown out brought the dog to a sitting position, his tail flickering while he assessed the situation. He tipped his head to the side, his hopeful gaze drifting between the two women.

Jules laughed. "Looks like he's ready to go right now."

As she held her breath, Brittany bit at the bait. "Maybe I could take him out now. Just for a little bit to run off dinner. Would that be okay?"

"Did you hear that, Gene?" Jules bent at the knees and scratched him behind the ears. "This is your lucky day."

Brittany was already up from the table. "I'll go get changed."

A few minutes later, the two of them headed out the door. Jules's attention was glued to the security app on her phone until she saw them run off together. Then she raced up the stairs to Brittany's room.

Her eyes flew to the bed, but the bag was gone. "Damn," she said under her breath.

She opened the closet door and reeled back. Brittany's doll was perched over the bar staring down at her. She caught her breath and dug around, but there was no sign of the folder.

Jules let out a frustrated groan as her eyes scanned the room. The dresser. She rifled through the drawers, taking care to put everything back as she'd found it so it wouldn't be obvious she'd been snooping. It wasn't there.

"Did you hide it under here?" Jules muttered as she slid her hands under the mattress.

When she came up empty-handed, she opened the closet again and pulled out the suitcase. She threw the top open, but it was empty. With an aggravated sigh, she zipped it back up and slid it back against the wall.

What could be in the folder that Brittany had taken such pains to hide it? Jules's heart thumped in her chest, and then she had a fleeting thought. She'd wanted Brittany to go for a run so she'd have the opportunity to search her room, but what if she'd only agreed to set *her* up? To catch her snooping. Jules gave one last look to ensure she hadn't left anything out of place, then hurried out of her room, making sure to shut the door behind her.

After racing down the stairs, she was out of breath when she called Becky.

"You okay?" she asked.

"Fine." Jules lowered her voice, even though she knew she'd hear the front door when Brittany and Gene got back. Not to mention the dog would gallop up the stairs from the first floor, tags clinking as they bounced off each other. There would be no missing that racket. "Remember when Brittany came back after being with Cami and she had that plastic bag with her?"

"Yeah."

"I think maybe it was the stuff from her safety deposit box."

"Makes sense," Becky said. "Did Brittany show you what was in there after I left?"

Jules hesitated. "Um. Not exactly. But it was on her bed, and this folder slid out of it."

Becky let out a huff that said she couldn't believe Jules was trying to sell that scenario. "C'mon, Jules. It just *slid* out?"

"Well, it partially slid out. Okay, so I might have helped it the rest of the way." Jules glanced out the kitchen window even though she knew she'd never be able to see Brittany and Gene from there. "There's too much that's not adding up. I thought she would have shared what she found in the box. You know, ask for help deciphering what it all means."

"But you heard her." Becky's tone sounded slightly exasperated. "She doesn't need our help anymore. Brittany's starting to remember her past, and she has her family to help her figure it all out."

Jules gritted her teeth. "What if they're not telling her the truth? If the stuff in that folder was in a safety deposit box, it was because Brittany wanted to keep it … well, *safe*. But from who? She admitted she still doesn't remember everything, and she's assuming what people are telling her is the truth. But what if it's not? She could still be in danger." Jules's throat tightened as she said the words. Now she second-guessed her decision to let Brittany leave with the dog.

"Where is she now?" Becky asked.

Jules slammed her hand on the counter. How had she been so stupid? "She went out for a run. With Gene."

"But you just said …"

"I know. I didn't think it through, and now I'm starting to freak out. I'm going out to look for them." Jules hurried down the stairs toward the front door. "Can you do me a favor if you have time tonight? The only thing in the folder I had time to see was an obituary. Can you do a little research online and see if you can find it? The name is Judith Hunter."

"Okay. When did she die?"

Jules shook her head as she stepped outside. She hadn't had enough time to study it. "Not sure."

"How old was she?"

She glanced down the sidewalk, but there was no sign of Brittany or Gene. "Young. I think it said she was thirty-two." Jules remembered because it was always a little disconcerting when someone died so young. Not to mention Judith had been about the same age as she was.

"Oh, wow. That *is* young. How'd she die?"

"It just said unexpectedly at home. Also, I remember noticing it was a North Carolina newspaper."

Becky was silent for a moment. "Maybe a congenital heart problem or suicide? Or some sort of freak accident?"

"Not sure."

Jules made her way behind her next-door neighbor's town-house to give herself a better view.

"Hey, let me go," she said when her call-waiting beeped. "Jonas is calling."

Jules blew out an anxious breath as she answered. "Hey."

Off in the distance, she could see Brittany heading back with the dog. She put her hand to her forehead and breathed in relief that they were in sight.

"Jules. You okay?" Her brother sounded concerned.

"Yeah." She began walking back to her own townhouse. Brittany would be back any minute, and there wouldn't be time to explain. "What's happening with you? Did they find any fingerprints on the note attached to the brick?"

"Nope. Not a thing."

"Well, a lot is going on here. With Brittany." Jules ran a hand through her hair. "At lunch yesterday, we ran into someone who knew her. Someone she went to high school with."

"Oh?"

Jules could almost picture Jonas's left eyebrow shooting up in that way he had when she had news that caught him off guard.

"Yeah, she spent the day with this woman today, and apparently, Brittany was able to talk to her parents. Her sister, too, I think." Jules realized she'd gone up to take the phone call but never confirmed who'd been calling. "Anyway, she said she's starting to remember bits and pieces. She's from Tampa and supposedly moved here to be with some guy she met on an online dating site. I guess her name really is Brittany Mullins."

"Huh."

Jules heard the skepticism in Jonas's voice. "What? Were you able to talk to the detective on her case?"

"Yeah. This morning. He said one of the reasons they didn't think it was her real identity was because they checked into the social security number assigned to that name. It's never been used until just recently."

Jules struggled to understand. "But how's that possible? You think she stole someone else's information?"

"Maybe. She could have used a number from someone that passed away. Maybe a child that never had any employment history. Or, I guess there's always the possibility she comes from money and never had to work or apply for a loan or anything until recently."

That didn't match what Brittany had told them that afternoon.

Jules could now see she and Gene had slowed to a walk and were headed toward her.

"Crap, I can't really talk about it now. Will I see you at Erin's shower tomorrow?"

"Uh, isn't that just for the ladies?"

"I think you're supposed to swoop in at the end and help Erin haul off all her gifts." Jules laughed. "She's going to need your truck just for the stuff I bought."

"Ah, got it. Well then, I guess you'll see me. Should we talk more then?"

"I think we need to." Jules lowered her voice and whispered into the phone. "Hang on."

She lifted her free hand and waved at Brittany. "Hey, I'm talking to Jonas about Erin's shower tomorrow. How was your run?" She cradled the phone to her ear as Brittany let go of the leash, and Gene ran to her, panting as his tail wagged.

"She's right there?" Jonas asked.

"Yup."

"Okay, we'll talk more tomorrow. Something doesn't sound right."

"I agree."

As she hung up, Jules couldn't help but think about what Jonas had said. Was it possible the police had the wrong person? Brittany had told them she'd worked at a hospital in Tampa, but how could that be unless she'd worked under a different social security number?

CHAPTER TWENTY-ONE

Becky wagged her finger in the air at her best friend. "Keep frowning like that, and the wrinkle between your eyebrows is going to be permanent."

Jules groaned as her hand flew to her face. "I know, but I can't help it. I was so relieved when Brittany and Gene came back safely last night. But, Beck, she's expecting to go back to her apartment later after the bridal shower."

Becky shifted in her seat. It wasn't often she and Jules weren't on the same page about something, but her best friend's suspicions were starting to border on obsessive. "You heard what she said the same as I did. Brittany's paid up and doesn't want our services anymore. She *fired* us, remember? Besides, she's a grown woman. You can't exactly keep her hostage against her will."

Jules still wasn't prepared to let it go. "But what if she doesn't realize—"

Barb came up behind Jules and tapped her shoulder. "Hi, honey."

She got to her feet and gave her biological mom a hug. "Do you need help?" She glanced around looking for the rest of the bridal party, a guilty heat on her cheeks that she'd been hiding out with Becky.

Barb waved her hand. "Nah. Brittany jumped in to help. She made more punch, and now she's helping them set up the platters."

"I can't believe the wedding's almost here. Next week Jonas will be a married man."

"And then you after that," Barb said with a smile. "How's the wedding planning coming?"

When she shared that she'd booked The Colby Museum, Barb's eyes lit up.

Jules nodded. "Yup. Mark your calendar. April twenty-second."

Barb pressed her lips together. "So soon? That's a beautiful place, honey, but you've got your work cut out for you. That's not much time to get everything done."

Becky realized Jules hadn't brought up the wedding at all since she'd booked the museum. She studied her friend's face and was sure she saw it—a flicker of panic.

Just as quickly, it was gone, and Jules had plastered a confident smile on her face. "It will be fine. Once Jonas's wedding is over, I'll be ready to jump in with both feet."

Becky stood and put her arm around Jules. "She has me to help her. We'll get it all done, don't worry."

"You're a good friend. She'll need all the help she can get to pull this wedding off on time." Then Barb's attention was back on Jules. "Are you moving in with Tim, or is he moving into your townhouse?"

The anxiety reappeared in her best friend's eyes.

"I don't—we haven't figured that out yet."

"Well, you have a chance to get rid of all those stairs you have, and my vote says you should move to Tim's." Barb's laugh was hearty. "Purely selfish on my part, of course But you do need to start thinking about it. April will be here before you know it."

Becky gritted her teeth. She was sure Barb didn't mean to stress Jules out, but she needed to stop reminding her how little time she had until the wedding.

When the front door swung open, Barb lifted her hand in acknowledgment. "Oh, Enid and Bonnie are here. Let me go help them with their gifts."

As she headed off to greet her sisters, Becky reached for Jules's arm. Barb's comments had left her looking panic-stricken. "You don't need to freak out."

She rolled her eyes and let out a whimper. "You can tell?"

"I know you, Jules. Sit back down before you fall over."

She gratefully sank to the couch. "It's just—you know I love Tim, and I do want to marry him. But *everything's* about to change and much sooner than I expected."

"Just breathe. It will be okay." Becky settled back down next to her on the couch. "You know I'll help you with whatever you need for the wedding. As far as where you live ..." She tossed her hands up in the air. "You and Tim will just have to figure out whose place makes the most sense. And if that's his place, Bryan and I will help you move and figure out how to sell your townhouse."

Jules dipped her head and wrapped her hands around it. "I feel like I might throw up." She looked up and forced a smile. "Or is that bad luck for a bride if someone vomits at your shower?" She moaned. "I could never do that to Erin."

"You're not going to be sick. Just breathe." Becky settled in next to Jules and changed the subject, hoping to give her something other than her queasy stomach to think about. "So, I think I found the obituary you asked about." She reached for her purse and pulled out the copy she'd printed.

The distraction worked. As Jules skimmed the paper, she sat up, and her shoulders weren't hunched up around her ears anymore. "Yeah, this is it." She dipped her head appreciatively. "Very impressive, considering I didn't give you much to work with."

Becky didn't mention she'd spent hours looking for it the night before, but she'd been determined to find it and give Jules some resolution. "Well, I still have no idea about the connection to Brittany. Judith Hunter lived in Shelby, North Carolina, and it looks like she died a little over a year and a half ago."

"Maybe she was a relative of Brittany's?" Jules blew out a frustrated sigh. "I wish her DNA results would come in already. That might help us figure it out."

"I guess, but—" Becky knew once her friend set her mind to something, it was hard to change it. But this had to be different. Brittany didn't want their help. End of story. "Jules, she doesn't want us to keep working on her case, so there's nothing to figure out." Becky caught her eye and gave a slow nod. "You have to let it go." Her voice was soft but firm, and she hoped the message was clear.

Her words hung heavy in the air, but finally, Jules squared her jaw with that determined look Becky knew well. "I can't. My gut is telling me something is very wrong here. What if something's going on that Brittany doesn't remember. What if she's just blindly trusting these people? The ones who are"—Jules made air quotes—"filling in the pieces?"

"Why are you so convinced they're not telling her the truth?" Becky asked, stealing a glance into the kitchen where Brittany was bustling around helping the maid of honor.

Jules tapped her lips repeatedly with her index finger. "Well, let's see. Her friend from high school claims Brittany Mullins is her real name, but I don't see how that's possible."

"Well, Cami actually said her name was Brittany Schroeder. We *assumed* her married name was Mullins. But we did ask Brittany if that was her married name, and she said it was."

"Maybe because that's what she was *told*." Jules shook her head as she tucked her leg underneath her and shifted her body toward Becky. "I keep trying to make all the information they gave her fit, but it doesn't. I mean, come on. If she's really Brittany Mullins, she's *twenty-five*. Do *you* think she looks twenty-five, Beck? Not to mention, we know the person who matches that date of birth has a social security number that hasn't been used until just recently. If it's true that Brittany used to work at Tampa General, then it *can't* be her."

Becky tipped her head against the back of the couch as she considered what Jules was saying. She couldn't deny some of what Brittany had been told didn't make sense. "Do you really think her family is feeding her misinformation, and she's just accepting it as truth because she doesn't remember anything different?"

"Who knows? It's possible." Jules leaned closer and dropped her voice to a whisper. "Maybe they're not even her real family."

Becky let out a frustrated groan. "Do you really believe that? Come on, that's crazy."

Her best friend's eyebrows shot up as if nothing was off the table at this point. "Is it really? Then tell me why they're backing up the name she's using when I know it's not really hers. And Cami too." Jules narrowed her eyes as she shook her head. "What if she really is running from her husband? Maybe Cami knows him, and he's using her to lead him to Brittany. What if it's a trap, and we're letting her walk right into it?"

Becky crossed her arms in front of her and tried to think. Jules's theories were making her head spin. "But her parents said she was divorced—"

"Her *parents* said." The tone Jules used mocked the words as if they weren't to be believed. "You're assuming they're telling the truth about it." Jules gripped Becky's arm in her bid to make her point. "Or what if Brittany didn't tell them what was really going on with her abusive husband because she didn't want to worry them?"

"But she said her family met the Bumble guy."

Jules rubbed her hand over her face and issued a sigh as if Becky's refusal to see her point was exhausting her. "Okay, let's say that story about her online boyfriend is true. We still don't know for sure that's the guy I saw at the apartment. What if she's assuming it was him because she doesn't know any better? Maybe this guy—Derek, right? Maybe Derek decided Brittany ghosted him and went back to his life. If it wasn't him, then who *was* looking for her?" Jules's voice was escalating. "Brittany could be using a fake or stolen ID for any one of a number of reasons, including trying to get away from a bad situation. Are you saying we should just give up and hope for the best? Hope she wasn't trying to hide from someone who could now find her because she has *no idea* he exists? Because no one has bothered to tell her the truth?"

Becky waved her hand in the air to get Jules to lower her voice. They were at Erin's bridal shower talking about abusive husbands, for Pete's sake. "Okay, but there could still be some sort of rational explanation with her ID that changes the entire situation. A screw up with social security. Maybe her parents somehow got two numbers—one with a middle name and one without. Maybe—"

When Jules's gaze traveled urgently above her head, Becky knew even without looking that Brittany had to be standing there.

"Hey," she said as she perched on the arm of the couch. "I can't even imagine what's got you two holed up in here looking so intense. We're getting ready to play some shower games. Are you coming?"

CHAPTER TWENTY-TWO

As she pushed open the door to her apartment, Brittany froze, a chill running through her at being back. Everything in her wanted to whirl around and tell Jules she'd changed her mind. Instead, she drew in a deep breath and forced her feet to move forward.

After Erin's shower, they'd stayed at Barb's well beyond the point when most of the guests had collected their parting gift and gone home. It was late when they'd finally gotten back to the townhouse, and Jules had convinced her to stay one more night.

Over breakfast, she'd tried once again to persuade her to stay longer. Brittany had been tempted to reconsider, but she knew it wasn't an option. Still, after being part of everything over the last few weeks, the transition back to these meager surroundings was downright painful.

That morning, she'd packed up her things. The doll she'd brought had watched over her, her painted stare seeming almost apologetic as Brittany piled her clothes and toiletries back into the suitcase she'd had when she arrived. When she finished, all that remained hanging in the closet was the dress Jules had lent her to leave the hospital. She didn't feel right taking it. She'd slipped the baggy with her rings from Jules's coat pocket where she'd stashed it. They were now tucked safely inside her purse.

Her throat had grown tight when she took one last look around to ensure she hadn't forgotten anything. Then she'd clutched the doll to her chest and sunk down on the bed. She'd sat there, in the room Jules had so graciously offered her, and wept.

It was only as they loaded the car that they realized Brittany had nothing to wear for Jonas's wedding. When Jules insisted they hit the mall to find her a dress, the excursion merely postponed the dread of returning to her old life. After shopping, they'd had lunch, and then Jules stopped at the supermarket.

"I don't want to leave you without everything you need," she'd said.

But now that temporary reprieve was over. Back in the apartment, reality punched Brittany right in the gut.

"You're sure you don't need me to take you to get anything else?" Jules asked as she unpacked groceries in the small kitchen.

Brittany forced a smile and shook her head. "I don't think so. Really, I appreciate everything you've done for me."

Jules's phone rang, and she glanced at the screen and silenced it. "My cousin, Lucy. I can call her back. So, about Saturday," she said, emptying the last grocery bag and setting the contents on the counter. "I can pick you up for the wedding if you don't mind getting to the church a little early. I have to be there by eleven for bridesmaid pictures. If not, I'm sure Becky—"

"I don't mind. Really." Brittany set the package of Mega

Stuff Oreos on a shelf in the cupboard. She'd never even known they existed but had discovered they were Jules's weakness. Now they were hers too.

Brittany wanted as much time as possible to be part of the festivities. It would most likely be the last time she saw them all.

After this weekend, Jules's life would go back to the way it had been before she met Brittany. She'd have her townhouse back to herself and time alone with Tim. They had their own wedding to plan.

Jules and Becky would simply mark Brittany's case closed. Move on. It had to be that way, but damn, she hadn't expected it to hurt so much. When the time came, she knew she wouldn't be invited to Jules's wedding. She'd be long-forgotten by then—just another former client on their list. It was for the best, but it was a bitter pill to swallow. Brittany had finally found a group of people she cherished—a feeling of belonging she'd never had. But now, she had no choice. She needed to walk away from all of them and never look back.

"Well, the dress you picked out is amazing. I hung it on the back of your bedroom door and put the shoes you got in the closet." She offered a bittersweet smile. "At least you don't have to worry they'll be a dog treat before this weekend."

Brittany felt her eyes well up. "I already miss Gene."

"Listen, I told you, if you want to come running by the lake, you're more than welcome. He loved it the last time you took him."

Brittany gave a half-hearted nod. "Okay, I'll let you know." She knew she wouldn't. Going back to Jules's place for any reason was out of the question.

She would have loved nothing more than to feel the sun on her face as she ran the trail around the lake again. To be able to look down and see Gene, his pink tongue hanging out of his mouth as he trotted along gleefully beside her. But that would just prolong the inevitable. Not that she wasn't already pushing her luck by attending the wedding.

Brittany was grateful Erin had welcomed her as part of their group and graciously invited her to be part of the celebration. She couldn't hurt her feelings by refusing to attend at the last minute. It was an excuse, and she knew that. She just needed one last gathering to look forward to before she said a final goodbye and tried to put the pieces of her life back together.

Jules paused by the front door, almost as if she was hesitant to leave. "If you think of anything else you're missing this week, let me know." Her eyes lit up. "Oh, maybe a purse? I have a little bag that will look darling with your dress. I'll bring it when I pick you up, and you can borrow it."

Brittany's throat tightened. She nodded, afraid if she tried to speak, she'd cry.

Jules didn't appear fooled as she studied her, her face full of concern. "Are you *sure* you're comfortable being back here? You know, if you don't feel safe, we can pack this all up and go back to my place."

Brittany pressed her lips together. If only it were that easy. "I'll be fine here. Besides, I need to start looking for a job and a car."

Jules tipped her head to the side, her brows pulling together as she studied her. "You can do that from my place too, you know."

Brittany hesitated, biting at the inside of her cheek. She was afraid if Jules offered one more time, she'd weaken, and they'd be in the car heading back to her townhouse.

"My sister is going to come down and stay with me next week. It's just—I'm going to miss you. And everyone else." Brittany couldn't resist a wistful smile. "Especially Gene, the flip-flop thief."

"He's hard not to love, even with his expensive shoe fetish." Jules's expression turned serious as she placed her hands on Brittany's shoulders. "Listen, I'm not trying to scare you, but I still think there's more to your story than you know. Or that you remember. If your Bumble guy shows up and there's any sort of problem, Tim and I can be here in a flash. Or Jonas." She wrinkled her nose. "Well, I guess if it's after Saturday, he won't be able to get back from Hawaii that fast. My point is, you're not alone just because you moved out of my place."

Brittany managed to nod. "Thanks, that means more than you know."

"Well, the offer stands, and when your sister comes, I'd love to meet her." Jules leaned in and gave Brittany a hug. "The wedding will be fun, and now you've met a bunch of people at the shower that will be there." She smiled as she shook her head. "I still can't believe my brother's getting married, and he couldn't have picked a nicer bride. Getting Erin as my sister-in-law is a nice bonus."

"You were lucky," Brittany said in a soft voice. Then louder, "You got the fairytale."

Jules cocked her head and looked puzzled. "What do you mean?"

Brittany lifted a shoulder. "Your adoption. You were placed with loving parents who got you when you were only a few days old. Then you found your birth mother, and she welcomed you with open arms. You have aunts, uncles, cousins, a new sister-in-law. You found Jonas, and it's like you've known him your whole life." She held up her hands. "You're even a bridesmaid in his wedding."

Jules stood silent for a moment before she responded. "Well, not all of that is true."

Brittany crossed her arms in front of her. "Which part did I get wrong?"

Jules took a deep breath, and Brittany wondered if she'd hit a nerve, maybe gotten the whole thing wrong. But she'd seen Jules with her new family at the shower. There was no mistaking how much they all adored her.

"When I found Barb, she wasn't sure she even wanted to meet me. I was *crushed.*" Jules pressed her palm to her forehead and let out a laugh that said she still couldn't believe it. "Here I thought she'd be swinging from the chandeliers at the chance to be reunited with the daughter she'd given up." Her face grew serious as she looked Brittany in the eye. "It took *six months* before she was ready. Six months of wondering if the woman who'd given birth to me would ever deem me worthy of meeting."

Six months? That was nothing. Brittany huffed, and her hand flew up into the air. "Okay, but still. She came around eventually."

Jules dipped her head in agreement. "She did." Then she gave a slight shrug, her lips pressed together in a firm line. "The first time we met, she also told me my birth father asked her to abort me."

Brittany's cheeks burned. She hadn't seen that coming. "Oh, Jules, I'm sorry. I didn't know."

"That's why I haven't met anyone on his side. The cousin who called before—Lucy? Her birth father and mine are half-brothers. Apparently, my biological father wants me to call him so we can talk, but I'm—I'm not ready." Jules's lip curled, and Brittany wondered if she was on the verge of tears. "I'm not sure I'll ever be ready. I have a great father, and I don't know that I need another one. Especially one that never wanted anything to do with me. What, almost thirty-two years later, he changed his mind?" Her voice had an edge Brittany hadn't heard before.

"Maybe he *did* change his mind about being your dad. Maybe that's the real fairytale ending," Brittany said in a soft voice.

Jules shook her head, her face hardening to match her tone. "He's no part of any fairytale in my life. I mean, Barb explained why she was so hesitant. We're great now, and well, you know how I feel about Jonas. I'm also looking forward to meeting Lucy. When you're adopted, it's always cool to meet someone who's biologically related to you. She's had a rough time too."

"Was she adopted?"

"No, just lied to her whole life. She took a DNA test and found out the dad that raised her wasn't her biological father. Just like that lady, Elise, we told you about. It's more common than you think, and that's how people find out they're not who they think they are. By spitting in a tube." Jules shook her head. "For some people, it's life-changing. Not always in a good way, I guess."

Brittany's face warmed as she considered her own test. "Maybe those DNA tests aren't all they're cracked up to be."

"Well, they certainly have a way of dragging the truth out of the shadows. And I'm not sure that's a bad thing, necessarily. I think everyone deserves to know their story … if they want to, that is."

Brittany swallowed hard. "Uh, huh."

Jules tilted her head as she studied her. "You're sure you're okay here?"

She nodded, not trusting herself to speak.

Jules hesitated for a moment, then hugged her again. "Okay, call me if you need anything. Otherwise, I'll see you Saturday morning around ten-forty-five. We can hop on the highway to get to the church, so it shouldn't take too long."

"Okay, I'll be ready."

Brittany wrapped her arms around her middle and fought back tears as she watched Jules get in her car and drive away. For a brief moment, she'd wanted to tell her the truth. If anyone might understand, it would be Jules. But how could she drag her into the middle of the mess she'd created?

As Brittany stood staring out at the dingy parking lot, she was sure of only one thing. She wished she'd never remembered a single moment from her past.

CHAPTER TWENTY-THREE

When Becky opened her front door, Jules blew in sputtering.

"It was horrible. I felt *awful* leaving her there like that." She collapsed dramatically onto the couch. "I could tell she didn't want to be back there, but I—I felt like she didn't think she had a choice."

Becky dropped down beside her. "You didn't tell Brittany she had to leave."

Jules held her head in her hands. "I know, but—"

"There is no but," Becky said in a firm voice. "Brittany wanted to go back. It was *her choice.*" She stretched out the two words for emphasis. "Besides, it's not like we won't see her this weekend for the wedding."

"But until then, she's there alone. In that depressing apartment. You've seen it." Jules's hands dramatically cut through the air as she emphasized her point. "It's horrible, and let's say she needs something. She doesn't have a car, so she has to walk. Right past the spot where she got robbed, where those lowlifes smashed her over the head."

"I guess the other option is to go past the cemetery." Becky cringed at the thought. "You couldn't pay me to stroll past there after dark. Maybe not even in the daylight."

Jules threw up her hands again. "Exactly."

"Okay," Becky said, her tone calm in hopes Jules would follow. "But you said Brittany's sister's coming to stay with her. She won't be alone then, and I'm sure her sister will have a car."

"But she's not coming until next week."

"Brittany will be *fine* until then. I think you're making more of this than she is, or she wouldn't have wanted to go back. She probably just wants to put the attack and everything that went with it behind her now that she has the answers she was looking for."

Jules's eyes narrowed, her face serious as she stared at Becky. "But does she really? Have answers? I can't help but feel there's more to this. Things her family hasn't told her."

Becky threw her head back and let out an exasperated sigh. "You keep saying that. But there's no *proof* that's true."

"Well, there's the obituary for Judith Hunter. Why did Brittany have that? Who is she?"

Becky drew in a breath and tried to reason with her friend. "She could be anyone. A friend. A co-worker. We don't necessarily know she's related to Brittany."

Jules cocked her head to the side. "Then why was the obituary in her safety deposit box?"

Becky pressed her hand to her forehead. "You don't know it was. You only know Brittany had it when she came back from Cami's." She gave her friend a hard stare. "Did she tell you the stuff in the bag was *all* from the box?"

Jules hesitated before responding. "Well, no. But where else would it have come from?"

"Who knows? Maybe Cami printed it for her. Maybe it was someone they both went to high school with. You know, a classmate who died."

Jules pursed her lips and then leaned her head against the back of the couch. The words came out reluctantly. "I guess it's possible." Then she sat up. "But wait." She wagged her index finger in the air in front of Becky. "It's not possible if you believe she's twenty-five-year-old Brittany Mullins. I doubt she and Cami went to high school with Judith Hunter, who was thirty-two."

"Okay, so maybe she *didn't* go to high school with them. Maybe they knew Judith some other way. My point is you're assuming there has to be some sinister reason why Brittany had a copy of her obituary. There could very well be a simple and *innocent* explanation." Becky let out a weary moan as she stared at her friend. "Brittany is going to be fine, Jules. And now that she's back in her apartment, there's a chance Derek will come back again looking for her. She fell for him once; she could fall for him again. Her parents said he was a good guy."

"And what if he isn't the guy stalking her? What if it's someone else who's *still* looking for her." Jules hung her head. "And now she's there alone. Like a *freaking* sitting duck."

"Well, the guys who attacked Brittany are in jail now, and there was nothing to suggest it was anything more than a random robbery. If someone had put them up to it, I'm sure those two would have ratted them out to save their own necks."

Jules sat quietly and then let out a loud, prolonged sigh. "You could be right."

She hoped she'd finally gotten through to her friend. While they were somewhat in agreement, Becky took the opportunity to change the subject. "So, I saw we got an inquiry about a new adoption case. You want to meet at the office in the morning?"

She gave a slow nod, but Becky could see the distracted look on her face. She was still thinking about Brittany.

"Hey, Jules," Bryan said when he came into the living room. "You want to stay for dinner?"

"Nah, I need to go." Jules pulled her phone from her purse and glanced at the time. "Shoot. I'm late." She jumped up from the couch. "Tim's probably already there waiting for me."

"A little celebration at having the place to yourselves again?" Bryan grinned. "Tell my boy I said congrats."

Becky rolled her eyes and before turning her attention back to Jules. "See, Brittany going back to her apartment isn't *all* bad."

Jules's lips lifted into a slight smile, and Bryan headed into the kitchen to start dinner. "Well, that is one benefit for sure, and Tim and I could use the alone time. I guess I should tell him I'm running late, so we don't start the night off on the wrong foot." She dialed her phone, then scowled. "Voicemail. Maybe he's on a work call."

"Can't you check the security camera to see if he's there?" Becky asked.

"I suppose I could. I guess now that Brittany's gone, I can also turn the notifications back on." Jules pressed a few buttons on her phone. "He's not there yet, but I'd better get going." But then, instead of moving, she stood rigid as she stared at the screen.

Becky got to her feet. "What is it?"

Jules's forehead creased. "Looks like there was a notification last night. At one in the morning."

Was that all? Becky's shoulders relaxed as she nudged Jules's arm. "Maybe the neighborhood cat was out on the prowl again."

Jules didn't respond. She was fixated on her phone, and then she took in a sharp breath. "Seriously?"

Becky moved to peer over her shoulder and instantly saw what had her friend so concerned. "That's your front door. But who's that guy?"

Jules shook her head in disbelief. "That's the man who ran at the apartment. I'm sure of it. What's he doing at my place?"

Bryan reappeared in the living room and moved to Becky's side. "Did I hear you say the man you've been looking for was at your townhouse?"

The three of them huddled together, their eyes anchored on Jules's phone.

A deep-set frown formed on Bryan's face. "I don't like this. Why would he be in front of your townhouse in the middle of the night?"

Becky shushed him, and they watched as the man lingered outside Jules's front door. His hands were stuffed into the front pockets of his jeans, and he seemed to be waiting for something. As they all stared at the small screen, the door opened from the inside.

"That definitely wasn't me," Jules said, her phone now shaking as she held it.

Becky reached out her hand to help steady it. She squinted at the screen, then her mouth fell open when Brittany stepped out in her pajamas. "It almost looks like she knew he was coming."

Jules huffed. "It sure does."

Just as the mystery man reached for Brittany, the footage froze, and the recording was over.

"That was from last night?" Becky asked.

Jules doublechecked the video. "Yup. Last night at 1:03 a.m."

Bryan shook his head and frowned. "I'm sorry to say this because I know you both care about Brittany, but I'm glad she's not staying there anymore." He gave Jules a knowing stare. "I have no doubt Tim feels the same way. It's exhausting to worry about the two of you all the time."

Becky stared off as she tried to make sense of the footage. Surprising, yes, but what had really happened that was so horrible? "So, she met a guy. That doesn't mean Brittany's *dangerous*. Besides, I thought you said you liked her."

"I do, but that's not the point here."

"So, what is the point?" she asked.

"You two don't know the first thing about Brittany's life before you met her. And even now, you only know what she *wants* you to know." Bryan turned to his wife. "You told me she admitted to you both that she still doesn't remember everything about her past. Some people have skeletons in their closet, and you two have no idea if that applies to her."

He waved his finger in the air between Becky and Jules. "I'm telling you both, after this weekend and the wedding, let it go. Let her move on with whoever that guy is at the front door. It's really none of your business anyway. She's not even your client anymore."

Becky gave Bryan a half-hearted nod, but as she walked Jules to the front door, she whispered, "Do you think that was the Bumble guy? But how would he even know where she was?"

Jules had a vacant stare on her face, as if she was running through the events of the previous night in her mind. "I don't remember Brittany taking any odd calls last night after we got home from Barb's. I guess she could have stepped into the backyard at any point during the shower to make a call or take one. It's not like I was watching her all day." Her shoulders hitched up. "I didn't think I needed to if we were all together."

"You're not supposed to be babysitting her anymore." Becky opened the front door, and they stepped onto the porch. "She must have gotten in contact with the Bumble guy somehow." It was the only explanation. "What about when you dropped her off at the apartment? Did she say anything about him then?"

Jules rubbed her temple thoughtfully. "I don't think she

brought him up, but I did tell her if it didn't work out with him or there was a problem, she could always call one of us."

"When you said that, she didn't admit she'd seen him?"

Jules met her friend's gaze and shook her head. "Nope. Not a word." She blew out a puff of air. "She definitely didn't mention they had a rendezvous outside my front door in the middle of the night."

Becky shrugged. "Maybe she's embarrassed."

"If she's not careful, she could have a much bigger problem than being embarrassed." Jules pursed her lips, then cast her eyes down at the porch. "Last night, there's a chance I might have heard Brittany if she screamed." She brought her gaze back up, her shoulders lifting as she eyed Becky. "But now she's back at the apartment. Alone. If it all goes horribly wrong, she'd better hope someone else can hear her if she yells for help. Someone who's also willing to save her."

CHAPTER TWENTY-FOUR

Brittany had just dragged her suitcase into the bedroom when her cell phone rang.

"Is the coast clear?" the voice on the other end asked when she answered.

Five minutes later, there was a rapping on the door.

She pulled open the door and gestured with her chin toward the bedroom. "I'm still unpacking."

He followed her, stopping short in the doorway. "What's this?"

She feigned innocence, even though she knew damn well what he was asking about. "What's what?"

"This dress hanging on the back of the door."

"Oh, that," she said dismissively. "Jules took me shopping for a dress for the wedding. It's this weekend."

He frowned. "You're still going? To her brother's wedding? You really think that's a good idea?"

Brittany shrugged. It was a terrible idea, but she didn't care. She wanted to go and be part of it. One last hurrah. After Saturday, she was well aware she needed to move on.

"It will be fine," she said. "It's just one day."

She tried to walk away, but he reached for her arm and pulled her toward him. "You're playing with fire. For no reason. The whole point of Cami was to get you out of this situation."

"I know." She pressed her lips together, felt her eyes go damp with tears. "They've just all been so nice to me. I've never—"

"Shhh." He pulled her close and wrapped her up in his embrace. "It will all be okay. I'm here now. I'm sorry about everything that happened, but that's in the past now. It's time for a fresh start."

That was the problem. Brittany had gotten used to the new existence she'd found, and she didn't want to leave it in the past. The more she thought about it, the more she was sure she didn't want any part of her old life back, and that had to include him.

If she stayed with him, he'd be a constant reminder of everything she wished had remained locked away in the deep recesses of her memory. If she'd never seen him, maybe none of it would have come back at all. She could have simply forgotten it ever happened.

She needed to tread carefully. He was in this with her, almost deeper than she was, and that could work against her. He wouldn't be willing to let her walk away so easily.

"I was so worried," he murmured as he stroked her hair. It was the way someone comforted a child, and she realized that was his nature. To make things better, no matter what it took. "When I didn't hear from you, I wanted to come right away, but I knew I couldn't just up and leave work or my class. How would that look? I had to stay and cover to keep anyone from suspecting, but I was going crazy without you. Then, I got here, and you were nowhere to be found. I didn't—"

Brittany pulled back from his tight embrace. "I know. I can

only imagine you were a bit concerned about what that meant—"

"It wasn't that, necessarily. I mean, I did start to wonder, but I was worried something might have happened to you. Even after everything ..." He left the thought unfinished as he cupped her face in his hands and brought his lips to hers.

She closed her eyes to see if she still felt anything. It might be easier if she didn't. Less ... messy.

She pulled back, and his eyes searched hers as he brushed her cheek with this thumb. Gentle strokes as he looked for confirmation her commitment to him hadn't changed. "It feels so good to be able to hold you again." He pulled her tight against his body and ran his hands down her back, his breath hot on her neck.

She felt his heart thumping against hers, her ear filled with his soft moan of contentment.

"You have no idea how much I missed you, Claire."

She flinched. She'd gotten so used to being called Brittany that it caught her by surprise to hear her real name slip from his lips.

CHAPTER TWENTY-FIVE

Becky had tossed and turned the night before, but she knew she had to speak her mind. She didn't have to wait long. As they trudged up the stairs to the office, Jules brought up the surveillance video.

"We need to figure out who he is because I don't like the idea that he was waiting for her."

Becky took a deep breath. "Jules, even if that guy was the reason Brittany was hiding—whether he's Derek, the Bumble guy, or someone else—it's her business if she wants to go back to him."

When they got to the top of the stairs, she pulled on Jules's arm and spun her around. "We both saw the same footage. It was a little disconcerting at first, I'll give you that. But he didn't seem like he was trying to hurt Brittany, and she was fine the next morning, right?" She gave Jules a demanding stare even though she already knew the answer. "She had no unexplained bruises or anything at all that gave you a valid reason to think she'd been battered in front of your townhouse."

Jules scrunched up her mouth. "No. Mostly she just seemed miserable at the idea of going back to her apartment. If she's into this guy, you would think she'd be happy about going back to her own place." She rolled her eyes as she waited on Becky to unlock the door. "Despite its generally depressing décor and morbid surroundings. What I can't figure out is why she'd lie about him."

Becky pushed the door open and hit the switch to turn on the lights in their office. "She didn't *lie*. She just didn't tell you about him. Who knows, maybe she ran into the Bumble guy when she was out with Cami, and they rekindled their connection. She probably figured you'd give her grief about wanting to go back to him, especially since he bolted when you saw him." She raised her eyebrows and gave Jules a hard stare. "You ever think of that?"

"No, that's not it." Jules's words were clipped. She shot Becky a look that said there was more to this than Brittany's need for privacy about her love life.

Becky unloaded her purse and computer bag onto her desk. "I hate to say it, but I'm starting to get a little worried about what you're going to be like when you have kids. I'm thinking you might be quite the helicopter parent."

That was something Becky never imagined she'd say about her best friend. She was usually the one that worried unnecessarily. Jules was the calm, cool, and collected one. But there was something about Brittany and this case. Jules was acting like a dog with a bone. She refused to let it go, despite the fact that they'd both been unceremoniously fired.

Jules continued to babble as she sat at her desk and powered on her laptop. "Even the bank where Brittany had her safety deposit box. We checked all the ones by the apartment, but if she didn't have a car, then how did she get a box clear across town?"

Becky rolled her eyes as she logged into her computer. "She said her parents took her there when they moved her into the apartment, remember?"

Jules waved her hand dismissively. "I think she heard us talking, which is why she told us that."

Becky groaned. "And I think you're grasping at straws."

"Maybe I am, but it makes *no* sense. If Brittany had no car and no way to get back to it, then why choose to have a box there? Why that bank?" Jules made her way to Becky's desk and perched on the edge. "Remember the day she spent with Cami?"

Becky sighed and leaned back in her chair. Jules was on a roll, and there would be no stopping her. "Yeah. I was there with you when she got back."

"Right. But after you left, we ordered dinner, and Brittany said she was starving."

Becky hung her head and brought her hand to her forehead. This conversation was starting to give her a headache. She and Jules had never veered in such different directions about a client before, but her partner wasn't even making sense anymore. She glanced up, sure her frustration was etched on her face. Jules didn't seem to notice or care.

"I said the same thing to Bryan when I got home. So, Brittany said she was hungry. What exactly does that prove?"

"When I asked her if she ate lunch with Cami that day, she said they got sandwiches from a deli right near the bank. Last night, after Tim went to sleep, I went out and drove there. Just to see." She tapped her finger hard on Becky's desk as if she was trying to drive home her point. "She lied. There isn't a deli *anywhere* near that bank."

Becky scooted forward in her chair and threw up her hands. This had moved beyond Jules's stubborn streak. "Do you hear yourself? Sneaking out in the middle of the night to check up on her story about what she had for *lunch*? And you wonder why she didn't want to tell you the truth about what's going on in her love life."

Becky ran her hand over her face and then eyed her friend.

"Did you ever think maybe Brittany meant the deli at the supermarket? I'm sure Cami knows not too many places can compete with a Publix sub. Maybe she took her there. I'm sure there's one of those near the bank. Or maybe they didn't eat lunch, and she didn't want you to demand to know why Cami hadn't fed her." Becky took in a breath and reached for her best friend's hand. "You're far too invested in this. You have to stop."

Jules yanked her hand back and ran it through her hair. She blew out a long breath, then hopped off Becky's desk and began to pace. "I know what it feels like to want answers about who you are. When Jonas told me the story of my adoption, it was like a giant weight lifted off my shoulders. I'm happy for Brittany that she's starting to remember. That she found her family." She spun around to face Becky. "I just can't ignore the feeling I have in my gut that's telling me something's *not right*."

Becky pushed herself up from her chair and placed her hands on Jules's shoulders. "Listen, I get it. This one feels personal to you. But Brittany *doesn't* want our help, and you've got to respect that. Her case is *closed*."

Becky didn't intend to wait for a response and instead changed the subject as she sat back down in her chair. She rolled it closer to her desk, then opened her email and scanned her inbox. "So, the email I got yesterday was from a guy who's looking to find his wife's birth mother." She offered Jules a slight smile. "He wants them to be able to meet as, sort of, his Christmas present to his wife."

Jules snorted in disgust as she headed back to her desk. "You can't give someone who's adopted a birth parent as a holiday gift. But he's probably not adopted, so of course, he has no idea what it feels like."

Becky gritted her teeth. She'd never seen Jules like this, but she decided to let it go. "I think a new case is just what you need," she said as she opened the email. "His wife already took a DNA test. It's just that neither of them knows what to do with her results. So, he was thinking *if* he could surprise her … you know, *if* her birth mother was willing …"

She hit the key to forward the form to Jules, then typed in her email address and pressed the send button. "Okay, it should be coming to you." Becky watched the screen to confirm it had gone through, then drew in a sharp breath when she noticed the new message now sitting in her inbox.

Jules hadn't missed the startled expression on her face. "What?" She jumped up from her seat and was looking over her shoulder before Becky could even close her inbox. "Hey, Brittany's DNA results are in."

"Right, but we don't need them anymore." Becky's voice was firm.

"The heck we don't." Jules was already back at her desk typing on her computer.

"Jules," Becky said, her tone a warning. "Brittany is *not* our client anymore."

"I know, but she never said she wanted us to delete her results when they came in." Her eyes pleaded with her partner. "I just need to figure out if everything she was told is true. Then I'll be able to let it go." She held up her hand. "I promise."

Becky racked her brain, trying to remember if Brittany had signed a contract with them. Since she wasn't paying them at first, she was sure she hadn't. They'd both strayed far from being professional with Brittany, a lesson they needed to learn from going forward. But this? Now Jules wasn't just crossing a line. She was driving a bulldozer over it.

Becky ran her hand over her face and remained seated at her desk—her way of letting her partner know she was unwilling to be any part of this. Her lips pressed together in a firm, disapproving line as Jules logged into Brittany's account.

With her elbows on the desk, palms pressed against her

cheeks, Jules stared at the screen. Her expression was unreadable.

Finally, Becky couldn't stand it. "What is it? Does Brittany have any close matches?"

The snort Jules let out seemed to have an *I told you so* wrapped up in it. "Uh, I'd say so."

"A parent/child match?"

Jules shook her head. "Closer."

With that, Becky was out of her seat. "What do you mean *closer*?"

Jules looked up from her computer. "It looks like Brittany's DNA was already in the system." She rubbed her chin thoughtfully. "At least I think that's the case. She has a self/twin match."

Becky groaned, and her pulse quickened. "Oh, don't say that." She moved to peer over Jules's shoulder at the results on her screen. "Remember at the hospital? Brittany said she felt like she had déjà vu when she took the tests."

"I think she was right," Jules said, pointing at the match at the top of her list. "She already tested, but under the name Claire Butler. And look at her second match. It's 2815 cMs."

"A full sibling. That must be her sister."

"Looks like it is a female, but she's listed with only a first initial. L. Doyle."

Becky huffed. "Of course she is. Does this L. Doyle or Claire Butler have a tree attached?"

Jules shook her head. "Nope."

"Maybe Doyle is her sister's married name. Did Brittany happen to mention if she was older or younger than her?"

"She didn't say." Jules leaned back in her chair, a pensive expression on her face. "I told you something wasn't right. Why would she have a test under another name if she really is Brittany Mullins?"

Becky couldn't argue Jules might finally have a point. "Did

she ever mention being adopted? I mean, why else would she do DNA testing?"

"People test for a ton of reasons. It's possible she and her sister both tested for fun." Jules shrugged. "Or maybe they were suspicious one of them had a different father."

"Which they don't. They share too much DNA to be half-siblings."

"But maybe they weren't sure." Jules glanced up at Becky. "Besides, Brittany knows my story. We talked about my adoption more than once, and she asked me questions about it. You would think if she remembered she was adopted, or her family or sister told her she was, she would have mentioned it to me."

Becky rubbed her chin as she considered it. "That could be *why* she was asking you questions. Or maybe she suspects she might be, but her family hasn't gotten around to telling her yet. That could be why her sister is coming down to stay with her. You know, to tell her in person."

Jules gazed off thoughtfully. "You think the parents kept one of them and put the other one up for adoption?"

"You know as well as I do, anything's possible." Becky shrugged. "Maybe they were *both* given up for adoption."

"I'm going to look at the shared matches and see if I can start building a family tree," Jules said, turning her attention back to her computer. "Why don't you take the name on the other test—Claire Butler—and do some digging. See if you can find anything that makes sense."

Becky went back to her desk. She was fully aware she'd just committed to going down the rabbit hole with Jules, who didn't seem quite as unreasonable now.

They worked silently, the only sound their fingers hitting keys on their computers.

Becky hit one dead end after another. She didn't know enough about Brittany to determine if Claire Butler was her name at birth or a married name. She considered it could even be an alias she'd used just for her DNA results.

Finally, Jules broke the silence. "There's not a single Doyle surname in Brittany's matches, so I'm thinking it must be her sister's married name. I think I found a common ancestor for two of her shared matches. It's still a couple of generations back, but I can build on that and see what I find." She spun in her chair so she was facing Becky's desk. "What about you?"

"I guess I can stop searching Claire Doyle then, but do you know how many Claire Butlers there are in the world?" Becky rubbed her eyes, relieved to stop staring at her computer for a minute.

"Maybe Butler was her married name. See if there's a mention of a Claire Butler in an obituary or a record of her getting married. Maybe you can find a Mullins that married a Butler or even a Butler that married a Mullins." She shrugged. "I suppose you could also search using her potential maiden name. Cami said it was Schroeder."

"Right, but she also said she knew her as Brittany." Becky arched an eyebrow in Jules's direction. "Are we believing what Cami told us now?"

She threw up her hands. "I have no clue what to believe anymore. But let's explore everything. Maybe she went by her middle name in high school. Who knows? Teenagers are a weird lot."

Becky searched every variation of the names she and Jules had discussed but came up empty for one that fit. When she glanced at her phone, she was shocked to see the time. No wonder she was starving.

She leaned back and stretched in her chair. "Can we take a break and get some lunch soon? How's the tree coming?"

"Slow going, but I'm making progress." She looked up from her computer. "How about you?"

Becky shook her head, then sighed. "No luck at all. I

haven't been able to find any of the names we have that matches Brittany's date of birth."

"Well, maybe it's because what's on her license isn't accurate. We've always said she doesn't look that young."

Becky's forehead creased. "Right, but—"

Jules held up her index finger. "Hang on." She hit a few keys, then bobbed her head. "Very interesting."

"What's so interesting? Did you find something?"

"Claire Butler has a profile attached to her account. It doesn't have much information, but it does have her age bracket listed." Jules turned with a satisfied smile. "Thirty to thirty-nine."

"Well, that changes things." Becky rubbed at her neck as Jules started typing.

"Here's something, I think. A Claire Mullins married an Alex Butler in 2011," Jules said, staring at her screen. "Unfortunately, it's just a record of the marriage, so there's no other information."

"Does it say where they were married?"

"Townsend, Tennessee." Jules pursed her lips and stared off as if she was trying to figure something out.

"What? Does that location make sense?" Becky asked.

"Maybe. I'm pulling up a map of Tennessee."

"Just because she got married there doesn't mean that's where she lived." Becky moved to Jules's desk and peered over her shoulder. "What exactly are you looking for?"

When the map appeared on her screen, Jules tapped the state's eastern border with her finger. "See, right here."

Becky squinted to see where she was pointing. "What am I looking at? Did Brittany ever tell you she thought she might be from Tennessee?"

"Not exactly." Jules spun in her chair to face Becky. "But remember that picture from the art show she said looked familiar?"

"The one of the mountains and all the leaves changing colors?"

Jules wagged her index finger in the air. "Not just any mountains. The Great Smoky Mountains." She turned back toward her computer and ran her finger up and down on the screen. "See here. They're right on the border of Tennessee and North Carolina." She leaned back in her chair. "It would seem to me that anyone who lived in Townsend, Tennessee would have a perfect view to watch the seasons change."

* * *

"I still don't understand why she'd use a different name," Becky said a couple of hours later as they tried to build Brittany's family tree.

"We could still be right that she's running away from a husband. I mean, if we're right about this, she has one she married in Tennessee." Jules scowled. "But now I'm even more worried about her staying by herself at the apartment."

"But she said she was only married briefly, and they got divorced." Becky hesitated. "Maybe that part was true. Why don't you add Alex Butler as her spouse on the tree and see what it pulls up? Do you need me to look up the wedding date again?"

"No. I saved it." Jules created a record for Brittany and added empty boxes where her parents and grandparents would go. "I just added her under this set of great-grandparents, but I have no idea if they're the right ones. I haven't finished building everything under the great-great-grandparents, but that's the shared ancestor I feel good about."

"For now, it will work. Just to see if we can find anything." Becky's stomach growled loudly. "I'm officially ready to chew off my own arm. Should we just get something and eat here? Order some lunch and see what pops up?"

"We won't have to wait that long. I think I found something." Jules nodded. "It looks like they did get divorced."

Becky tipped her head to the side. "How do you know?"

"There was a hint on Alex Butler, and it took me to an obituary for his mom, Carol Butler. She died two years ago."

"You're sure it's the same guy?" Becky asked.

The printer came to life, and Jules gestured at the piece of paper it spat out.

As Becky reached for it, it occurred to her this might be the same way Brittany had ended up with a copy of Judith Hunter's obituary. Maybe it had been research of some sort.

She laid it on the desk and read out loud. "Carol Butler, survived by her son Alex, daughter-in-law Barbara, and two grandchildren. It says she was buried in Maryville, Tennessee."

Jules pulled up the map on her computer again. "Maryville isn't very far from Townsend."

"Okay, but what does this really tell us?" Becky asked, her shoulders lifting. "Brittany said she got married young, and it was brief. If this is her ex-husband, he's remarried with two kids, so it seems like that could fit. But then why would she be running from him?"

"Just because he has two kids doesn't mean they're with his new wife. They could be Brittany's. Claire's." She threw up her hands with a huff. "Whatever her name really is."

Becky exhaled her frustration. "Can we just call her Brittany until we know for sure? I'm already confused enough. Were there any hints on the Claire Butler you found?"

Jules consulted her screen. "There's a couple of potential public records hints." She took in a sharp breath. "Ah. This one has a date of birth—July 12, 1990. That makes her thirty-one." Jules looked up with a satisfied smile. "Which fits her profile." She turned her attention back to her computer. "It says here she lived in a city in Tennessee, but it's not

Townsend. There's also another record for Shelby, North Carolina."

"That could make sense since Tennessee and North Carolina are right next to each other. Does it say when she lived there?"

"It's a range of years. Recent but nothing exact."

Becky planted her elbow on the desk and nibbled on her fingernail as she stared at Jules. "Why does Shelby, North Carolina sound so familiar?"

"It doesn't mean anything to me, but I can pull up the map again." Jules shrugged. "Looks like it's about an hour from Charlotte."

Becky ran her hand over her face. "I know I've heard the name of that town before. Just recently."

"Any chance Brittany mentioned it to you?" Jules crossed her fingers in the air and gave Becky a hopeful lift of her eyebrows.

"I don't think so. Hang on, let me check something." Becky pulled up her search history, and there it was. "Judith Hunter, the obituary you asked me to look up. That's where she died. In Shelby, North Carolina."

CHAPTER TWENTY-SIX

"WELL, now we know Brittany lived in the same town as Judith," Becky said, staring at the obituary. "They're about the same age, so they were probably friends."

"Not necessarily." Jules tapped her finger against her lips. "We could still be right that they're related."

"But there was no mention of her in the obituary." Becky read from her screen. "It says Judith was survived by her husband, Charlie, her father, James Davies, and sisters Meredith and Holley. She was predeceased by her mother, Maureen McGraw Davies." She glanced over at Jules. "Any of those names sound familiar from Brittany's matches?"

"Not that I remember."

Becky rubbed her stomach as it growled. They still hadn't discussed lunch, and pretty soon, it would be closer to dinner time. "I know she didn't want us to continue working on her case, but maybe we should just ask Brittany."

"And say what?" Jules asked as she threw up her hands. "So far, the only thing we know is she has a second set of DNA results under another name. We believe she has a full sister with the last name Doyle, and we think she's currently using someone else's name. Someone younger. Brittany's older than she thinks by what, six years?" She winced. "That information might sting a little. If our research is accurate, we'll need to let her know her real name is Claire Mullins, not Brittany Mullins. Married and divorced from Alex Butler, hence the name Claire Butler she used on her other DNA results."

Becky wrinkled her nose. "Yeah, that might be a lot to take in at once."

"But what I still can't make sense of is Cami." Jules massaged the back of her neck. "Why would she tell Brittany her name in high school was Brittany Schroeder? And that she lived in Tampa. Did you ever find anything at all on a Claire or Brittany Schroeder?"

Becky shook her head. "Nothing I could connect definitively. Any other hints we can use?"

"Nothing." Jules turned to face Becky's desk. "We could try her ex-husband. See if he can shed any light on the situation."

"Sure, why not." Becky had a feeling she wasn't getting lunch anytime soon.

Alex Butler was easy to track down, and several minutes later, Jules had a cell phone number. A voice with a southern twang answered. "Hey, this here's Alex. What can I do you for?"

Jules pressed the speaker button on her cell phone. "Hi, Alex. My name is Jules Dalton. I was looking for some information on someone and wondered if you'd be able to help me."

"Oh, yeah?" His voice took on a hard edge. "Who y'all looking fer?"

"Uh, her name is Claire Mullins."

"My ex-wife?" He let out a hiss. "You ain't the only one lookin' for her. I ain't seen her in years, and I got no idea where she's at. Sorry, but I'm workin'. I gotta go."

After the call disconnected, Becky scowled. "Well, that was odd."

"It doesn't bode well if someone else is trying to track her down. I wish I had seen more of what she had in that folder." Jules leaned back in her chair. "Maybe we try Judith Hunter's husband. Charlie, right? He could probably shed light on her relationship to Brittany."

Becky still wasn't sure there was a worthwhile connection, but it couldn't hurt. "I guess it's worth a try. Let me see if I can find a phone number for him." She shot Jules a stern stare. "But after this, we're getting something to eat."

Becky recited each of the numbers she found, but Jules shook her head after trying each one.

"That one's disconnected too," she said after trying the last number. She pressed her lips together and stared off thoughtfully. Finally, she glanced back at Becky with a slight smile. "Charlotte's a quick, cheap flight. Maybe I'll just go there and see what I can find out."

Becky let out a sigh, then shook her head firmly. "Jules, no. If you really want to know about Judith, just ask Brittany when you see her on Saturday. If you're not willing to do that, I think it's time to think about letting this go."

"I don't think I can." Her expression was serious as she stared at Becky. "I can't help but feel like Brittany's being fed a bunch of bull. And part of me needs to know why that is. Why would the people who are supposed to love her fill her head with lies? I'm worried she could be in trouble because they haven't bothered to tell her the truth."

Becky could tell this was a battle she wasn't going to win. "When do you think you're even going to go? The rehearsal dinner's tomorrow night, and the wedding's Saturday. You can't just be running off—

But Jules wasn't listening. Her focus was on her computer, and it appeared she was already searching for a flight. "It's only an hour. I can fly out early tomorrow morning and make it back in plenty of time." She pulled her credit card from her wallet. "Can you make an excuse to spend the day with Brittany? I don't like the idea of her being at the apartment by herself."

Becky had no idea if she could pull it off, but she heard herself agree to it.

A moment later, Jules nodded when she glanced up. "Okay, I'm booked."

Becky shook her head incredulously. "You really think this trip is necessary? That you need to go *tomorrow*? You have enough on your plate with your brother's wedding this weekend. You don't need to do this, especially now."

"I just know that if something happens to Brittany, I won't be able to forgive myself." Jules stood. "Come on, let's go get something to eat."

Becky reached for her purse and followed Jules. "I want my opinion on the record that I think flying to North Carolina tomorrow is crazy."

"We're missing an important piece of the puzzle, and my gut tells me it has something to do with that obituary. Why did it appear after she spent the day with Cami? I have to go find out."

When they got outside, Becky jabbed her finger in the air at her best friend. "You'd better be back in time for that rehearsal dinner tomorrow night, or Erin's going to lose her mind."

"I will, don't worry." Jules turned and locked the office door. "All I need to do is figure out what part Judith Hunter plays in all of this, and I'll be back on the plane heading home."

CHAPTER TWENTY-SEVEN

JULES PULLED the rental car to the curb in front of a gray two-story house. She glanced at the address she'd written down for Judith Hunter's husband, Charlie, and compared it to the number on the mailbox at the curb. She was at the right house.

She didn't need to wait long to confirm someone was home. Halfway up the driveway, the front door flew open.

A tall, imposing man stared her down from the porch with eyes narrowed into slits. "Get the hell off my property, you blood-sucking leech." His voice was controlled, measured, but it was the eerie way he punctuated each word that made the hair on the back of Jules's neck stand up.

She reeled back, then stood paralyzed, her heart thumping wildly in her chest.

The man lifted a baseball bat that had been propped beside the door. He gripped the handle in his right hand and tapped the end against his left palm. Slow and precise. A warning. "Exactly which part of that did you not understand?"

"Sorry." The word squeaked from Jules's throat. "I'm—I'm going." The man's menacing stare left Jules with no reassurance he wouldn't hesitate to make good on his threat, but she couldn't imagine why his wrath was aimed at her. It wasn't like she'd shown up with bad intentions, but this wasn't the time or place to argue.

Jules turned and scurried back toward her car, the heels of her sandals clicking against the concrete. When she'd dressed to catch her early flight, she hadn't considered she'd need appropriate footwear to flee from a crazy man. Becky had been right. Coming to North Carolina to find out more about Judith had been a bad idea and a complete waste of time.

When Jules reached the street, she heard the man's front door slam with an angry thud. She stole a quick glance over her shoulder and noticed he was still watching her from his front window. His angry scowl hadn't lessened in the slightest. Jules had no doubt he'd be back out that front door in a flash if she didn't keep her promise to be on her way.

She clicked the button on the fob for the rental car, but as she pulled open the driver's side door, she heard a female's voice call out, "You a reporter?"

The question seemed to come from the next-door neighbor's house, but a long row of shrubs divided her property from Charlie Hunter's. Jules stole a peek at his house, relief loosening her shoulders that he was no longer visible in the window. She eased the car door closed until she heard a soft click. With one last look to ensure Charlie hadn't returned, Jules left the safety the car offered and peered around the hedges. A woman was unloading groceries from the trunk of her car.

"You a reporter?" the woman asked again.

Jules brought her palm to her chest. "Me?" She shook her head as her shoulders lifted. "No, I'm not a reporter."

With her hands full of grocery bags, the woman aimed her chin at the house next door. "What do you want with Charlie, then?"

"I just—" Jules strolled closer to the woman, her stomach

twisting at the possibility of being overheard. For all she knew, Charlie could be listening on the other side of the tall hedge. "I was looking for some information about his wife."

The woman tilted her head, eyes narrowed. "Did you know her?"

"Yeah," Jules said with a quick nod, even as she hoped she wouldn't get caught lying. She didn't know the first thing about Judith, certainly not enough to fake her way through pretending they'd been friends.

The woman let out a prolonged sigh. "I knew her too. The whole thing was horrible. I mean, the media *just* stopped coming around. I guess they're all distracted now by that small plane that went down a couple of days ago." Her eyebrows shot up as she bit back a smile. "Supposedly, it was one of the candidates for the upcoming local election, and he crashed with his *mistress* on board. I can only imagine the circus they've got going on." With the latest gossip relayed, her smile faded. "But before that, they were camped out here for weeks, when, you know …"

Jules didn't know, but if there was someone who might be happy to share information, it seemed to be Charlie's neighbor.

The woman squinted at Jules as she looked her up and down and must have decided she seemed harmless. "I'm Helen." She aimed her chin at the remaining groceries still in the trunk. "Why don't you grab the rest of those bags and come on in?"

With plastic bags slung over both arms, Jules followed her through a side door that led them into her kitchen. She slid the bags onto the counter.

Helen nodded in appreciation, then gestured at the table. "Have a seat." She began to unpack the grocery bags, then glanced briefly over her shoulder. "How did you say you knew Claire again?"

Jules felt her breath catch in her throat. Why was she asking about Claire?

"We, uh, used to run together. At the park." Jules knew she didn't look like a runner, but she'd been caught off guard, and it was all she could think of in that instant.

"Yeah, Claire was always out jogging. No matter the temperature or the weather. Day or night. Rain or hot as hell. It didn't matter to her."

"Yeah, well, it's that runner's high." Jules forced a laugh. "We used to run together all the time. Then I hurt my knee and had to stop for a bit." She crossed her fingers in the air. "I'm hoping to get the all-clear from my doctor soon that I can start up again." Jules had a thought and threw it out as she fished for any insight Helen might have. "We even did that life-saver 5K together."

If Helen knew anything about the race, she didn't say. "I always saw her running alone. It must have been nice for her to have someone to go with. God bless ya for being able to keep up with her. I would never have even tried, but I always liked Claire. We became friendly. You know, some people just wave in the street, but she was always real nice to me. Of course, I liked Judith too."

Jules decided to play dumb to see what she could find out. It wasn't like she'd be getting any information from Charlie. "Judith?"

Helen spun around, her head tipped to one side. "Claire didn't tell you? Judith was Charlie's first wife."

First wife? Jules pressed her lips together and worked to conceal her shock. Did that mean Claire was *married* to Charlie?

"She—well, she died." Helen slipped into the seat across the table from Jules. "Took a nasty spill down their stairs." She made air quotes. "An accident."

"You don't think it was?"

Helen lifted her shoulders. "I did at the time. But now, I

don't know what to think." She leaned in. "And I'm not alone. I'm a hairdresser over at Salon Deja Vu. We're in the plaza by the new CVS. Anyway, as soon as I pick up the scissors, gums start flapping. I hear it all." Her expression turned serious as she studied Jules. "You have great hair. That your natural color?"

Jules fluffed her hair with her fingers. "Almost. I do some auburn highlights a few times a year, but I'm horribly overdue."

Jules held her breath, praying Helen wouldn't ask where she got her hair done. She didn't know enough about this town to even think about throwing a salon name out there. As her heart skipped in her chest, she was prepared to say she did her own hair when Helen stood and returned to her groceries on the counter.

"You know, there was a time I blamed myself for what happened to Claire." She turned away from Jules to unload canned goods from one of the bags.

Jules had no idea what Helen could be referring to, but she was determined to find out. "Here, let me help you." She rose from her chair and moved to the counter. "Why would you blame yourself?" she asked as she helped unload items from the grocery bags.

Helen silently shelved canned vegetables before finally responding. "Claire told me Charlie made a comment that he wished she were more like Judith." Her face went dark as she shook her head in disgust. "He was always saying crap like that to her. It was sad, really. Poor Claire actually thought maybe if she looked more like his first wife, Charlie would love her. Anyway, she came over and pleaded with me to color her hair that day. I even stayed late after the shop closed for the night, but I still didn't think she'd actually go through with it. I just couldn't believe she'd want to dye that beautiful blond hair of hers brown."

"But you did it?" Jules asked, even though she already knew the answer.

Helen met her gaze, nodded, and then let out a deep sigh. "I tried to talk her out of it, but Claire wouldn't take no for an answer." She reached out and gripped Jules's forearm. "But then, after it was done, she got real nervous. She was worried it might actually make Charlie mad. She thought maybe her plan would backfire because—" She pulled her hand back and shrugged sadly. "I guess she realized just changing her hair color wouldn't magically turn her into Judith."

Jules pulled a half-gallon of milk from the last bag and handed it to Helen. "So, Charlie really loved his first wife, huh? That must have been hard for Claire to feel like she had to compete with a ghost."

Jules knew nothing about Judith, except that she was either extremely clumsy or she'd angered her husband enough to get herself pushed down a flight of stairs. If there was any chance of the latter, it was no wonder Brittany had gone into hiding.

Helen snorted as she pulled on the handle to the refrigerator. "That man doesn't love anyone but himself." She placed the milk on the shelf and slammed the door with an angry huff. "I think the comments he made to Claire about Judith were just a way to keep her on her toes, but she took them to heart. When I was done, she didn't look like Judith, of course, but Claire looked *drastically* different." Helen pressed her lips together and gazed off, her eyes growing glassy. "I figured maybe it caused a fight when she went home, and well, you know."

"You really think her husband would have hurt her over the color of her hair?"

Helen lifted her hands in the air, but the knowing look that accompanied the gesture told Jules it was clear that was precisely what she thought.

"Aside from Charlie, I was probably the last person to see

Claire alive." She hesitated, then rubbed her temple. "The night I colored her hair was the night she went missing." Helen took in a deep breath as she collected the plastic grocery bags and tucked them into a bucket underneath the kitchen sink. "I wouldn't put anything past that monster. Especially after what happened to Judith. It's all my clients have been talking about since Claire went missing." She grabbed a can of Coke from the refrigerator and nodded at Jules. "Thirsty?"

"No, thanks." She followed Helen and sat back down at the table. "Your customers don't think Judith's fall was an accident?"

She shook her head. "Not anymore. I think the police are reconsidering too." Helen leaned in and lowered her voice as if she was worried someone might overhear her. "I heard they're going to dig her up to see if they missed something."

Jules reeled back in her seat. "Really? Exhume her remains. Why?"

Helen sipped from her soda can and eyed her with a curious stare. "You must not watch the news."

Jules shrugged. "I don't really watch much television. I'm more of a reader. You know, mystery and suspense novels."

"Hmm. I've never been able to understand how people read a whole book. I mean, read because they *want* to. In school—"

"What's been on the news?" Jules asked. "Do the police think Judith's death has something to do with Claire? I mean, technically, she's just missing. She's not dead, right?" Jules already knew the answer. Claire was alive and well and living as Brittany Mullins.

Helen set her can down on the table. She met Jules's eyes and dipped her chin. "I'm sorry to have to be the one to tell you."

Jules frowned. How could anyone think Claire was dead if they hadn't found a body? "Tell me what?"

"Officially, yes, Claire's still a missing person, but—I can *feel* things." Helen clasped her hands over her chest. "In here. I just *know* she's gone."

Jules felt the air escape her lungs in a slow hiss. "So, you mean you *believe* she's dead?"

Helen nodded. "That Charlie's a son of a bitch. You know, Claire used to come over. Sit right where you're sitting now and tell me her troubles. They weren't married but a few months when she went missing."

"That's all? Just a few months?"

Helen pursed her lips. "I thought you said you were looking for Charlie's wife?"

Jules shifted in her seat, her cheeks hot as she tried to recover from her slip-up. At the time, she'd thought she was asking about Judith, not Claire. "I mean, last I saw her, she was sure Charlie was getting ready to propose. You know Claire. When she wants something, she gets it. I just figured ..." She let the thought drift off and hoped she'd covered appropriately.

Helen offered a bittersweet smile. "Yeah, you're right. I still don't understand why she was so determined to marry him. It was a whirlwind—her and Charlie." She shook her head in disgust. "He certainly got right back in the saddle after Judith died. That threw the town gossip into overdrive, which is probably why Claire didn't mention his first wife to you." She lowered her voice. "Some of Judith's friends weren't very happy when Charlie took up with her. Claire was probably a little embarrassed, but it was Charlie that shoulda been. He was supposed to be the grieving widower. Not gallivanting around town and then racing down the aisle again so soon."

"I wonder what the big hurry was all about," Jules said thoughtfully, more for herself than Helen.

"Claire told me he took out an insurance policy on her. She said Charlie insisted when they got married. And she just—"

Helen drew in a deep breath. "She just always went along with what he said."

"You think Charlie killed her? For the insurance money?"

"Oh, I know he killed her." Helen leaned across the table. "One of my clients has a sister who's married to a cop. She said they sprayed this stuff in the house that looks for blood."

"Luminol?"

"Yeah, that sounds right." Helen's face twisted in disgust. "She told me the downstairs lit up like a Christmas tree."

Jules flinched. "Oh my gosh. That's terrible."

"There was way too much blood." Helen lifted her eyebrows and gave Jules a knowing stare. "Almost too much to be from one person. There's no way Claire could have— Anyway, at this point, supposedly they're looking for her body. Linda Martin, who lives across the street, has one of those Ring cameras on her front door. It also happens to catch the end of Charlie's driveway." Helen cocked her head, a smirk lifting her lips. "It seems he went out for a little ride the night Claire went missing."

"Did your neighbor tell the police that?"

"Yeah, Linda gave the footage to the cops, which is why I can't believe he hasn't been arrested yet." Helen shot a look in the direction of his house. "But it's only a matter of time before they put that bastard behind bars. They'll get him for Judith too, and who knows who else?" She threw her hands up in the air. "It's like I'm living next door to a serial killer."

Jules's head was spinning. The blood wasn't Claire's, so whose was it? Maybe Charlie was more dangerous than anyone imagined. What if she'd walked in on him hurting someone else? It would explain why she'd changed her identity and run off to keep him from silencing her, from making her his next victim.

"Do you think Charlie ever told Claire the truth about what happened to Judith?" Jules asked.

Helen shrugged. "She never did say it outright, but I know she was afraid of him. Claire told me more than once she made a mistake when she married Charlie. I asked her one time why she didn't just tell him it wasn't working out. File for divorce. Trust me, I wouldn't have blamed her." Helen sipped her soda, then leaned closer to Jules. "Claire just got this real scared look in her eyes, and then she whispered, 'Well, you know. *Judith.*' Like that explained it."

"Oh, man. Maybe Judith asked for a divorce before she died. Did you tell the police any of this?"

Helen raked her hands through her hair and leaned back in her chair. "I tried, but no one ever called me back. Maybe they already have enough to lock him away. I just hope they figure out where that bastard took Claire's body so we can have a decent burial and say a proper goodbye."

"Do you think that's why they haven't arrested him yet? Because they haven't found Claire's body?"

Helen lifted a shoulder. "I heard all that testing takes time. DNA and stuff. But I know they're building their case against him. I mean, supposedly, they found Claire's purse and phone in a dumpster right by where Charlie works." She let out a disgusted snort as if the police were inept for not arresting him on the spot. "I mean, come on, that's *not* just a coincidence." She gave a slow shake of her head. "Maybe they're waiting until they have the results back from Judith, but I'm telling you, Charlie's days are numbered. I've got my eye on him, and I'm surprised he showed his face to yell at you today. He barely leaves the house anymore. One of my clients told me they heard he lost his job. Who wants a murderer working for them, right?"

Jules nodded in agreement. "No kidding."

"You know, I actually felt bad for him after the car accident. But now, of course, I'm starting to wonder about that too."

Jules cocked her head. "Car accident?"

"Yeah. You know where Trudy's is? That little dive bar on Dixie?"

Jules had no idea, but she nodded anyway. "Yeah."

"A woman ran the red light at that intersection." Helen smacked her hands together. "Charlie T-boned her with his Bronco, and she died."

Jules's hand flew up to cover her mouth. "Oh, that's awful."

"*Supposedly*, the girl was loaded. She'd been drinking at Trudy's, and the accident was said to be her fault. At the time, Judith said Charlie took it real hard. But now, you know, I don't know what to think, especially since then Judith had an accident of her own a few months later." Helen used air quotes again to indicate she didn't believe for one second Judith falling down the stairs wasn't the result of her husband pushing her.

Jules nodded. "Of course."

"She was a pretty little thing, that girl he killed. Blond hair, blue eyes. If it really was her fault, what could be so wrong in her young life that she'd drink and drive like that?"

"It's hard to imagine," Jules said, shaking her head.

"I have two kids, and I don't know what I'd do if I lost one of them like that. Her parents were on the news when it happened. Just heartbroken. They live right in Danville, not far from where the accident happened. Can you imagine driving around the wreck and not knowing it was your own daughter?"

"That happened?" Jules cringed at the horror of it. "How awful."

"The whole thing was so sad. One of my clients goes to the same church as the Doyles. She said two years later, they're still on the prayer list every single Sunday."

Jules sat up straight in her chair. "The Doyles?"

"Yeah, you know them?" Helen asked. "It was their daughter, Laura, that Charlie killed."

CHAPTER TWENTY-EIGHT

Jules left her phone number with Helen and promised to see her when there was a funeral for Claire. Of course, there wouldn't be a service because she wasn't actually dead.

As she slid into the rental car, her heart raced. She glanced over at Charlie's house and half-expected him to come hurtling toward her car with his bat. Jules was grateful and a little surprised he hadn't flattened the tires while she was inside talking to Helen. Still, the information she'd gotten from his neighbor might have made it worth it.

Jules reached for the rental car agreement laid on the passenger seat and located the return time. With a frown, her gaze lifted to the clock on the dashboard. She wasn't going to be able to get it back on time. Or make her flight. But there was no way she could leave without trying to talk to the Doyles.

Jules started the car and drove down the street until Charlie Hunter's house was out of sight. She pulled back over to the curb in front of a house with no cars in the driveway, turned off the car, and dialed Becky's number.

"Hey, just say yes or no. Are you with Brittany?" she asked when Becky answered.

"Uh, yeah."

Of course, she was. Jules had made Becky promise to spend the day with her. "Can you go somewhere to talk?"

"Yeah, give me a second." There was silence, and Jules imagined her friend trying to figure out a way to get some privacy. "It's, uh, in my car," Becky said a moment later. "Hang on."

Keys rattled, and then Jules heard her talking to Brittany. "Be right back. Bryan needs some information I left in my car."

There was the sound of the front door as it creaked open and then shut.

A few seconds later, Becky was back. "Okay, I'm inside my car in the driveway."

Jules took a deep breath. "There's something really odd going on here."

"What do you mean? Like what?"

"I'm not even sure where to start, but I'm pretty sure we have the right Claire Butler. What we didn't count on is that she *married* Charlie Hunter after his wife, Judith, died." At the mention of his name, Jules cast a nervous glance into her rearview mirror. He hadn't followed her. There was no sign of him or anyone else on the quiet suburban street.

"So, I guess that explains why Brittany had her obituary. She was probably just curious—"

"Oh, no. It's way bigger than that." Jules considered for a moment what would have happened if she had listened to Becky and not made the trip to North Carolina. They'd still be in the dark about Claire being married to Charlie Hunter. "I went to the husband's house, but I didn't get very far. He told me to get the hell off his property and threatened to clobber me with a baseball bat if I didn't."

Becky let out a gasp. "Geez. Are you okay?"

"I'm fine, though I did start to question my decision to try and talk to him."

"No kidding. It sounds like going to see him wasn't the best idea, but it also means we might be right about Brittany being married to someone abusive. Looks like she had good reasons to run from him."

"Charlie thought I was a reporter."

"A reporter?"

Jules lowered the driver's side window to let in some fresh air. "Yeah. Apparently, the media's been a regular fixture in the neighborhood. I never actually talked to the bat-wielding husband, but I had a nice chat with his neighbor. Turns out Brittany—Claire—went missing about six weeks ago."

"Well, that lines up if you add in the time in the hospital."

"Right. But his neighbor also said she heard there was so much blood found in the house, there was no way Claire could still be alive."

There was silence on the line for a moment, and then Becky asked, "But how could that be?"

"I don't know." Jules raked her hand through her hair. "Maybe Charlie killed someone else, and that's why Brittany ran? Apparently, Helen—the neighbor—was all sorts of chummy with both of his wives. And get this. Charlie took out a life insurance policy on Claire. Maybe he had one on Judith too. The neighbor told me Claire was scared of Charlie and his first wife died under *suspicious* circumstances."

"Suspicious? There was nothing in Judith Hunter's obituary that said that."

"She died from a fall down a flight of stairs, but they ruled it an accident." Jules couldn't help but think of the air quotes Helen had used when she told her that.

"So, it *wasn't* considered suspicious?" Becky sounded confused.

"Well, not at the time. But I guess after his second wife went missing and they found all this blood in Charlie's house, they're thinking of taking another look. There's apparently talk of exhuming Judith's remains."

Becky took in a sharp breath. "Oh, wow. But it couldn't have been Claire's blood because we know she's alive and living as Brittany. So, whose was it?"

"Not sure, but clearly, Charlie hasn't been arrested yet, or he wouldn't have been there to threaten to bash in my skull with a baseball bat." Jules checked the time on the dashboard. She needed to get moving.

"So, a dead wife, a missing wife, and a house full of somebody's blood. Why haven't the police arrested this guy yet?"

"Maybe they're waiting to exhume the first wife. I mean, they can't *prove* he killed Brittany—I mean, Claire. How could they? We both know she isn't dead."

"Right," Becky said. "But it sure sounds like *someone* was killed in that house. So, who?"

Jules shook her head and started up the car. "I have no idea. But I did get another nugget of information from the neighbor that's very interesting. I need to catch a later flight, so I can go check into it."

"Jules, no. You can't do that." Becky's tone was adamant. "The rehearsal dinner's tonight. You *have* to get back here."

Jules stared up at the dark clouds and prayed the weather would cooperate. "I'll make it to the church on time, don't worry. It shouldn't take me that long to have the chat I need, and then I'll head to the airport. I promise." Jules had no intention of disappointing Jonas and Erin, but she couldn't leave when she was so close to figuring it all out. "I think something Helen told me might be a big piece of the puzzle. Apparently, Charlie Hunter's had a string of bad luck."

"You mean, beyond his dead first wife and missing second wife?" Becky asked with a hint of sarcasm. "Is there more?"

"Yup. He was in a car accident, and a young woman died."

There was silence. "Okay," Becky said finally. "Was that considered suspicious too?

"No charges were filed. The girl he hit had just left a bar, and apparently, she was tanked. She ran the red light."

"I don't understand," Becky said. "If the girl he hit was drunk and didn't stop at the light, then it wasn't his fault. So, what does that have to do with—"

Jules didn't let her finish. "The woman who was killed, her name was Laura Doyle. L. Doyle. Remember Brittany's DNA match?"

Jules heard an intake of air on the line and then, "Wait, so you're saying—"

"Yeah, exactly. Brittany married the man who killed her sister."

"And then took off when she realized he was violent?" Becky asked. "I'm not sure what to make of why she would *want* to marry Charlie if he was the one who hit and killed her sister. Do you think they formed some weird bond over her death?"

Jules couldn't imagine anyone bonding with the man she'd seen wielding a baseball bat. "I have *no* idea, which is why I don't think we should mention it to Brittany. See why I can't leave yet? I need to try to talk to Laura's parents. They might be able to shed light on how it went down. And why."

"Is it possible it's just a weird coincidence?" Becky asked. "We have no way of knowing when they submitted their DNA, so her sister might have already died by the time Brittany did hers and got her as a match. But wait—"

There was silence on the line, and Jules could only imagine Becky's wheels were spinning the way hers had. Or maybe Brittany was wondering what was taking her so long.

"You still there?" Jules asked. "Did Brittany come looking for you?"

"No," Becky said. "And by the way, it was like pulling teeth to get her to agree to spend the day with me. She's watching a movie right now, so I guess she's not too concerned about why I've been out here so long. I'm just trying to wrap my head around the situation with her sister. After Brittany met with Cami, she talked to her sister on the phone. She called while we were sitting at the kitchen table, remember?"

Jules turned off the car again. She couldn't leave Becky hanging, but she really needed to get to the Doyles, or she was going to miss the rehearsal dinner. "I realized later she never actually confirmed that's who was calling, but yes, she did say she left a message for her sister and was waiting for her to call back."

"Well, she must have spoken to her because she told you her sister's coming to visit next week and staying at her apartment. So, if Laura is dead, is there *another* sister?"

Jules considered the question. "When we asked her about her siblings, she told us she only had one sister. The one from the picture."

Becky let out a groan. "Maybe she meant she only had one sister that's *alive*. Or if she didn't really know Laura, it could be Brittany doesn't count her."

"All I know is Laura Doyle, the full sister Brittany matched through DNA, appears to have died in a car accident. Maybe she was adopted out, which is why they both tested. Helen said the Doyles live nearby, so my plan is to find an address and go talk to them."

"Okay, go quickly, and then get yourself on a plane home. Do you need me to do some research on the computer for you? I can try and figure out where they live."

"Nah. I got this. Besides, you need to keep an eye on Brittany, and I don't want her to see you looking up information about the Doyles. Not yet anyway. I still don't understand all the blood at the house, but now that I've seen Charlie, I'm positive he's not the guy I saw following her. He's a big guy. Tall and muscular." Jules closed her eyes and visualized the thin guy standing at her front door, his hands stuffed in his pockets. "He's definitely not the guy we saw on the surveillance camera."

"So, maybe that *was* the guy from Bumble."

"Listen, for all we know, Charlie could have sent someone to find her and bring her back. He might have no idea Brittany lost her memory." Jules's stomach was in knots. She needed to figure this all out before something terrible happened. "Just keep her close for now. Don't let her out of your sight."

Becky exhaled loudly. "I'll try. Just hurry back. Let me know when you rebook your flight."

After Jules hung up, she used her phone to locate the nearest public library.

When the woman at the front desk told her she needed to obtain a library card to use the computer, she quickly filled out the required form and thought of Brittany. Could this be the reason she'd gotten a card? She had no computer of her own. Wouldn't she have wanted to search online for information about her status as a missing person? Try to gain insight into what the police suspected had happened?

Jules found an overwhelming number of articles about Charlie's suspected role in Claire's disappearance. She only had time to scan a few. Then it wasn't difficult to find a local address for the Doyles and a newspaper article about the car accident. Helen had been right. No charges had been filed against Charlie. It had been ruled Laura's fault, her blood alcohol well over twice the legal limit.

Jules skimmed the article, looking for any information she could use.

According to her parents, Kyle and Nancy Doyle, Laura had struggled with alcohol issues in the past. They had thought she had her sobriety under control but discovered she'd started drinking again after being fired recently from her job.

Jules tucked away that little tidbit of information.

A call to Laura's parents mentioning she'd been a friend of their daughter's was all it took. She was on her way to meet the Doyles.

CHAPTER TWENTY-NINE

When Mrs. Doyle answered the door, Jules leaned in to give the woman a hug. "I was so sorry to hear about Laura."

"Thank you. Won't you come in?" she asked, stepping out of the doorway.

A man approached them, and Mrs. Doyle rested her hand on his arm. "This is Laura's father."

Jules extended her hand. "It's nice to meet you, Mr. Doyle. I'm so sorry for your loss."

"Please, call me Kyle." He gestured at his wife. "And this is Nancy."

Jules followed them into the house, and Nancy Doyle waved her hand at an armchair in the living room. "Please, sit."

As Jules took a seat, Laura's mother settled on the couch beside her husband. She reached for his hand as if she anticipated their visit would be difficult.

"I'm glad you called, Jules, and that you were able to stop by before you went out of town. It's nice for us to meet Laura's friends." She pressed her lips together and glanced over at her husband. "It's been a rough couple of years. You said you just heard about her death?"

"Yeah, I had lunch with a mutual friend, and she told me about the accident. We all worked together." Jules leaned forward in her chair. "You know, when Laura got fired, I thought she got a raw deal. It wasn't fair."

Nancy dipped her head. "You probably didn't know she was drinking again. She hid it well, but I—I understand why the department store fired her."

Jules winced and then shook her head. "Oh. No, I didn't realize."

Her gaze drifted around the room. When she caught a glimpse of a family photo, she had confirmation. The young woman in the framed photograph Brittany had brought with her was the same person in the picture displayed on the Doyle's bookshelf.

Jules sighed as she glanced subtly at the other photos displayed around the room. "Laura was beautiful. It's just so sad." None of the pictures in the Doyle home also included Brittany.

"She'd had a little … upheaval in her world." Nancy stared off wistfully and lifted her shoulder. "I guess Laura didn't handle it as well as we thought."

She let go of her husband's hand to reach for a photo sitting on the end table beside her. "This one was taken only a few months before she died. She was fine. Happy."

Laura stood between her parents, her arms around their shoulders. They all wore smiles. She *looked* happy, but Jules knew better than anyone that appearances could be deceiving. The view presented to the outside didn't always reflect the turmoil happening on the inside.

"May I?" Jules asked as she reached for the photo. She could see the resemblance to Brittany. Jules pushed down the familiar pang of jealousy ingrained in her, despite having found her birth mother who looked just like her. "This is how I remember her. Smiling."

As she stared at the photograph, Jules caught her breath. The ruby ring Laura was wearing on her finger was the same one taken from Brittany when she was attacked. When she glanced up, Nancy was staring at her curiously.

Jules felt her cheeks warm that she'd been caught studying the photo so intently. "I always loved that ring she had. The ruby one."

"Oh," Nancy said with a nod. "Laura did too. I guess she didn't tell you she bought it herself to celebrate getting sober." Her gaze drifted to her lap, and she took in a deep breath before lifting her eyes to meet Jules's. "When she started drinking again, it went missing." Nancy traded a glance with her husband, then gave a sad shrug. "Or she sold it for the cash. She'd never taken it off before, so when it disappeared, I guess that should have been a sign something was wrong."

Jules knew exactly where it had ended up, but how *had* Brittany gotten her sister's ring? She considered the timing of the DNA test as she handed the photo back to Laura's mother.

"Can I ask you something?"

Laura's mother bobbed her head. "Of course."

"Was Laura … adopted?" Jules asked in a soft voice.

Her parents exchanged a glance, then Nancy nodded. "Actually a foster to adopt. When we first got Laura, she was about ten months old. Her mom had substance abuse issues. Alcohol. Drugs." Mrs. Doyle shook her head. "She would disappear for long periods of time, and a neighbor finally called children's services on her."

Jules's mouth fell open. "Oh, that's terrible."

"The mother drank while she was pregnant. Who knows what else she did?" Nancy sighed. "I always felt there had to be permanent damage. Even genetics at play. You know, we tried to give our daughter everything, but sometimes …"

"It's okay, honey." Mr. Doyle rubbed his wife's arm.

She ran her finger under her eyes to wipe at her tears. "You love your kids, but sometimes it's just not enough."

"I'm sorry," Jules said, her tone gentle before she asked what she really wanted to know. "Do you know—did Laura have a biological sister?"

Nancy flinched, and her face fell, which gave Jules the answer she needed even before the woman confirmed it.

"She—she did. Older. The sister was six when we got Laura."

"Did you foster both of them?" Jules asked.

"No. We—we—" Nancy let out a deep breath. "We only took Laura."

Jules could tell from the flush across the woman's cheeks that a six-year-old hadn't fit into their adoption plans.

Nancy tipped her head to the side and eyed Jules. "But how did you know Laura had a sister?"

"Did you know she did DNA testing?"

Nancy traded a glance with her husband. "What?"

"DNA testing," Jules said again. "Was Laura *aware* she had a sister out there somewhere?"

Nancy was silent for a moment, her lids fluttering as she fought a new round of tears. "In the beginning, they had regular visits. The sisters. But Laura was so young. It wasn't like she knew …"

She choked up, and her husband took over. "After the adoption was final, we moved several hours away. Their visits didn't continue." He rested a reassuring hand on his wife's leg.

Jules let her gaze drift back to Mrs. Doyle. "Then how did Laura know …"

Nancy swallowed hard. "She found a file—paperwork from one of the visits. She demanded I explain what it was. By that time, she was in high school. I mean, I told her the truth, but she didn't take it well. She was furious when she found out she had a sister and we hadn't adopted both of them." She bowed her head and cast her eyes downward as she wrung her hands together. "It wasn't a very good time for us as a family. I think that was when the drinking really started."

"So, eventually Laura decided to take a DNA test to try and find her sister," Jules said, more a statement than a question.

"She never mentioned it to us, but that might explain a lot." She turned to her husband. "Don't you think, Kyle?" He nodded, and then Nancy pinned her gaze on Jules, her shoulders lifted and rigid as she asked the question Jules knew was coming. "Do you know if Laura found her sister?"

Jules pressed her lips together as her gaze drifted between the two of them. She dipped her chin. "I'm pretty sure she did."

"Oh." The word escaped Nancy's lips in a moan as she slumped down into the couch. "At one point, Laura demanded we tell her where her sister was, but I mean, we had no idea. It wasn't like we refused to give her the information. We just didn't know."

Her husband spoke up again. "The social worker told us that because their mother was absent so much, Laura's older sister had tried to take care of her when she was an infant. She didn't get the chance to just be a kid, which was why I think they made the decision to put them in different foster homes."

"And then, well, we fell in love with Laura, and our family felt … complete," Nancy said. "We decided it was perfect the way it was, but we felt confident her sister would get adopted as well. Then as my husband told you, we moved, and it just wasn't convenient to get them together anymore." She held up her hands as if she hadn't had much choice in the matter. "You know, time flies when you have a young child. We simply got busy and never followed up."

Jules gritted her teeth at the matter-of-fact way she justified her role in separating the sisters. "You never even tried to look for her?"

Nancy lifted a shoulder and shook her head. "We didn't. I think we always figured she probably had a new name, like Laura."

Jules's forehead wrinkled. "You mean a new last name?"

"Well, maybe her first name too. Her sister's name was Claire, but it could have been changed. She was six, but sometimes—sometimes adoptive parents do change it. Even at that age."

"Really?" Jules was horrified, but Nancy shrugged as if it wasn't a big deal.

"Sometimes they want a family name," she said. "Or they've just always liked a name and thought they'd use it when they had kids. Some adoptive parents feel like it gives the child a clean break from a traumatic past."

Jules reeled back in her seat. Stealing someone's identity at six years old didn't change where they came from. She pressed her lips together and tried to keep the judgment from her voice. "So, when you adopted your daughter, you gave her a new first name too?"

"Well, she was so young. Not even talking yet, and it wasn't as if she *knew* her name." Nancy's tone became defensive as she looked over at her husband for support. "It wasn't like there was anyone in her life who knew her by the name she had when she was born."

"Which was?" Jules's heart thudded so loudly she fully expected they could hear it. She took in shallow breaths and pinned an expectant gaze on Nancy.

"Well, her name at birth, the one she had before her adoption was final, was Brittany Mullins."

CHAPTER THIRTY

"YOU'RE lucky that standby flight worked out." Becky had met Jules at the Chick-fil-A, located around the corner from the church where Jonas and Erin would exchange vows the next day. "I was worried I might have to go fill in for you," she said as she pushed open the door of the women's bathroom.

"I appreciate you going by my place and getting my stuff. If you hadn't done that, I would never have made it on time." Jules pulled her phone from her purse and glanced at the time. "I'll be pushing it as it is."

Becky handed her a dress pulled from her closet, still on the hanger.

"This is perfect." Jules pushed open the door to the largest stall and disappeared with it inside. "I wasn't sure if Brittany would be with you when you met me. Did you tell her I had a photography job today?" Jules's voice was muffled as she changed.

Becky leaned against the counter. "I did, but right after we spoke, she insisted on going home. What was I going to say?"

"I get it, but at least now we know she's using her dead sister's identity. Well, the identity she had before her adoptive parents decided she wouldn't remember her name anyway and changed it."

Becky was grateful they were alone in the restroom for this conversation. "So, Laura *was* adopted?"

"Yeah." Jules smoothed down the front of her dress as she emerged from the stall. "Don't even get me started on her parents, but I'll have to tell you the rest later. As long as no one figures out Brittany's in Florida, we have a little time to try to put all the pieces together. I learned an overwhelming amount today, but there are still a few things I don't understand. Tomorrow after the wedding, I plan to sit her down to get some answers." Jules's gaze searched the floor near Becky. "You brought me shoes, right?"

"I just hope she's not mad we inserted ourselves into her business." Becky set the strappy sandals she'd chosen from Jules's extensive shoe collection onto the floor. "She did fire us, after all."

Jules smiled as she slipped her feet into them. "Exactly the pair I would have chosen to go with this dress." She stepped back into the stall and grabbed the shoes and clothes she'd worn to North Carolina. "I think what Brittany's going to be mad about is that she wasn't told the truth about *anything*."

"Well, after I dropped her back at her apartment, I did take a look at her matches to see if I could pick up where you left off on her family tree. You know, now that we're sure of her real identity."

"Anything interesting?" Jules glanced at the empty counter. "Did you grab my makeup bag?"

Becky pulled it from the tote hanging over her shoulder and handed it to her. "I think I might have found a half-aunt. I'm still not sure if it's on her maternal or paternal side."

Jules stared into the bathroom mirror as she applied a fresh coat of mascara. "She was a DNA match? I didn't think—"

"No, her son was the match," Becky said. "I figured out his

mother from his Facebook page. Looks like they're both from Tennessee, so that seems like it fits."

"Did you call her?"

"No, I had to run to your place to get your stuff. When I get back home, I'll see if I can find a phone number for her."

"It might be worth it, just to confirm Brittany's parents really do live in Tampa. I don't know who that girl Cami was, but for some reason, I don't trust her." Jules puckered her lips and carefully applied a dark, wine-colored lipstick. "Or anything she says."

"Okay, I'll see what I can find out."

"Any chance there's a brush and hairspray in that bag?"

Becky lowered the bag from her shoulder and handed it to her best friend.

"Oh, fabulous, you even brought my flat iron. Do I have time?" Jules asked as she glanced around searching for an outlet. "I was actually worried I was going to get caught in the rain while I was there. That would have been hard to fix in a fast-food restaurant bathroom."

Becky glanced at the time on her phone. "You're supposed to be at the church in ten minutes."

"Everyone will just be chit-chatting for a little bit anyway." Jules plugged in the appliance and stuffed everything else into the oversized tote. "I'll call Tim when I get in the car."

After several swipes with the flat iron and a bit of hairspray, she was ready to go.

Becky shook her head as she stared in awe at her best friend. "How do you do it?"

Jules frowned. "Do what?"

"Look so stunning with so little effort. Especially after two flights and almost getting beaten with a baseball bat."

"Right now, I'm running on adrenaline and the peanut M&Ms I bought at the airport. I hope they're serving something good at the dinner tonight. Then tomorrow, after the wedding, I fully intend to get to the bottom of this." She lifted her shoulders. "Even if Brittany's not a client, I consider her a friend, and as her *friend*, I want her to have answers. Not to mention the truth, which I don't believe she's gotten from anyone yet."

Becky wasn't sure why Jules was so convinced there wasn't an explanation that meant Brittany's family hadn't lied, but now wasn't the time to get into it. "Okay, go practice walking down the aisle. After tomorrow, the next time will be at your wedding."

Jules rolled her eyes at her. "Seriously? I'm already a bundle of nerves about Jonas's wedding. Let's not bring up mine until after I get through tomorrow. The wedding *and* what's going on with Brittany. If you could talk to the aunt and figure out this mess by then, that'd be great."

Becky gave her a salute. "I'm on it." She propped open the restroom door with her foot. "Come on, you'd better get going." She turned as Jules followed her out. "I'll see you at the church tomorrow. You're picking up Brittany, right?"

"Yup. Although keeping what I know to myself until after the reception is going to be hard." Jules pushed open the door to the parking lot and strode in her high heels toward their cars parked side by side. "Can you get to the church by eleven-thirty to keep an eye on her while I'm taking pictures?"

"What do you think could possibly happen at the church?"

Jules lifted her eyebrows and eyed her best friend. "At this point, who knows? Just come early, okay?"

"All right, I will. I'll have to break it to Bryan, but don't worry, everything will be fine tomorrow. At least now you know Brittany's husband is in North Carolina." As they stood next to Jules's car, Becky rubbed her arm reassuringly. "Besides, what could possibly happen at a cop's wedding with all of Jonas's police friends there?"

* * *

"Jules's flight make it back on time?" Bryan asked when Becky strolled through the door.

"Yup. And she headed off to the rehearsal dinner looking absolutely gorgeous."

"Not as beautiful as you." He leaned down and kissed his wife. "Was the urgent last-minute trip worthwhile?" Bryan hadn't been at all happy when she told him she'd be spending the day with Brittany because Jules had jetted off to North Carolina.

"You two just can't let it go, can you?" he'd asked.

The day before, Becky would have agreed and understood his frustration with Jules's dogged pursuit of Brittany's truth. But when Becky had explained about the second DNA test, her husband had been intrigued as well.

"There wasn't enough time for Jules to tell me everything she found out. We're not exactly sure why yet, but it does look like Brittany is using her dead sister's identity. A sister who was given up for adoption. But we're fairly certain Brittany's real name is Claire Hunter."

Bryan's eyebrows shot up. "Hunter? I thought the last name on the other DNA test was Butler?"

"Right. It was, but that was before she married the man who killed her sister in a car accident. The dead one whose identity she's using."

Bryan pressed his lips together and tapped two fingers against them. "So, let me see if I have this right. Brittany, whose real name is Claire, had a sister who was given up for adoption. She was killed in a car accident, and then Brittany married the man who caused it and started using her identity?"

He was so matter-of-fact about following along that Becky bit back a smile at how well he'd managed to jump in. "Well, supposedly the accident was the sister's fault, but yeah, that's pretty much the gist of it."

Bryan cocked his head. "But wouldn't the husband think it's odd she had the same name as the girl who died in the accident?"

"Brittany used her real name when she married Charlie Hunter. Now, she's using the name her sister was given when she was born, but no one would make the connection. Her adopted parents changed her name. We're not positive Brittany even met her sister before she died." Becky opened the refrigerator and pulled out a Diet Coke. "There's a lot we still need to figure out."

"I would say so. Specifically, why Brittany has a husband in North Carolina, but she's living in Florida under a different identity."

"We're pretty sure she only started using her sister's name when she moved here. And she probably came to Florida to get away from her husband." Becky hesitated, then decided to tell Bryan about Charlie. "He threatened Jules with a baseball bat today, so I'm pretty sure he's not the nicest guy around."

Bryan's expression hardened, his intrigue with the story coming to a screeching halt. "See, this is why I warned you both that you didn't know enough about her past. Is Jules okay?"

"I know, but obviously, she's fine if she's on her way to the rehearsal dinner." Becky's eyes widened. "Oh, and supposedly the police found blood in Charlie Hunter's house, *lots* of it. Everyone thinks it's Brittany's, which it *obviously* isn't, because she's not dead, as you know. So now they're getting ready to dig up the first wife—the one before Brittany—because there's suspicion Charlie Hunter might have killed her."

Bryan held his head in his hands. "I don't even know where to start." His eyes narrowed into slits as he stared at his wife. "Oh, I know. How 'bout that some guy came after Jules with a *baseball bat,* and neither of you seems to think that's a big deal? Or maybe we should discuss that people are bleeding and dying in his house, and Jules could have been next. Geez, Beck. This is why Tim and I—"

"He didn't really come after her with the bat. And when Jules went there, we had no idea he was married to Claire—Brittany. She just wanted to talk to him, to see if we could figure out the connection between Judith Hunter and Brittany. Now we know. They had the same husband." Becky took a sip of her soda, then wrinkled her nose. "A mean one."

"So, you and Jules think Brittany ran to get away from him? Somehow got a fake ID with her sister's name and tried to start over?"

"Well, that theory is our lead contender, especially when you stop to wonder whose blood was in Charlie's house." She blew out a loud puff of air. "If I saw that, I'd run too. And if what Brittany's been told is true, her parents and sister live in Tampa, so maybe that's why she came to Florida."

Bryan cocked his head and studied his wife. "You don't think it's true?"

"Jules doesn't." She shrugged. "I'm not sure what to believe. I was working on Brittany's DNA matches earlier, and I think I found a half-aunt. I'm going to see if I can find a phone number. I'm hoping she can back up the story Brittany's been told."

Bryan let out a defeated sigh as if he knew she wouldn't be able to just let it go. "I'll start dinner if you want to see what you can find."

She stood and wrapped her arms around him. "You're the best, babe."

Becky's laptop was still on the coffee table in the living room where she'd left it earlier. Though she'd found the Mullins name amongst Brittany's matches, there'd been no one with the Schroeder name, which didn't make sense if it was

Brittany's maiden name. But then again, Cami had also said her real name was Brittany, not Claire.

Maybe Jules was right that Brittany had been lied to—by Cami and potentially her family in Tampa, who might not be who they claimed they were. Or maybe Brittany had been adopted out as well, and no one in her family wanted to tell her the truth.

Becky pulled up the Facebook profile for the woman she suspected of being Brittany's half-aunt. Autumn Duffy appeared to be in her forties. Her name was unique enough that it didn't take long to find a phone number, and when Becky dialed it, the message on her voicemail announced she'd found the right person. She left a message and hoped for a return call. One that might yield answers.

From what Becky could tell, Brittany had spent time in Tennessee. That's where the half-aunt lived as well as her ex-husband, Alex—the one who'd had no interest in talking to them. Now she knew why. When his ex-wife went missing, the media must have hunted him down the same way she and Jules did.

Then, at some point, Brittany had moved to North Carolina. That's where her sister Laura had lived as well as where she'd married Charlie. Becky pulled up the map of North Carolina and located Shelby. According to the neighbor, Claire had moved into the same house where Judith lost her life. The same place the police had found evidence of other people being hurt, maybe even killed.

She googled Charlie's name and found a litany of articles. None of them mentioned the additional blood found in the house, and Becky wondered if the police were keeping that information to themselves until they knew whose it was.

Were there other women missing in Shelby, North Carolina? Or had the neighbor just repeated idle gossip that wasn't true, like the old game of telephone?

Still, she couldn't help but notice the articles didn't seem hopeful Claire Hunter was still alive. There was no mention of any extensive search for her. Maybe they did assume there was too much blood in the house for her to have survived. Except the blood couldn't have been hers. Wouldn't the police have been able to figure that out?

Becky exhaled loudly. The news had died down around Charlie in the last week or so, but she set a Google alert. If anything happened that concerned Charlie Hunter, his missing wife, or the town they lived in, Becky wanted to know about it as soon as possible.

As she was about to close her laptop, she had another thought. She typed *lifesaver 5K races in Shelby, North Carolina* in the search box. As she skimmed the results, she drew in a sharp breath. Finally, there on the screen was a match to the logo on Brittany's T-shirt.

As Bryan called out that dinner was ready, Becky stared at the computer screen. Her mind was reeling.

Had she just found the answer to the biggest question of all?

CHAPTER THIRTY-ONE

THE NEXT MORNING, Becky had just poured herself a cup of coffee when Bryan nudged her arm. "Your phone's already ringing."

"Probably Jules," she said with a yawn. "She has to be at the church early for pictures."

She hurried back into the bedroom and scooped up her cell from her nightstand. It wasn't Jules or a number she recognized.

"Hi, this is Becky," she said when she answered.

There was no response.

"Hello?" she said again.

"Um, yeah, hi. My name is Autumn Duffy, and you left me a message last night about my niece, Claire."

Becky's heart thumped wildly in anticipation as she perched on the edge of the bed. "Right. Thanks so much for calling me back. I'm a partner in a small detective agency in Florida. We're trying to help your niece, Claire, and I wondered if you might be able to help."

"Help with what? Is she okay?"

"Actually, she was in an accident. She suffered some memory loss as a result."

"There's probably a lot she'd *like* to forget. How can I help?"

Bryan came into the bedroom and handed Becky the coffee mug she'd left on the kitchen table. She mouthed a grateful *thank you*.

"Well, her parents are also trying to help fill in some of the gaps. I believe they're in Tampa, Florida, right?" She took a long sip of coffee while it was still warm.

There was silence on the line for a moment. "Honey, you sure you have the right person?"

Becky swallowed hard. Had she messed up? "Brandon Duffy is your son, right? And he did a DNA test?"

"Yeah. Yeah, he did." Now the woman sounded suspicious. "Why?"

Becky let out a breath. "My partner and I specialize in using DNA results to solve family mysteries. Your son was a match to our client, Claire Hunter." She wasn't officially still a client, but Autumn didn't need that minor detail.

"Hunter? She got married again?"

"Oh, sorry. Yes, she did. Fairly recently. Her married name before that was Butler, and her maiden name was Mullins, right?"

"Well, I guess you do have the right person because Claire Mullins is my niece, but ain't no way she has parents who live in Tampa, Florida."

"No? Oh, I must have been mistaken. Where do they live?" Becky asked.

"Well, Claire's mom is actually my half-sister, but honestly, I have no idea if Rita's even alive anymore. Last I heard, she was living on the streets. I told Claire the same thing when I saw her a year or so ago."

"What about her father?"

"That good-for-nothing Dean Tuggle?" It was clear Autumn had no affection for Brittany's biological father. "I have no clue where he ended up. Rita got pregnant when she was eighteen, and her mom threw her out of the house. She came to live with us for a bit until she had the baby."

"You said you were half-sisters. You and Rita share a father, I take it?" Becky sipped her coffee and screwed up her face as it went down. It was cold.

"Right. Rita didn't marry Claire's father, but they did try to make a go of it after she was born. No big surprise it didn't work out. Dean wasn't really father material, if you know what I mean. He was a year older than Rita and out drinking with his buddies every night." She let out a disgusted huff. "When Claire was about a year old, my sister came home from work one day, and shocker, Dean was gone."

Becky considered that Dean could have matured and finally gotten married. Maybe those were the parents who lived in Tampa. Then she remembered Claire and Brittany were full sisters. But if he'd left Rita, how was that possible?

"That's terrible, but Claire has a younger sister, doesn't she?" Becky asked. "Wasn't she Dean's child too?"

Autumn sighed loudly. "Rita worked hard to get her life together after Dean ran out on her. She wasn't even doing too bad for herself, and then that loser just showed back up one day, acting like he'd never left. Claire was in kindergarten, and next thing you know, my sister's pregnant again. But Dean had spiraled out of control while they were apart, and this time he took Rita down with him. Drugs. Drinking."

"Oh, how awful."

"When the little one was born, it was the wake-up call my sister needed. She wanted to keep her family together for the sake of the girls, but Dean was just there for the free ride." Autumn hesitated as if still hurt all these years later. "Rita got in too deep with him." She sighed. "Then she had a hard time trying to get out."

"Wasn't there anyone who could help her?" Becky asked in a soft voice. "Family, maybe?"

Autumn let out a groan. "My dad refused to let her move in with us again. My sister stole from him too many times to count, and he didn't trust her anymore. I was much younger than Rita—just about to finish high school when she had Brittany. It wasn't like I could have done anything to help her, not that my dad would have let me. He hoped tough love would work, but instead, Rita cut us all off. For a long time, I had no idea where she was."

"So, you didn't get to see your nieces at all?" Becky asked.

"Nope, the last time was when Brittany, the little one, was just a baby. Rita did come back at one point, years later, and she had to admit she'd—she'd lost the girls." Autumn was silent for a moment. "I guess they weren't enough to make her realize she needed to get her shit together. At the time, she was about to be evicted from her apartment, and she begged me to help her. But it wasn't like I had money layin' around to give her. She asked if I could at least hold onto some of her stuff. Just until, you know, she could get on her feet. I said fine, but —" She released a heavy sigh. "That was the last time I seen her."

"I'm so sorry. When was that?" Becky asked.

"Oh, at least ten years ago. That's why I think life may have caught up with her. Living on the streets ain't easy, you know."

Becky slugged down the last sip of cold coffee and grimaced as she set her cup on the nightstand. "Do you still have the stuff Rita gave you?"

"I did. I held onto it all those years, just thinkin' maybe she'd come back someday. It wasn't much, but when Claire found me, I gave it all to her. She said she had a storage unit, and she'd keep the boxes there until she had time to go through them."

The mysterious storage unit. "You never looked to see what was in them?"

"I did. Crazy what my sister kept." Autumn released a soft laugh. "She couldn't take care of herself, but she somehow managed to keep a file with the girls' important papers—birth certificates, hospital records, social security cards. Stuff like that. She also saved their baby blankets. Some children's books. There were a few photo albums and a couple of school yearbooks. The rest was mainly toys and stuff from when Claire was little. I'm not even sure why she wanted to keep it all. Not like the kids had any use for it at that point."

"Sentimental value, I guess."

"I suppose. I'm sure the state just couldn't track her down, but she told me she had no idea what happened to the girls after they were taken from her. She figured they'd probably been adopted." Autumn hesitated. "I felt awful when Claire told me what her life was like after she went into foster care. If I had known—when I got older and was better equipped—" Her voice shook. "But by that time, the system had already broken her. Sounds like Claire was in and out of trouble. Bitter, and who could blame her? I was happy when she told me she reconnected with her younger sister, but that had to have been hard. To know her sister got adopted and she never did. Especially with the way some of those foster families treated her."

Autumn recounted some of the horrors that had befallen her niece as a young girl and then as a teenager.

Tears slipped down Becky's face. "That's just awful," she said, reaching for a tissue. "I understand she had problems, but how could anyone treat a child that way?"

"I agree, but now you understand. If Claire forgot it all, you should just let it be. She doesn't need those memories back." Autumn's tone was firm. "She was finally happy when she came to see me. Told me the only thing that mattered was having her sister back."

Becky didn't have the heart to tell her Laura was dead and everything that had transpired since then. "Well, we're working to get Claire back on track, so I'll have her call you when she can. But I'll keep in mind what you said. About, you know, not reminding her of the past." Becky then thought about Cami. "So, Claire never did live in Tampa, did she?"

"Not that I know of, unless it was after she turned eighteen and aged out of foster care. But I'm pretty sure she told me she got married right after that and stayed in Tennessee. At least until that busted up."

Becky thanked her for calling and hung up.

She tapped the side of her cell phone against her lips as she stared out the bedroom window. She couldn't stop thinking about how hard Brittany's life had been.

Bryan came back to check on her to find she was off the phone but still perched on the side of the bed. "You probably need to start getting ready." He studied her face and noted the crumpled tissue in her hand. "Hey, you okay? Who were you talking to?" He pulled up the quilt and made his side of the bed.

"Brittany's aunt."

"Oh, she called you back? That's good, right?" He tossed his pillow into place against the headboard and then made his way around the bed to her side. He sat down beside her. "Did she tell you anything you could use?"

Becky sniffled. "Just that Brittany had it rougher than we'd ever imagined."

"Well, that's not good. I'm sorry to hear that."

"I know, and I think she just added another mystery to the pile."

"You can tell me about it on the way to the church, but

right now, you might want to get in the shower, or we're going to be late." He grabbed her coffee cup off the nightstand.

"Right." Becky left her phone on the bed and wandered into the bathroom. As the hot water poured down on her, she couldn't stop her brain from spinning.

Just who the hell was Cami? And why had she told Brittany she recognized her from a high school in Tampa, Florida?

According to Autumn, there was no way that was possible. Brittany hadn't been anywhere near Florida. She'd spent the majority of her childhood in the foster care system in Tennessee.

CHAPTER THIRTY-TWO

CLAIRE STOOD in front of the bathroom mirror. All dressed up, she felt like a princess. All that was left was to slip into the high heels she'd bought at the mall with Jules.

Peter came up behind her and wrapped his arms around her. "You look far too beautiful to leave this apartment today."

"Jules is going to be here any minute."

Claire pulled out of his embrace and strode purposefully into the living room, her eyes scanning the room as she walked. She was looking for any evidence that would betray his existence in her apartment.

The day before, she'd managed to meet Becky in the parking lot when she got picked up. She'd been so insistent about spending time with her that Claire had been afraid she'd just show up at the apartment anyway if she declined. But after today, no more. Her heart couldn't take it.

Peter frowned as he hurried along behind her. "What are you looking for?"

Claire scooped up a shirt he'd left hanging over the arm of the couch. Next, his wallet and keys sitting on the kitchen table.

He followed her back into the bedroom. "Hey, what are you doing with my stuff?"

Claire slid open the closet doors and tossed the shirt onto the pile of laundry that sat beside his duffel bag and her empty suitcase.

"I don't want Jules to know you're here." She set his wallet and keys on the top shelf, then turned to ensure he was paying attention. "Don't forget this is where I'm putting these." She wagged her index finger at him. "But you need to be careful if you go out. You can't be coming back at the same time she drops me off later."

His forehead wrinkled as he studied her. "What? And why are you *hiding* my stuff?" He grabbed her arm. "What does it matter if she knows I'm here?"

Claire yanked herself out of his grip and looked him directly in the eye. "Jules thought she was protecting me. From you. I can't tell her—" She drew in a sharp breath.

He'd reached for her again, but this time he moved quickly to pull her close to him. He wrapped his arms around her waist and held her tightly. It was as if he thought he could make her see his point of view if she couldn't wiggle away.

"Claire, you're being silly," he said. "Why would Jules care? How is our relationship any of her business? Or anyone's, for that matter."

He was being naïve. "Peter, you ran from her. Twice." She rolled her eyes and jerked out of his grasp. "You threw a damn brick through Becky's window with some sort of mafia note attached. I mean, seriously, what the hell were you thinking? Those aren't the actions of a man with nothing to hide." She held her hands up in a grand gesture. "But sure, pull up a seat, and I'll introduce you to Jules. Maybe I should just bring you to the wedding."

He swayed on his feet, his eyes begging her to understand. "I'll admit I acted a bit paranoid, but I had no idea what was going on. When I didn't hear from you, I thought maybe..." His voice trailed off as if he didn't want to say the words and accuse her out loud.

She gave him a stern stare. "We talked about this—how important a little distance between us was going to be."

"But still, under the circumstances. The way you left—"

She groaned in frustration. "You knew I returned the rental car. I took a damn bus to the library so I could send you an email. I told you I would call you as soon as I got a phone."

His eyes narrowed as he dipped his chin. "But then you didn't."

"Well, okay, you got me there." Claire threw her arms up, annoyed they were wasting time rehashing what had been out of her control. "But it's not like I asked to be mugged. It isn't like I planned to lose my memory."

"Still, I was worried about you. I couldn't help but wonder if you'd tell someone what happened. You can't even imagine how I felt watching the news. Knowing—"

"That's why it doesn't make sense for anyone to know you're here. Especially Jules. She's very smart. She is a detective, you know." Claire drew in a breath and expelled it as a long sigh. "Besides, this is it. After today, I'll disappear from their lives, and you and I can be together. We'll put it all behind us."

She still hadn't decided if that was the path she wanted to take with Peter, but she didn't want him to know that. She knew she needed to tread carefully.

He hesitated and then put his arms around her. "That's all I want. For us to be together. You can trust me, Claire. I don't intend to ever let anything happen to you again. I love you."

He put his lips on hers, and she kissed him back. "I love you too." But did she?

When she pulled back, his eyes searched hers. "Our time is coming," he said with a nod. "I finished teaching my class, and no one said anything about the missing equipment. I have a couple of leads for a job here, and I have someone covering the mobile unit until Monday. When I get back, I'll put in my two weeks, and we can finally make plans to start our new life." He kissed her again and then scowled. "You spent most of yesterday at Becky's. We only have a few days, and now you're leaving again to go to this stupid wedding. I still don't think it's a good idea. Why did you even say you would go—"

He was interrupted by the sound of knocking.

Claire whipped her head toward the front door. "That's her." She slid her feet into her heels and made her way out of the bedroom. In the doorway, she stopped short and wheeled back around. The look she shot him was meant to leave no room for further discussion. "Do not leave this room until we're gone, Peter. Under any circumstances. Do you hear me?"

He let out a puff of annoyance, then gave her a single nod. "You need to make this up to me later. And I want you to call me from the wedding to let me know everything's okay."

Claire rolled her eyes. "Everything will be fine. Please don't start losing it on me now." With an aggravated grunt, she shut the bedroom door behind her.

She drew in a deep, cleansing breath before she answered the door. When she saw Jules standing there, she lifted her hand to cover her mouth. "Wow. You look incredible."

Jules twirled on the concrete walkway. "Erin did a great job picking out the bridesmaid dresses. I love it."

"It's beautiful. That color looks amazing on you."

"Sapphire blue." Jules posed with a foot out in front so it protruded from the bottom of the floor-length dress. A wide grin filled her face. "Shoes to match with a little extra bling by yours truly." She'd added rhinestones to the front of each shoe.

Claire crossed her arms over her chest as she gazed appreciatively, then stepped out of the doorway. "Sorry. Come on in. I'm all ready to go." She resisted the urge to let her gaze wander toward the bedroom and prayed Peter wouldn't decide to pull anything stupid.

"It's a good thing Gene didn't get a whiff of those shoes." Brittany laughed, and she felt her body relax. She'd missed Jules in the past week and was looking forward to spending the day in the world she'd just left. She felt more comfortable there than in the one that would be waiting for her when she got back to her apartment later that night.

"Tell me about it. I kept them on the top shelf of my closet until the last possible minute this morning."

Jules stepped back and gave Claire's appearance an approving nod. "I told you that dress would look amazing on you." She handed her one of the small clutches that had been tucked under her arm. "I was right. This purse is perfect."

"It's so tiny." Claire carried it into the kitchen and pulled her regular purse off the back of one of the chairs at the table.

Jules gestured at her own bag. "So is mine, but you just need the essentials. Lipstick and a compact. Your phone."

As Claire transferred a few items, she couldn't help but notice Jules was fixated on her hands. "What?" she asked.

Jules's lips pressed together. "Your ring. I'm just glad you got it back."

"Oh." Claire forced a smile. "Me too."

Jules cocked her head and stared at her. "Do you remember where you got it? Who gave it to you?"

Claire hesitated. The truth was too complicated, so she shook her head. "I feel sure it was important to me, which is why I wanted to get it back from the pawnshop, but no, I don't remember where I got it. At least not yet."

Jules nodded, but her expression had changed. Hardened.

She then meandered into the living room. Claire's heart pounded at the thought she might try to continue into the bedroom, but instead, Jules paused by the windows.

"It's like a tomb in here. You should really let some light in."

As Jules reached for the string that would lift the blinds, Claire rushed toward her and put up her hand. "Oh, no, please don't." She shrugged, her cheeks hot at the idea of anyone seeing Peter in her apartment. "I guess I'm still a little paranoid, but can we leave them closed?" It wasn't such an outrageous request considering Jules thought someone had been spying on her at one point through those same windows.

Jules seemed to accept her anxiety about it, and when she strolled away from the window, Claire's chest deflated with relief.

"Okay, but maybe I can at least help you decorate in here. Make it a bit homier if you're going to stay." She gestured at the couch. "We could get some pretty throw pillows. Maybe some nice frames for more pictures of your family." Jules picked up the photo of Claire and Laura displayed on the end table. "This is the sister that's coming to visit, right?" She glanced up from the picture and pinned Claire with a stare that reeked of more than mere curiosity.

Claire swallowed hard, then strode over to where Jules stood. "Yeah. That's her."

Jules had seen this photo before, but now, she stared at it intently as if she was looking for something incriminating. Claire felt her armpits dampen.

"Hey, look at this." Jules's breezy tone seemed fake. Contrived. As if she'd found exactly what she'd gone looking for in the photograph of the two sisters.

Claire's pulse quickened. "Look at what?"

Jules held the framed photograph in one hand, but her index finger on the other now hovered over Laura.

Claire's breath hitched in her throat. Why had she left their photo in the living room? Her stomach lurched when Jules tapped the glass of the frame over her sister's right hand—the one holding up a drink with a tiny umbrella perched on the side.

"In this picture, your sister is wearing the exact same ring." Jules seemed to stretch out the last three words for emphasis. She tipped her head to one side and stared at Claire expectantly as she waited for a response.

Claire took the photo from Jules's hand and pretended to give it a cursory glance. "Not the exact ring, but it looks similar, for sure." She set the photo back down on the end table. "We probably need to go. Let me just get that cute purse you brought me."

Jules's phone rang. She reached in her purse, gazed at the caller ID, and silenced it.

"Becky looking for you?"

"Nope. Still playing phone tag with my cousin, Lucy. She left me a message last night, and when I tried to call her back on my way here, she didn't answer." Jules's lips were set in a firm line as she eyed Claire. "When we get back later, I think we need to sit down and have a talk."

Heat blazed up her neck. "Sure. What about?"

"I don't want to get into it now. Let's go to the wedding and have a good time. But I went to North Carolina yesterday, and I think there's more to your story than you've been told by your family."

So much for the photography job Jules supposedly had the day before. Becky had lied to her.

Claire's chest tightened at the implication of their coordinated ruse. She hoped Peter wasn't listening at the bedroom door. All she needed was for him to come rushing out and ruin everything. If she had time to think this through, she could handle Jules. Whatever she'd discovered could be explained. Claire would make sure of it.

"Oh, wow. North Carolina, huh?" Claire tried to breathe normally. "Okay, I can't wait to hear what you found out." She staggered toward the kitchen, her gait awkward until she got to the tile. She let out a nervous chuckle. "Apparently, I'm not used to wearing heels. I guess I'm more of a sneakers and flip-flops kind of girl."

She sucked in a deep breath, grateful Jules couldn't see her face. Then, with her fingers wrapped around the clutch Jules had lent her, she spun back around, a smile plastered on her face.

"Okay, I'm ready. Let's get out of here before you're late for pictures." She managed a thin laugh. "I don't want to have to answer to the bride." Claire began to make her way to the front door but stopped short. "Almost forgot my keys. Need to be able to lock up the apartment, right?"

She retrieved them from the kitchen counter and took small, quick steps as she hurried toward the front door and her desperate attempt to get Jules out of her apartment. "I just hope they'll fit in this teeny-tiny purse."

"You can leave them in my car since I'll definitely be driving you home later. We're going to need time to talk, remember?"

Claire turned the button to release the deadbolt and bobbed her head. "Oh, right." Like she could have forgotten Jules's ominous promise to fill her in on how her family had deceived her. It would be all she'd be able to think about at the wedding and reception, the wait hanging over her like a ticking time bomb. "Okay, let's go. We've got a wedding to get to."

She swung open the front door, but in an instant, a crushing pressure hit her in the middle of her chest. Claire opened her mouth to scream, but nothing came out, the sudden impact stealing the air from her lungs.

There was a loud grunt as she stumbled backward, her high heels frustrating her attempt to regain her footing. Her body tumbled into Jules, who let out a yelp of surprise. The two of them toppled like dominoes into a heap on the carpet.

When Claire stared up at the source of the sharp, hot pain now stabbing her insides, the eyes she looked into were as black as a moonless night. He tossed the baseball bat to the side and slammed the door behind him.

"You fucking bitch. I knew you were still alive."

CHAPTER THIRTY-THREE

"You," Jules said, her tone accusatory as she crawled on the carpet to get away from Charlie. She tried to stand, but the long bridesmaid dress she had thought exquisite for gliding down the aisle now did her no favors.

Once on her feet, she reached for Brittany's hand. "Are you okay?"

Brittany let out a whimper as she tried to stand, her arms wrapped around her middle.

Jules glared at him, her need to protect overcoming her fear. "You probably broke her ribs. I don't know what you're doing here but get the hell out before I call the police."

She reached into her purse for her phone, but before she could dial, Charlie knocked it from her hand with an angry growl. Jules watched with dismay as her only means of communication slid across the carpet and hit the baseboard with a thud.

He picked up the bat and waved it in their direction before using it to gesture at the couch. "You won't be calling anyone just yet. Sit down. Both of you. Me and the missus need to have a little chat."

Jules leaned into Brittany. "Just do what he says," she whispered. "We need to get him to calm down."

When they were seated side-by-side on the couch, Charlie kicked the coffee table out of the way. He stood in front of Jules, his head cocked to the side. "You know, something didn't sit right about that visit of yours yesterday. Then I heard you talking to that busybody neighbor of mine. I was all ready to use your windshield for batting practice until I saw the contract on your seat and realized you were in a rental car." He gave Jules a slow nod. "That really got me wondering who you were. So, I did a little digging of my own." He huffed. "Imagine my surprise when I found some of your recent photographs online, including one of this one here, alive and well and enjoying a lovely afternoon at the art festival."

He glared at Brittany, his face turning red. "My wife. The one everyone thinks I murdered." He shook his head. "Trust me, I didn't feel like making that long drive last night, wondering if the cops would pull me over to try and stop me."

He drove the bat down hard on the cushion next to Brittany, and his eyes blazed with anger. "I just want to know *why*. I thought you loved me."

"Loved you?" The laugh that erupted from Brittany was almost maniacal, but it was followed by a moan of pain. "I loathe you," she managed to choke out.

Jules's nervous gaze went to the bat in Charlie's hand to see if he'd raise it again, but instead, his shoulders sagged, confusion flooding his face as the bat slipped from his hand to the floor.

"Every time you touched me, it made my skin crawl." Brittany's voice was slow and stilted. "Luckily, I've had plenty of practice going somewhere else when I need to. Why do you think I insisted we didn't need a honeymoon?"

Charlie's hands flew up in the air. "Then why did you marry me? Just to steal from me and set me up for murder? I was grieving for Judith, and you told me—you made me believe—"

The shrug she gave him was matter-of-fact, but the stare that followed was cold and hateful. "I had to. For my sister."

Deep lines formed on Charlie's forehead. His eyes narrowed as he stared at her like she'd lost her mind. "Your sister? What the hell are you talking about?"

Brittany turned to Jules as she struggled to breathe. "My sister is the real Brittany Mullins. But I guess you already figured that out."

"I don't even know anyone by that name." Charlie leaned down until his face was inches from hers. "What kind of game are you playing?"

Across the room, Jules's phone began to ring. She wasn't surprised someone was looking for her. She should have been at the church by now.

Charlie pulled back and searched the room for the sound, but the ringing had stopped.

"You probably know my sister by her adopted name." Brittany took in a shallow breath. "The one she was using when you killed her."

"You've lost your damn mind," Charlie said, his voice rising. He stood, raked his hands through his hair, and began pacing.

"Have I?" Brittany asked. "Her name was Laura. Laura Doyle." She leaned forward, her face contorting in pain. "Now, does the name ring a bell?"

Charlie wheeled around. "All this because of the accident? That wasn't even my—"

"Shut up, you liar!"

When Brittany winced, Jules put her hand on her shoulder. "You're hurt. We need to call an ambulance."

She put up her hand and whipped her head back and forth. "I've endured *way* worse than this, and he needs to understand what he took from me." She anchored her gaze on Charlie. "Do you know how long I had my sister back? Eighty-two days. That's it. I thought all those years of wondering, of missing her, were over."

Brittany looked away, her eyes glazed over as if her mind was elsewhere. "We even took our first vacation together. We flew to Miami and watched movies on the plane. Spent our days shopping and lying on the beach. The things sisters are *supposed* to do together. We wanted to make up for all those years we'd missed."

She refocused her attention on Jules. "That trip was when Laura *gave* me this ring." Brittany held up her right hand. "Right after we toasted that we were back in each other's lives."

"So, *after* the photo was taken."

"She took the ring off her finger and told me she wanted me to have it," Brittany said, her voice insistent. "To celebrate that we were together again." She pressed her lips tight, tears falling from her eyes. "Finally, I had *my* fairytale," she said in a soft voice.

Just as quickly, the anger was back in her eyes as she fixed her attention on Charlie. "But you took her from me and just went on with your life. Like it never happened. You need to be behind bars." Brittany leaned forward, her eyes narrowed as she stared at him. "Because that's where *murderers* belong."

Just as it was all starting to make sense to Jules, her phone rang again. She swallowed hard, her pulse racing as she considered what had to be happening at the church.

They'd keep calling. Erin needed her for pictures. Tim would be wondering why she hadn't shown up. Jules had asked Becky to come early to keep tabs on Brittany, but she'd most likely have arrived by now to find they were both nowhere to be found.

Fear twisted Jules's insides at the thought that her best

friend might come to the apartment looking for her. Charlie had slammed the door shut, but it wasn't locked. Becky could walk right into all of this without any warning.

"You need to let us go." Jules glared at Charlie. "I'm supposed to be at my brother's wedding. People will come looking for me." She waved a hand between her and Brittany. "For both of us."

"You think I'm worried about people showing up here?" Charlie asked.

"My brother's a *cop*, you know." Jules's chin jutted out, but she didn't feel as brave as she hoped she sounded. "You sure you want him wondering where I am? On his wedding day?"

Charlie shot her a look as air hissed through his lips. "Please. I'm surprised the cops from North Carolina didn't follow me here." He aimed his chin at Brittany. "I kind of wish they had, so they could see how wrong they've been." He let out a loud huff. "Accusing me of killing my wife, when clearly, she's not dead. She's alive and living the good life here in Florida."

"And you should be behind bars," she said, seething through gritted teeth.

"Brittany," Jules said in a loud voice. She needed to make her understand the truth as much as she needed to diffuse the situation with Charlie.

His eyes blazed in Jules's direction. "Her name is *Claire*."

Jules held up her hand to appease him. "Okay, *Claire*." She shifted on the couch to face his wife, to try and help her understand. "The accident wasn't Charlie's fault, which is why he wasn't charged. While I was in North Carolina yesterday, I went to see Laura's parents. They admitted to me she was an alcoholic. Well, she'd been a recovering alcoholic." She glanced down at Brittany's finger. "That ring she gave you—her parents told me she'd bought it to celebrate her sobriety."

She flinched and shook her head. "No, that's not true—"

"It is, and her parents confirmed she'd slipped. Laura had started drinking again—" Jules hesitated, but Brittany needed to understand she'd most likely played a role in what had really happened. "Maybe it started on your trip to Miami. I'm sure your sister wanted to be able to celebrate, to toast that you'd found each other. It just wasn't that simple for her," Jules said, trying to be gentle. "Before she died, she ended up getting fired from her job because she was drinking excessively. Her parents were really worried about her." She met Brittany's eyes and gave her a slow nod. "Isn't it possible she didn't handle your reunion as well as you thought she did?"

Brittany glared at Jules, her jaw set defiantly. "No. She would have told me. Laura never said anything about it—"

She was interrupted by the shrill ringing of Jules's phone again.

"Where the hell is that thing?" Charlie followed the sound until he found Jules's phone behind the empty television stand. He punched the button to power it down and tossed it across the room. "Enough already."

The silence was immediately followed by the muffled sound of Brittany's phone ringing. It was still inside the small purse that lay on the carpet.

"Are you kidding me?" Charlie sneered at his wife. Then he lifted his foot and used his heavy boot to stomp on the purse until the ringing stopped.

Her eyes blazed with hatred. "That wasn't even mine, you asshole."

Jules rested her hand on Brittany's arm. "It's fine, but I'm sure that's Becky wondering why we aren't at the church yet. She left me a message this morning that she talked to your Aunt Autumn."

Brittany's face paled. "What?"

"Did you tell Laura you aged out of foster care?" Jules asked in a soft voice. "That your anger issues had you in ten different foster homes in twelve years? Did she know that some of those people—the ones who should have loved you and kept you safe—didn't do anything even close to that?"

Brittany bit her lip. "She was my sister," she said, the words coming out strangled. "I wanted her to know how lost I was growing up without her."

Jules tried to reassure her with a nod. "I know, but it was likely hard for Laura to hear what you went through. She got adopted, and you didn't. Maybe she felt guilty, and that's why—"

"Enough of the sob story," Charlie cut in, his words tinged with disgust. "Your poor pathetic childhood is no excuse for what you did. You had me questioning my *sanity*. You left me wondering whether I could have done what they accused me of because I couldn't imagine how else it could have happened in my own house."

Brittany's mood shifted as she offered him a smug smile. "You were worried about me, Charlie? That's sweet."

"I might have even convinced myself." He gave her a hard stare. "If it wasn't for the money. You emptied the safe in the house on your way out." His eyebrows lifted. "A dead woman can't steal, so I knew you had to be alive somewhere."

She cocked her head to the side, her index finger tapping against her lips. "And how'd that go with the police? You have no proof I took anything."

Charlie snorted. "How do you think? And how the hell was I supposed to explain the amount of blood they found in my house?" He reached for the bat and held it in the air. "Who the fuck's blood was that, Claire? They tried to tell me they found not only yours, but there was blood from three other people. Did you really kill people in my house to try to blame it on me? Were you trying to convince them I was a damn serial killer?"

Brittany offered him a matter-of-fact shrug. "I needed there to be enough to convince the police I was dead. Bleach was supposed to kill the DNA, so they'd only know there'd been blood there. I didn't count on them knowing whose it was." The corners of her mouth tugged upward into a smile." I guess you being a serial killer is just a bonus prize."

Just then, Jules realized what else Becky had left in her message. She'd figured out the Lifesaver 5K Brittany had run and who it had actually supported. It all made sense now.

"You're a *psychopath*. And why the hell would you want to frame me for murder? Did you know they want to dig up Judith? My wife? Now the police think I might have *killed* her." Charlie ran his hand over his face and bowed his head. When he glanced back up at her, there were tears in his eyes. "I would never have hurt Judith. I loved her."

Brittany smirked. "Exactly."

Charlie's eyes narrowed. "What the hell does that mean? Is that what all this was about? You were *jealous* of Judith?"

"No, not at all. I just wanted you to know how it felt to lose someone you love."

"You *knew* how devastated I was losing her. When we met, I told you everything. I bared my soul to you."

"Right." Brittany bobbed her head. "When *we* met." She bit back a smile. "But you see, Charlie, I met Judith first."

He reeled back, his brow furrowed as he seemed to be trying to make sense of her admission. "What?"

"We only met once, but it was under rather unfortunate circumstances. Well, for her anyway. She was a trusting woman, wasn't she, Charlie? Never felt the need to lock the doors even when she was home alone. I mean, what could happen, right?"

Charlie held his breath as the color drained from his face.

"Don't worry, I know you didn't kill Judith." A small smile lifted the corners of Brittany's lips as she locked her eyes on his. "Because I did."

CHAPTER THIRTY-FOUR

BECKY REACHED for Bryan as they strolled toward the church. "You're looking mighty handsome there, mister," she said, giving his hand a squeeze. It had been ages since they'd gone out all dressed up.

He smiled at her. "Only because I need to keep up with my beautiful wife. Should I assume you'll be deserting me to run off and fill Jules in on your call with Brittany's aunt? I suppose I should say *Claire's* aunt."

"She still believes her name is Brittany, which I guess is how I'll always think of her. It's hard to switch gears. I already left Jules a message with the highlights of our call, but I'll have to fill her in on the rest later." Autumn's words still rang in her head. "That poor girl. I feel terrible for what she went through. I'm not sure what we want to tell her, but Jules was right. She *was* lied to about her past."

"It would seem she was," Bryan said as they ascended the steps to the front of the church.

"I just don't understand who that woman Cami is and why she would fill Brittany's head with all that information that's not true." Becky frowned. "And Brittany told us she spoke to her parents in Tampa. Another lie."

Bryan cocked his head and glanced down at her. "I thought you said it could be her biological father and a stepmother."

"It is possible, I suppose." Becky shrugged. "Just not sure how likely it is. He sounded like a bit of a loser. The aunt gave me his name, but I didn't have time to look him up."

Bryan pulled open the door to the church, and Becky lowered her voice as they entered. "Although, they could have another daughter who Brittany considers to be her sister, and maybe that's who's coming to visit. But if her father never rescued her from foster care, would she really consider them to be her parents?"

"All good questions." Bryan glanced around. "Uh, are we early?"

"Jules wanted me to keep an eye on Brittany. It was also probably her sneaky way of making sure I wasn't late." Punctuality wasn't always Becky's strong suit.

Bryan stifled a laugh. "Well, she is your best friend after all. She knows you well."

Just then, Tim came down a set of stairs and held up his hand as he hurried toward them.

"Well, don't you look dapper?" Becky gave him an approving nod. "Nice tux."

"Thanks. Hey, Jules isn't with you, is she?"

"With us?" Becky shook her head. "No. She had to be here even earlier than she told me. For pictures."

"Huh." Tim wore a confused frown. "I tried calling her, but she didn't answer."

"I'm sure she's with the bridal party. Probably distracted knocking back a few mimosas and didn't hear her phone. I'll go find her. I need to let her know I'm here anyway." Becky gave her husband a pointed look. "Not that I'm that late, mind you." She glanced around before giving Tim a helpless look. "Where are the bridesmaids?"

He gestured toward a second set of stairs on the other side of the entrance. "The women are that way."

When she got upstairs, Becky tentatively opened the first door and peeked inside. The room was empty.

Then she heard voices. Female voices. She knocked on that door and pushed it open. When she did, the bride's eyes were anchored on her. Becky caught her breath, her hands lifting to cross her chest.

"Oh, Erin, you look stunning."

The bride shimmied toward her as fast as her fitted dress would allow. "Thanks, but where's Jules?"

Barb was right behind Erin. "She isn't here yet. Have you spoken to her?"

Becky's gaze drifted around the room at the sea of blue bridesmaid dresses. "I haven't talked to her yet today, but she should have been here almost an hour ago."

"I tried calling her a little while ago," Erin said. "She didn't answer, and no one has seen her."

Becky's brow furrowed. "That's not like Jules." She reached into her purse and grabbed her phone. "She was supposed to pick up Brittany and be here by eleven. At least that's what she told me last night. Maybe they had car problems on the way." She hit the button for Jules's number. "Let me try to call her."

After it rang several times without being answered, Becky frowned. "No answer. Let me try Brittany's phone." Again, the call went to voicemail. "I don't understand. Did you ask Jonas? Has he heard from her?"

Erin's maid of honor stepped forward and waved her index finger in the air. "Oh, no. The bride's not allowed to talk to the groom before the wedding."

Becky nodded with an amused smile. "Right. Okay. I'll go check with him. Where are the guys getting ready?"

"Go back down to the main level and take the other set of stairs," Erin said. "They're in the first room on the left."

"Should I go too?" Barb asked. "I was with Jonas earlier, but then he told me it was okay to hang out with the women."

Becky patted her shoulder. "I got this. Stay here with Erin and hang tight. I'll be right back."

She hurried as fast as her heels would allow, down the hall and to the bottom of the staircase. Bryan and Tim were exactly where she'd left them.

"Well, Jules isn't with the bridesmaids. Did you check to see if Jonas has heard from her?"

"I haven't," Tim said, glancing at his watch. "I've been watching the parking lot and waiting for her."

"Well, let's go ask." Becky gestured at him to lead the way.

Jonas's eyes lit up when she rushed into the groomsmen's suite. "Hey, Beck."

"Look how handsome you are, and just wait until you see your bride. She looks absolutely stunning." Bryan nudged her arm, and Becky felt the heat of Tim's stare. "But I'm really here to find out if you've heard from Jules."

"Heard from Jules?" Jonas's eyes drifted around the room until he found a cooler containing bottles of water. He twisted the top off one and took a swig. "I haven't seen her, but she should be with Erin. Did you check the women's suite? It's on the other side—"

"I've already been there," Becky said, shaking her head. "She was supposed to pick up Brittany and be here an hour ago. Nobody seems to know where she is, and she isn't answering her phone. You know as well as I do, that's not like her."

"Let me try her again." Tim dialed his phone, and when he held it to his ear, a deep divot formed immediately between his eyebrows. "It's not even ringing anymore. It went right to voicemail." He shook his head, his mouth pinched tight. "I don't like this. I'm gonna take a ride over to her townhouse." He nodded at Jonas. "Don't tell Erin I left. I'll be back as soon as I can."

As Tim raced out of the suite, Becky rubbed the back of her neck and tried to loosen how tight it now felt. "I don't like this either." She gave Jonas a quick rundown on what Jules had discovered in North Carolina as well as the conversation she'd had that morning with Autumn. "Nothing is what it seems with Brittany, so I have no idea what the actual truth is anymore."

"Why don't you try Brittany again?" Bryan asked. "Maybe Jules just forgot to charge her phone."

That would have been just as surprising as her being late for her brother's wedding.

Becky dialed and then flinched. Her nervous gaze volleyed between Bryan and Jonas. "Now Brittany's phone is going right to voicemail too."

Jonas pulled out his cell. "Hey, Anderson," he called out to his best man. "Steve working today?"

"Yeah. He has to pull a double since so many of us are here."

Jonas scrolled through the contacts in his phone and dialed. "Hey, buddy. Yeah, I'm actually at the church right now, but I need a favor. My sister, Jules, hasn't shown up, and we're starting to get a little worried. Can you find out if there's been any traffic accidents?"

When Becky winced, Bryan reached for her hand. "I'm sure she's fine. He's just covering all the bases."

Jonas recited Jules's address into the receiver and then turned to Becky. "She was supposed to get Brittany, right? You know where she lives?"

She pulled up Brittany's contact information and held it up so Jonas could read the address.

"Yeah, so that's her route of travel," Jonas said into his

phone. "Can you see what you can find out and call me back? As quick as you can, please. I'm supposed to be getting married soon."

Becky drew in a deep breath. "I should go back and tell Erin. Maybe she wants to get started on pictures."

Jonas frowned. "Without Jules?"

Becky shrugged, feeling completely helpless. "Well, maybe there's some she can get done now. You know, while they're waiting. It might take her mind off wondering where Jules could be."

Jonas ran his hand over his face, and it was clear he needed a distraction as well. "Okay. Tell her I love her."

"I will." Becky turned to her husband. "Stay with Jonas, and I'll call you if I find out anything. You do the same."

Bryan nodded, then leaned over and kissed her.

Erin let out a small whimper when Becky pushed open the door to the bridal suite and she saw Jules wasn't with her. "Still nothing?"

"What did Jonas say?" Barb's eyes pleaded for good news.

"He hasn't heard from Jules either. He, uh, made a call to a buddy. Another cop." She hesitated. "He's got him looking into whether maybe she broke down or had an accident—"

Erin bent at the waist and let out a moan.

Becky reached for her arm and forced her to stand back up. "Okay, don't do that. You'll wreck your headpiece." A beaded tiara sat atop Erin's short blond hair, and the veil flowed down her back. Becky carefully fixed the tulle so it wasn't bunched up around her bare shoulders. "Listen, I'm sure there's a reasonable explanation, and Jules is fine. Why don't you start taking pictures now, and when she gets here, she can just slip into the group shots." Becky tried to sound calm, but her stomach was in knots.

Erin sniffled, then nodded. "Okay, but let me know the

minute you find out anything." She took in a deep breath and ran her finger under each eye. "Do I look okay?"

Becky placed her hands on Erin's shoulder and looked her in the eye. "Absolutely gorgeous. And I told Jonas just that when I saw him. He's a lucky guy."

"I'm the lucky one," Erin said, and then she nodded at her photographer. "Okay, I'm ready."

Just as he began to set up his first shot, Becky's phone rang. She drew in a deep breath when she saw it was Tim. She stepped out of the bridal suite so she wouldn't distract Erin.

She didn't even say hello. "Please tell me you found her."

"Her car's not here. I wish I knew how to pull the footage from the new security camera to see when she left. Any idea?"

Becky brought her palm to her forehead. "Not a clue, and I haven't heard anything back from Jonas yet. He has someone checking to see if maybe—maybe her car's broken down on the side of the road." Becky didn't want to bring up the possibility that Jules could have been in a wreck. Tim wasn't naïve. He could figure that out himself.

"Well, then I'm heading over to Brittany's apartment next," Tim said in a determined voice. "Can you text me the address?"

Becky's eyes grew glassy as she typed it into a message and hit send.

"Call me back when you get there." She hesitated. "Or if you see anything on the way. Please." She hung up, her chest so tight she felt like she couldn't breathe. Where the hell was Jules?

Becky stepped back into the suite and watched as Erin smiled for the camera. Becky felt terrible she had to deal with this on her wedding day. And Jonas and Barb would be a mess if anything happened— She stopped herself. Now wasn't the time to think the worst.

She stepped back out of the room into the hallway and called Bryan. "Nothing?"

"Not yet. Jonas is just pacing like a crazy man here."

"I finally convinced Erin and Barb to start on pictures, but Tim just called and said Jules's car isn't at her townhouse."

Bryan was silent for a moment. "Okay, so she's either on the road to Brittany's, or they're both somewhere between Brittany's place and the church."

"Or they could be at Brittany's apartment, but it doesn't make sense they'd still be there. Or why they're not answering their phones. Tim's leaving Jules's place and heading there now. He's taking the route she would most likely have used, and I told—I told him to keep an eye out on the way there. In case he sees anything …" Becky let out a whimper.

"It will be okay. It's *Jules*." Her husband said her best friend's name like it was unfathomable anything could happen to her. Like she was a superhero or had magical armor that would keep her safe.

Becky understood. She'd always felt that way about Jules. She was strong and smart and always seemed to know just what to do in any situation. But right now, it was Brittany's situation that had her most concerned.

"What if someone really is after Brittany?" Becky swallowed hard, but the lump in her throat remained. "Since she was with Jules, what if they had no choice but to grab both of them?" She pressed her lips together hard and tried not to cry. "Otherwise, I can't think of a single good reason why both their phones would be turned off. It's her brother's *wedding day*. Jules would never not show up unless she didn't have a choice in the matter. Bryan, something bad *must* have happened."

"Okay, babe, calm down. We don't know that—wait, hang on a second."

Becky paced the long, carpeted hall until Bryan came back on the line.

"Okay, so Jonas just got the call," he said. "Unless Jules decided to take some weird, unexpected route, there's no indication she's been in a wreck, and they're not broken down on the side of the road either."

Becky blew out a deep breath and hung her head with her cell phone pressed to her ear. But the relief she felt with this update was short-lived. At least if Jules had a flat tire or was on her way to the hospital after a car accident, they'd know where she was. But this news still left Becky without an answer to the question that had her heart aching with worry. Where was her best friend?

She lifted her head when her call waiting beeped. "Tim's calling. He must have made it to Brittany's apartment. I'll call you right back."

"Well? Is she there?" Becky held her breath as she waited for Tim's response.

"I just pulled into Brittany's apartment complex. Jules isn't in it, but her car's in the parking lot."

Becky tipped her head back and exhaled in several stuttered breaths. "Oh, what a relief. At least we know where she is, but I can't understand *why* she'd still be there." She pulled the phone from her ear for a quick glance to confirm the time. "If she was on time picking up Brittany, she's been there almost an hour and a half. She should have just run in and out and then been on her way to the church. It doesn't make sense."

"Brittany's apartment is on the second floor, right?" Tim asked.

"Yeah, why. Do you see something suspicious?" Before he could answer, Becky heard voices on the stairs. "Hey, I'm outside the bridal suite, and Bryan and Jonas just walked up."

She turned to them. "I'm on the phone with Tim."

"Is he at Brittany's yet?" Jonas asked, his voice urgent.

She nodded. "He just got there, and Jules's car is in the

parking lot. She must be in the apartment, but at least we know where she is."

Jonas gestured at her cell, and she handed it to him.

"Hey, Tim, it's Jonas. I have a bad feeling about this. Just stay put. I'm going to see if I can get an officer to meet you there in the parking lot, and I'm going to head over there myself. My bride-to-be isn't going to be very happy with me, but I need to know what's going on."

"I'm going with you," Becky said, her voice determined as she took back her phone.

She spoke into the receiver. "Tim, hang on."

Jonas rapped his knuckles urgently on the door to the bridal suite. It opened slightly, and Erin's maid of honor appeared and shook her head emphatically. Jonas protested from the hallway. Then he backed away slightly, bowed his head, and stared down at the carpet. Becky saw Erin's white dress appear and realized her maid of honor must have consented to let her talk to her groom from the other side of the door.

"It's *Jules*, honey," Jonas said through the narrow opening. Becky couldn't hear Erin's half of the conversation, but a minute later, Jonas tapped gently on the door with his fingertips. "I know I'm not allowed to kiss you yet, but this is why I love you so much. We'll be back as soon as we can."

As he turned to leave, the door to the suite burst open, and Barb rushed out into the hallway. "Jonas?" She searched his face for reassurance. "I can't lose Jules. I just got her back. After all these years—"

"Don't worry, Mom. We're gonna find out what's going on." He leaned down and hugged her. "Keep my girl company until I get back, okay?"

He dipped his chin at Becky and Bryan. "Let's go."

"Tim, we're leaving now," Becky said into the phone as she hurried down the stairs behind Jonas. "Just wait for the police.

Let them be the ones to go into the apartment to see what's going on. We'll be there as soon as possible."

Tim's voice was choked with emotion. "I'll try to wait, but if anything happens to Jules, I'll never forgive myself for just sitting out here doing nothing. I can't live without her, Beck," he said in a soft voice. "You need to hurry."

CHAPTER THIRTY-FIVE

JULES WATCHED in horror as Charlie's face went dark. He shook with rage.

"*You* killed Judith?" He tossed his bat off to the side and lunged at Brittany. "I'd rather strangle you with my bare hands."

"Charlie, stop!" Jules leaped from the couch and tried to pull him off her. "You'll end up exactly where she wants you." She beat on his muscular back with her fists, but she was sure he didn't even feel it. "Do this the right way, or you'll be helping her win. You'll be behind bars." She tugged on his biceps. "You need to stop before you kill her. Is she worth going to jail for the rest of your life?"

He let out a frustrated grunt and released Brittany, his hands then clenching into tight fists.

Brittany gasped for air as she rubbed her neck, angry red marks where Charlie's fingers had just been. "See, I told you he was violent." She glared at her husband. "If they'd just arrested you after Judith died, I could have moved on. None of this would have been necessary." She baited him as if his hands hadn't just been around her neck trying to squeeze the life out of her.

Jules wasn't sure she could pull Charlie off her a second time. "Claire, *stop it.*" It was time to use her real name. This person was someone Jules didn't know. Someone evil.

Claire offered a nonchalant lift of her shoulders. "What? It's true. If my sister had gotten justice for her murder, none of this would have had to happen. Charlie would be in jail, and Judith would still be alive." She shrugged in his direction. "So, really, it was your fault that—"

"You're deranged," Charlie said, spitting the words in her direction. "You're the murderer." He grabbed Claire's wrist. "But now, you're coming back with me. You're going to tell the police *you* killed Judith. You're going to show them you're not dead." His eyes brimmed with hatred. "But, oh, how much I wish you were."

Claire wouldn't survive if he dragged her from this apartment. His fury and her arrogance would have fatal consequences.

"Charlie, we'll call the local police," Jules said as she tugged on his arm. "Let them deal with it."

He gave her an angry shake of his head. "No way. She's coming with me."

He yanked Claire toward the door, and she let out a yelp, her eyes pleading with Jules to intervene.

Jules couldn't let Charlie hurt her, but that was just human decency. As she looked at the woman she'd known as Brittany, nothing felt the same. This person begging Jules for help wasn't the same person who'd played with Gene. She didn't resemble the woman who'd discovered the foods she liked to eat and the ending to movies she didn't remember seeing. She wasn't the friend who'd taken joy in the simple task of picking out Becky's birthday gift. No, this monster didn't even feel like the same person who'd been living in her townhouse.

Jules had been duped. She felt betrayed, by Brittany and by her own lack of control. This is why she couldn't let down her guard and trust that people wouldn't disappoint her.

"Stop. You're *hurting* me. I'm not going anywhere with you, *Charlie*." Claire's voice was loud, her eyes repeatedly darting toward the bedroom door.

Jules frowned and followed her gaze. Was someone in there?

As if he'd been summoned, the door opened, and a man emerged.

She caught her breath—it was the man she'd seen running away the first time she'd been at Brittany's apartment. Now she was sure it was also the same man she'd caught on her surveillance camera. In her mind, Jules had pictured him differently, certainly not as clean-cut as he appeared now. In her imagination, he also hadn't been holding a revolver.

He had the gun pointed at Charlie. "Let her go."

"Who the hell are you?" he asked, his grip still tight on Claire.

"I'm the man who's going to make sure you never hurt her again." The man jabbed the air with his gun. "Now, let go of her."

Charlie screwed up his face, but he dropped Claire's arm and let her fall to the floor. She scuttled along the carpet until she was huddled next to Jules.

"I don't know what the hell you're talking about." Charlie's eyes narrowed. "I never laid a hand on her, although it's an eight-hour drive back to North Carolina, so I can't make any promises it's gonna stay that way."

The man with the gun shook his head. "Claire's not going anywhere with you ever again. I saw the bruises on her. Every time she came to donate blood, she was covered in them. She told me what you did to her."

Charlie snorted. "Not me. Once she conned me into

marrying her, the ice princess barely let me touch her in *any* sort of way, if you know what I mean." He managed a thin laugh. "She played you to get what she wanted. Just like she fed me a huge platter full of crap."

Peter's anxious gaze drifted to Claire. "What's he talking about? You told me he was hurting you. You said you were scared he was going to end up killing you if you didn't get away from him."

When she didn't answer right away, Charlie chimed in. "Yeah, Claire, the man wants to know if you lied to him too. I mean, do you even know how to tell the truth about *anything*?"

She narrowed her eyes, then shifted her attention back to Peter. "I *was* scared of him. That was the truth, and I needed your help to make sure he wouldn't be able to come after me. All that blood was necessary so the police would really believe—"

"And all those bruises I saw?" Peter asked, interrupting her. "Where did they really come from?"

Claire hesitated and then lifted her shoulders ever so slightly. "Makeup," she said in a soft voice.

"Makeup?" Peter repeated incredulously. "Everything I did to keep you safe was based on *makeup*?" The gun in his shaking hand now drifted from Charlie to Claire.

It was also aimed at Jules, standing beside her. Her breath hitched in her throat as she tried to strategize how she could get away from the target of this man's increasing anger.

But Claire wasn't accepting defeat so quickly. She shook her head, a look of desperation in her eyes. "No, Peter, Charlie *did* hurt me. That was the truth. He was just careful not to leave marks where anyone could see them. I only used makeup so you'd believe me. That's how desperate I was to get away from him." She sniffled dramatically. "I just wanted the abuse to stop."

As Claire tried to convince Peter she'd really been in

danger, Charlie moved slowly toward his baseball bat. When it was within reach, he moved quickly, and the color drained from Peter's face when he realized he'd let Claire distract him. Her husband was an imposing figure. He had at least thirty pounds and four inches on his opponent. Now he also held a weapon.

Charlie held the bat and glared at Claire, his eyes dark with hate. "That's bull, and you know it. I never laid a finger on you. Well, until five minutes ago, that is. But why don't you tell him why? Tell him what you did that left me with no choice but to try and strangle the evil out of you. Does he know you're a complete psychopath?"

The gun shook in Peter's hand, and Jules realized he didn't appear to have much experience handling a firearm. Still, he seemed to understand that if Charlie decided to lunge for him, it could change the entire trajectory of the situation.

Peter swallowed hard as his attention drifted back and forth between the two of them. "What's he talking about, Claire? I need you to tell me the truth."

He began to perspire profusely. He took one hand off the gun and wiped the sweat dripping from his forehead into his eyes. Then he wiped his hand on his jeans and placed it back on the gun. "While you've been hosting this little reunion with your husband, my phone's been blowing up. My boss is looking for me." Peter's voice cracked. "The police launched an investigation, Claire." He jabbed the gun in the air toward her.

Jules shrank back and braced herself. One slip of his sweaty finger, and she wouldn't make Jonas's wedding. She'd never see Becky again. Never get the chance to be Tim's wife.

"A hunter and his dog found everything in the woods. It's over, Claire." His face paled as he shook his head. "This is all about to go sideways, and I'm not going down by myself."

"What? No." Claire's eyes widened, and Jules could see the panic in them. But then, just as quickly, her expression changed as she regained her composure. "We're in this together. You and me, remember?" She extended her hand in Peter's direction. "You know I love you. Let's get out of here, and we can go anywhere, just the two of us. Somewhere no one will be able to find us."

Peter let out a nervous chuckle. "And what about them?" He gestured with the gun at Charlie and Jules. "You think they're really going to let us walk out of here?"

"Peter, that's your name, right?" Jules asked, her breathing rapid and shallow. "Why don't you put the gun down, and we can all talk about this rationally?" Her gaze shot over to Charlie. "He'll put down the bat too, right? We won't say a word about anything. Just grab Brittany—I mean Claire—and go."

Charlie held onto the baseball bat, and with his jaw set in defiance, he shook his head. "No way. If she walks out of here, I'll end up in jail."

"No, you won't." Jules worked to keep her voice steady. "He just said the police are figuring it out. They'll know Claire framed you and is still alive. And I'll tell them you didn't kill your first wife or anyone else."

She tried to send Charlie a telepathic message. Let the police deal with Peter and Claire, so at least the two of them would have a shot at getting out of this apartment alive. Didn't he realize Peter's shaky finger on the trigger and his nervous desperation could prove to be a lethal combination?

"It's okay, Charlie," Jules said, her eyes focused on the gun. "We can just let them go, right?"

When she gave him a reassuring nod, Charlie cocked his head as if he might consider her proposal.

Then, an urgent rapping on the door interrupted them.

"Hey, Jules. You in there? I saw your car out front. C'mon, you're late. We gotta go."

Her hand covered her mouth as her gaze flew to the door. Relief flooded through her at the sound of Tim's voice, but then her focus was back on Peter, his gun still pointed in her direction. Jules's heart hammered against her ribs as the doorknob twisted.

Tim stepped into the apartment, the front door left open behind him as he gasped. "Jules, what the hell is going on?"

He rushed toward her, then stopped short. His hands lifted into the air when he saw Peter, who stood by the bedroom door with a gun aimed at his fiancée.

"Whoa, easy there, buddy."

Tim locked eyes with Jules, his face flooded with fear.

Subtly, she shifted her gaze to the open front door, back to him, and then to the door again. Her eyes then met his with her silent question. Was there any chance they could both make it out before Peter started shooting?

Jules's shoulders heaved as she focused on Tim and took in long, deliberate breaths. She slipped out of her right shoe ever so slowly. Then her left. She hid them under the long skirt of her dress as she stood in her bare feet. She inched her hand down from her waist to hitch up the material to make it easier to run.

She then gave Tim a single nod. She was ready.

When he subtly dipped his chin in return, she took in a deep breath and raced toward him.

As she crossed the room toward the man she loved, she heard Brittany's scream. "No, Peter, don't!"

But it was too late. The deafening pop of the gun rang out just as Tim moved to protect her.

CHAPTER THIRTY-SIX

Becky peered through the opening between the front seats of Jonas's car and watched the speedometer. He might have been in his personal vehicle, but he was flying like he was in his police cruiser.

He'd made a call to another precinct to ask them to send an officer to Brittany's apartment, but Becky knew how much Jonas cared about Jules. There was no way he could get married until he saw for himself she was okay.

When her phone chimed, Jonas's shot a hopeful gaze over his shoulder. "Is it Jules?"

Becky shook her head. "No, it's a Google alert." She scooted back in the seat.

"A what?" Jonas asked, his voice testy and sharp.

Becky understood his disappointment that it hadn't been a message from Jules.

"I set my phone to notify me if anything popped up online about Brittany's husband or the situation in North Carolina. You know, the story that Claire's considered a missing person. Presumed dead, apparently."

Bryan shifted in his seat and craned his neck to see into the backseat. "What's it say?"

"It's the online version of the local paper that covers Shelby, North Carolina. That's where Claire lived." Becky drew in a sharp breath as she read, then glanced up. "It sounds like the police have figured out what I suspected the other day. That logo on the T-shirt Brittany had with her was related to being a blood donor." She looked down at her phone again. "They've confirmed one of the other samples they took from Charlie's place was from someone who's never been inside his house. A man who's also very much alive. Seems they've made the connection that he donated blood at the same mobile site Brittany did, so they're investigating the staff ."

"Do they suspect Brittany's alive too?" Bryan asked.

Becky nodded. "They do now. A hunter's dog dug up a doll buried in the woods. A dummy."

Bryan frowned. "A dummy? What does that mean?"

"It was one of those life-sized dummies you use to learn CPR. Someone had wrapped it in a bloody comforter, and it looked like it had been beaten with some sort of blunt object. They determined some of the blood belonged to Brittany."

Bryan scratched his head. "Okay, am I the dummy here, or am I missing something?"

Jonas let out a puff of air, then gave an appreciative chuckle. He shook his head. "She thought this out. I'll give her that."

"Who, Brittany?" Bryan asked, still looking confused.

"Claire. Brittany. Whatever name you want to call her," Jonas said, keeping his eyes on the road. "Sounds like she somehow got her hands on a few contributions from a blood donor location. Maybe she stole it. I have no idea how all that works. She also had a sample of her own and poured it on the dummy. Then, my guess is she used a blunt object—something in the house she wanted police to suspect was the murder weapon. She used that in the assault on the CPR doll."

"Okay, again," Bryan said with a scowl. "Am I the dummy here? Why in the world would she go to all that trouble?"

Jonas's palm went to his chest. "My guess? It was an attempt to mimic the blood splatter you'd get from beating a real person. She figured if the police found evidence she'd been attacked and lost a ton of blood, they wouldn't bother to look for her." He shot Becky a glance in the rearview mirror. "They'd be convinced she didn't survive, so instead, they'd be looking for her body." His eyebrows shot up. "Unless he had a rock-solid alibi, the husband would have a hard time proving he didn't have anything to do with it. Especially since it went down in his house.

Becky's brows knitted together. "But they were never going to find Brittany's body. She wasn't really dead."

"Plenty of murder cases without the body," Jonas said with a shrug. "Not that it's an easy conviction. There needs to be enough evidence that a jury doesn't believe there could be another reasonable answer."

"So, that's why she needed all the blood," Becky said with a slow nod. "And obviously, it couldn't all really come from her."

"Right. That's what I'm thinking. She just didn't clean it up well enough. If you use bleach, it destroys the DNA but still shows up with a luminol test. The problem is blood gets everywhere. Behind baseboards, underneath floors. It's hard to get to every last speck. I'm sure that was her downfall." Jonas's tires squealed as he took Brittany's exit off the highway. "She missed some that wasn't hers."

Bryan rubbed his chin thoughtfully. "So, she thought she could not only get away from her husband, but he'd most likely end up going to jail for her murder." He shook his head in disbelief. "It's like an episode of *Dateline*."

Becky glanced back down at her phone, and her stomach knotted. She let out a moan.

Bryan's gaze flew back to his wife. "Beck, you're white as a ghost. What else does it say?"

When she looked up, her eyes were filled with tears. "Jonas, can't you go any faster?"

The car lurched forward. "We're almost there. What does it say, Becky?"

"The article says the police have no idea where her husband is now. Charlie Hunter's gone missing." Becky held her stomach. "I think I'm going to be sick."

When Jonas took the turn and squealed into the parking lot, there was already a police car there. They could see an officer heading toward the stairs that would take him to the second floor.

Becky glanced up, her arms wrapped around her middle. "That's Brittany's door. The one that's open."

"Where's Tim's car?" Jonas asked, his eyes scanning the parking lot.

Becky looked around and pointed. He'd parked right next to Jules's car, but the driver's seat was empty. Tim was gone.

Jonas slammed the steering wheel with his fist. "Damn him. None of you ever listen." He shook his head and expelled a groan of frustration. "I don't get how no one understands the concept of staying put to let the police handle it."

Becky's shoulders hitched up in a helpless shrug. "I told him to wait, but Tim—" She held up her hands and glanced at the open apartment door. "He was worried about Jules."

Jonas shifted in his seat so he could see into the backseat. "We're all worried about her, but we need to be smart about this. Tim may have walked blindly into a bad situation." He shot a look at the apartment. "Especially if somehow Brittany's husband found her."

Jonas lowered his window, held out his badge, and flashed

his lights at the other officer sitting in the cruiser.

He drove closer and explained he had reason to believe this wasn't a simple welfare check anymore. He suggested they call for backup.

As Jonas pulled his car beside the police cruiser, Becky sucked in a gulp of air and reeled back against her seat.

"Did you hear that? It sounded like a gunshot." A whimper slipped from her lips as she watched the officer come out of the stairwell to the second floor. "Jonas, he needs to get in there and make sure Jules is okay."

The officer must have heard the same sound Becky did. He was making his way down the concrete walkway, but now, his gun was drawn.

"Beck, call 911 and get an ambulance here," Jonas said. "Just in case."

The policeman disappeared into the apartment, and Becky recoiled at the sound of a second shot. Then a third.

She was sobbing when her 911 call was answered. She tried to speak, but no words came out.

"911. Fire, police, or paramedics?" the operator asked again.

Becky shook her head and thrust the phone through the opening in the seats toward Jonas. She was too hysterical to talk to the operator.

Jonas grabbed the phone from her hand. "Paramedics." He recited the address. "Three shots fired. Police already on site, but we need to request an ambulance." He paused and ran his hand over his face. "Still unconfirmed at this time."

Becky wailed, and Bryan threw open the passenger side door and slid into the backseat. He threw his arms around his wife and pulled her close. "Shh. It's okay."

Becky lifted her tear-stained face from Bryan's suit jacket. "Jules is my best friend. What do I do if anything—"

Bryan shook his head. "Don't think like that. She's going to be okay."

"What about Tim?" Becky asked, her gaze drifting toward the apartment. "He's in there too. There were three shots fired, and Brittany's apartment is tiny. How would they—"

Another police car came flying into the parking lot. Jonas pushed open the car door and chased after them, holding up his badge as he ran. Becky watched as he nodded several times and then jogged back to the car.

He dropped into the driver's seat and spoke over his shoulder. "They need to make sure the scene is secure before we can get anywhere near it."

"But what did he say, Jonas? What happened up there?"

Becky knew he couldn't hear her over the ambulance that had swung into the parking lot. It pulled up near the staircase, and the siren went silent right before two paramedics jumped out and disappeared into the stairwell. A moment later, they reappeared on the second floor. With large black bags in their hands, they raced down the walkway toward the open door of Brittany's apartment.

"Jonas, what did the cop say?" Becky asked again. She wrapped her arms around her stomach and rocked in her seat. "Please just tell me what he said."

He took in a stuttered breath and met her anxious gaze. "Three people were shot inside the apartment."

"Three?" Becky's hand flew to cover her mouth. "If we know Jules, Tim, and Brittany are in there, then—"

Jonas held up his hand and traded a glance with Bryan. "We need to wait. Let's not make any assumptions."

"Why? What else did he say?" Becky needed reassurance Jules was okay, but Jonas's somber expression sent a shudder through her body.

When he didn't answer her, she pounded her fists on the back of his seat. "What did he say?" she asked again, her voice high-pitched and tight.

"He said—" The words came out raspy. Jonas cleared his throat. "He said two of the gunshot victims were male and one was female."

Becky fell back against the seat and bowed her head, her shoulders shaking as she sobbed. Bryan reached for her and cradled his wife's body in his arms. He held Becky tight, and all three of them sat without saying a word while they waited.

Finally, an officer approached the driver's side window of Jonas's car. "You can come up, but you absolutely have to stay outside the apartment. It's an active crime scene, and we've got a fatality."

Becky clutched at Bryan's arm and emitted a sound that resembled a wounded animal.

Jonas nodded at the officer, but the color had drained from his face. "I understand. I'll stay out of the way."

As the cop walked off, Becky's hand was already on the door handle. "I'm going with you." She sucked in a gulp of air. "I need to know Jules is okay."

Jonas shot Bryan a look and gave his head a slight shake. "Becky, no. Stay here for now, and I'll report back as soon as I know what happened."

He drew in a deep breath and opened his door. "Can one of you call Erin? Just tell her—I guess ask her to try and hold off the guests until we know more about what's going on."

Jonas hesitated a moment, then stepped out of the car. He wiped his hands on the sides of his tuxedo pants and then shuffled toward the building, his shoulders hunched as he stared down at the asphalt.

Becky had never seen him like this. Jonas was always confident and assured, but as he walked stooped over, elbows held tight against his sides, she knew. He was worried too. She wasn't the only one filled with dread about what he might find when he got to that apartment on the second floor.

CHAPTER THIRTY-SEVEN

The police officer glanced around and then pointed at a dent in the refrigerator. "Looks like the bullet might have ended up there."

"He's very lucky," the paramedic said with a nod at Jules. "The bullet just grazed him."

Tim winced as antiseptic was applied to the wound on his shoulder. "I need to check the rental agreement, but I'm pretty sure the bloodstains and bullet hole aren't going to go over well when I try to return the tux. I'm pretty sure I own it now." He reached for Jules's hand and gave her a smile. "Hey, hon, maybe I can just wear this one for our wedding."

"Dream on." She squeezed his hand. Though Tim was joking now that they knew he'd be fine, the idea that Jules could have lost him terrified her. He'd jumped in to protect her, and every doubt she had about marrying him had evaporated in that instant.

"Hey, sis."

Jules looked up and saw Jonas standing outside the door.

"Not really allowed inside." He wrinkled his nose. "Active

crime scene and all. But your best friend is in the car, and she's pretty worried about you. We all were."

Her mouth gaped. "But, Jonas, your wedding—"

"I picked myself an amazing bride. She knows how important you are to me. C'mon, how could I get married without my sister?"

"Well, your wife-to-be isn't going to be very happy you're down a groomsman," Tim said.

"Why's that?" Jonas eyed his shoulder as the paramedic cut a piece of medical tape. "That's nothing. He'll have you patched up in no time, and then you can be on your way. Besides, once we get to the reception, it's open bar." Jonas unleashed a wide grin. "If you plan it right and have a designated driver, you won't feel a thing."

"I also have a couple of Tylenol in my purse." Jules rolled her eyes. "I'll admit I was thinking more hangover and less gunshot wound when I threw them in there." She glanced down at her dress and cringed. There was a long tear down one side, and the front was splattered with Tim's blood. "We're going to be quite the pair on the dance floor."

Tim glanced over at his tuxedo jacket lying in tatters on the carpet beside him. The paramedics had cut it off him, then cut open the sleeve on his shirt to get to his shoulder. "My tux doesn't exactly look the way it did when I rented it." He grimaced. "Now, I kind of wish I'd left the jacket in the car before I headed up here."

Jules shrugged at Jonas and gestured at her dress. "I think you're going to need to tell Erin the bloody power couple is out for today. The bridal party will be better for it, trust me."

"No way," Jonas said, shaking his head. He lifted an eyebrow and offered a mischievous smile. "It'll make for interesting conversation when we break out our wedding pictures. Besides, Erin will just be grateful it wasn't me. She knew what she was in for when she agreed to marry a cop."

Jules snorted. Her brother was pushing his luck now. "Your bride is going to kill you herself if she has a wedding album that looks like she got married in a horror film."

Jonas threw off his jacket and hung it over the railing. He caught Becky's eye as she stared up at him from the car. He gave her a thumbs-up, then unbuttoned and removed his tuxedo shirt.

"I'm sure Becky and Bryan are wondering why there's a male burlesque show out here. He slipped his white T-shirt over his head and handed it to Jules. Make sure he's all cleaned up before he puts this on. We'll just staple the jacket back on him." He rebuttoned his shirt. Then he wound his bowtie around his neck and hooked it in the back. "Don't worry, I'll warn Erin before you come down the aisle. She'll just be relieved you're both okay." He craned his neck to peer inside the apartment. "They told me a female also got shot?"

Jules glanced over to where the paramedics were loading Claire onto a stretcher.

"Oh. Got it." He waved his hand toward the other side of the room. "What about them?"

"It's a long story that requires a few cocktails, I think. The dead guy somehow helped Brittany disappear and made it look like her husband killed her. Her husband's the big guy on the couch over there. Charlie."

"But he was abusive, right?" Jonas asked. "So, the other guy tried to help Brittany get away from him? From what I've heard, they went a little overboard, but desperation makes people do crazy things."

Jules glanced over at Charlie being questioned by a police officer. She thought back to how he'd almost cried when he mentioned his wife, Judith. Even though he'd come after her at his house with the baseball bat, she wasn't sure she blamed him after what Claire had put him through.

"Actually, I don't think he was abusive. At all. Brittany,

whose real name is Claire, had a vendetta against him for causing the car accident that killed her sister." Jules shook her head. "She tried to set him up. Make it look like he killed her, so he'd end up in jail."

"That sounds like quite the scheme."

"You have no idea, and the accident wasn't even Charlie's fault." Jules left the story of Judith's murder for another time. She still didn't want to believe it was true.

One of the officers tapped her on the shoulder. "She asked if she could speak to you before they take her to the hospital. You don't have to if you're not comfortable with it."

Jules hesitated then narrowed her eyes as she looked off in Claire's direction. She dipped her chin thoughtfully. This might be the only chance she had for any final words with the woman who had lived in her home. "I'm okay with it."

Brittany was sitting up on the stretcher when they wheeled her over. "A couple of broken ribs and a bullet in my ankle. I don't want to speak ill of the dead, but it's a good thing Peter was a lousy shot, huh, Tim? Unfortunately for him, the cop had much better aim." Her face grew serious. "I just wanted to tell you both how sorry I am for dragging you into this mess."

"To be fair, you didn't actually remember it was a mess when we met. I mean, that *was* the truth, right?" Jules gave her a pointed stare.

Claire bobbed her head. "It was. For a while anyway. I should have listened to you and stayed inside when you went to your dress fitting. But I—I went out, and that's when Peter found me. Seeing him, having him tell me how he'd staged Charlie's house the day I left. Everything came flooding back."

"I actually knew you went out that day."

Claire's head tilted as she stared incredulously at Jules. "You did?"

"You left your running clothes on the floor. When I got home, your shower was still wet."

Claire pressed her lips together, regret flooding her face. "I wasn't the perfect houseguest, was I? But I am sorry I lied to you." Her shoulders lifted. "There's a lot I'm sorry about."

There was a noise outside the door, and when Jules glanced over, Becky and Bryan stood beside Jonas. He shook his head and groaned. "These two were supposed to stay in the car, but they followed directions about as well as Tim did."

Becky nudged her way into the doorway so she could see Claire. "I've been listening, but I just have one question. Where did Cami fit in?"

Claire shrugged matter-of-factly. "She was a setup. Peter paid her to pretend she knew me. I was sure if you both looked at my DNA results, you'd see the other test I did. You two are smarter than anyone I've ever met. I had no doubt you'd put all the pieces together."

"I'll tell you about Peter later," Jules told Becky. "We did almost figure it out, right? Just not in time to prevent what happened today."

Claire cast her eyes down at her hands. "I'm sorry I didn't walk away when I had the chance. I just wanted to be able to go to the wedding—one last chance to pretend I belonged somewhere." She brought her gaze up, and her eyes met Jules's. "Trust me, I wish to hell I'd never regained my memory. I would have loved nothing more than to continue living as Brittany Mullins." A sob caught in her throat. "She had the friends I never had. She didn't have to remember her horrible childhood or what it felt like to lose her sister not once but twice."

"I talked to your Aunt Autumn," Becky said. "I'm sorry for what you went through. But, for what it's worth, she was thrilled for you that you found your sister." She lifted her shoulder in a half shrug. "I didn't have the heart to tell her what happened to Laura."

"That's okay," Claire said. "I didn't tell her I found her sister either."

Becky gawked at her. "You did? You found your mom, Rita?"

"She's actually the reason I came to Florida."

Jules traded a look with Becky. "So, you *do* have family in Tampa?"

Claire shook her head. "No, that part was a lie. My mom—my mom's actually here. Right down the street."

Becky narrowed her eyes. "Here? I don't understand."

Claire gave a slow nod, and her gaze drifted to the window. "Rita's in the cemetery. I have no idea how she got there, but I found a record of her death and saw that's where she was buried. So, I figured after all these years—" Her breath hitched in her throat, and she took a moment to regain control. "I thought we could finally be close to each other."

"Oh," Becky said, exhaling the word in a single breath. "I'm really sorry."

"Jules, do you remember when I asked if you were angry your mother gave you up?"

She nodded. "Yeah."

"You said you weren't angry, but you needed to know why." Claire's voice was soft. "I knew why I was given up. Some man convinced my mother that drugs and drinking were more important than her kids. But even after the crappy childhood I had, moving from one foster home to another, I never stopped loving her. Then, when I saw the stuff she left with my aunt, my toys and books, that doll I had, I knew she was sorry. She'd made mistakes, but she loved us too."

Brittany gave a slight shrug. "No one can change the past, right?" She gave them a bittersweet smile. "But for a little while, I almost did just that. I got the chance to start over. To have a blank slate." Her gaze drifted between Jules and Becky.

"Without my past weighing me down, I was able to be someone worthy of friends like the two of you."

Jules stared at her thoughtfully. With no memory of the trauma she'd been through, the woman she'd known as Brittany *had* been a good person. She couldn't deny she'd felt a certain kinship to her, especially with her need to know who she really was. Jules had wanted nothing more than to protect her and help her figure out the mystery of her past. She'd considered Brittany a friend.

Claire was a different story. She was hard around the edges, and her past had made her bitter. But if she'd grown up with her mother and sister in her life, would she be completely different? More like Brittany? Jules was torn. Maybe what Claire had done wasn't entirely her fault.

Then her gaze drifted over the bandage on Tim's shoulder and around the small apartment that had resembled a battlefield for those few tense moments. No, no matter what had happened in Claire's past, it couldn't provide her with an excuse. Not for murder. Not for what she'd put Charlie through. Not for the fact that Peter had been killed that day because of her.

She didn't say any of that. "I'm sorry you had a rough life," Jules said to Claire instead. "I know it wasn't easy, and I'm glad you got a small taste of what it felt like to have something better." She dipped her head. "I wish things could have been different." As she said the words, she realized how deeply she meant them.

Claire met her eyes and gave a slow nod. "I know. You wanted to believe in me, and I let you down." She gave Jules a matter-of-fact shrug. "Unfortunately, that's always been kind of my thing. Give that sweet Gene a kiss for me." She dipped her chin at the paramedic. "Okay, I'm ready."

He lifted his hand in the air to signal his partner. Becky,

Jonas, and Bryan stepped aside as they pushed Claire's stretcher out the front door. She rolled away toward the stairs where the two medics would need to carry her down the single flight to the ambulance.

A female officer tapped Jules on the shoulder. "We're going to need you to give a statement."

"Oh," she said, then looked helplessly at Jonas. "Can I come by the station tomorrow?" She asked, gesturing at him standing there in his tuxedo. "My brother's getting married, and the ceremony was supposed to start over an hour ago."

The officer cocked her head and turned to Jonas. "You're the cop, right? You'll vouch for her?"

He rolled his eyes but then nodded. "Yeah. But only because I'll be on a plane to Hawaii by then." He gave Jules and Becky a stern stare. "Do you think you girls can stay out of trouble? At least until I get back from my honeymoon?"

"I can promise they will," Tim said, reaching for Jules's hand. "I won't be letting my fiancée out of my sight. Christmas is coming, and besides, she has a wedding to plan."

Bryan rubbed Becky's shoulder. "How 'bout you lay low too, and we'll just work on your birthday wish for a while?"

She offered her husband a coy smile. "Well, I can't complain about that idea, but we did just get a new adoption case. Don't worry. It all sounds pretty straightforward, and they want it wrapped up by the holidays. No danger whatsoever." Becky eyed her partner. "Right?"

Jules bit the inside of her cheek and nodded. She hadn't even had a chance to tell her best friend about the voicemail she'd gotten from her cousin.

Jules was grateful Lucy wasn't still trying to convince her to talk to her birth father, but what she *had* said in her message had left Jules more than a little intrigued.

We'll be in Florida in mid-December, and I would love for us to meet finally. I also know you opened a detective agency specializing in DNA and family mysteries, and I have a friend who needs help. I can tell you more about it when I see you, but she thinks she might have been kidnapped as a baby.

AFTERWORD

I remember going for my annual bloodwork and watching the tech walk away with vials of my blood. Of course, only I would wonder if it could be planted at the scene of a crime!

I would be remiss in not acknowledging the liberties we take when we write fiction. Is there the smallest possibility broken protocol could allow my contribution at the lab (or any one of a variety of other places) to be used for nefarious purposes? Maybe, but I accept it's highly unlikely. Not to mention, we put our DNA out into the world in other ways as well. As my hairdresser likes to remind me, she's covered in DNA from her clients' hair every day. Just another reason to tip generously, lest a strand be relocated somewhere you wouldn't want it!

But in all seriousness, blood donation is much needed. Please don't let anything in this novel dissuade you from the generous act of donating like people's lives depend on it. They do.

ALSO BY LIANE CARMEN

Thank you for reading *Memory Hunter*.

If you've enjoyed this book, a rating or review would be much appreciated. Reviews and referrals help other readers find my novels and allow me to keep writing them.

My other novels include:

When Wings Flutter

The Investigation Duo Series

> *Where the Truth Hides* – Book #1
>
> *The Dark Inheritance* – Book #2
>
> *Memory Hunter* – Book #3
>
> *For Just a Minute* – Book #4 (coming in 2022)
>
> Growing up, Tess Riley never gave much thought to her identity. She was Frank and Evelyn's daughter, sister to Erik, and the family member responsible for feeding their cat. Now about to turn thirty, Tess has a good job, a husband she adores, and a baby on the way. Her life feels perfect until her brother has one drink too many at her birthday party. His shocking suspicion leaves Tess reeling.
>
> Jules's cousin, Lucy, begs the detectives to meet with Tess, who's now convinced she's been lied to by her parents. When her DNA results come in, Jules and Becky are inclined to agree. Convinced this is most likely a simple case of an unknown adoption, they agree to take on her case.
>
> But as they dig deeper, they begin to suspect Tess may hold

the answer to a decades-old cold case. If their client really is the baby snatched all those years ago, then what happened to the real Tess Riley? The answer is a secret someone's determined to keep hidden, no matter what the cost.

Unanimous Vote – working title (coming in 2022)

When 53-year-old true-crime aficionado, Maggie Turner, reports for jury duty, she's embarrassed to admit she's secretly excited. Then she's chosen for a murder trial and she's giddy with anticipation.

She sits through testimony convinced the defendant's guilty, but when deliberations begin, she's the only who thinks so. With insight gleaned from a steady diet of true-crime television, Maggie argues how she believes—no, she knows—the murder happened. None of the other jurors will budge. They convince her the evidence doesn't support her theory and begrudgingly, Maggie changes her vote. The verdict's delivered, and after a disgusted look aimed at the prosecutor, she goes home.

But Maggie can't stop thinking about the case—she believes they set a murderer free. Though the defendant can't be tried again, she's obsessed with knowing the truth.

She begins her own investigation but finds herself walking into a trap set by the former defendant. If she doesn't use what she knows to outsmart him, Maggie could discover not only was she was right, but he's willing to kill again.

She just won't be on the jury next time. She'll be the victim.

ACKNOWLEDGMENTS

To the readers who follow the trials and tribulations of Jules and Becky, I'm so grateful. You had to know it was Jules's turn to take one for the team, right? After spending time working on a standalone novel this past year, it felt like getting together with old friends when I began writing the next installment in the Investigation Duo series. I hope you felt the same when you began reading *Memory Hunter*.

To **Alexa** (yes, *that* Alexa) – I'd like to thank you for your concern. When I was on the phone discussing the plot for this book, including details about blood splatter, Alexa piped up out of nowhere. Worried I might be in danger, she offered to call one of my contacts for me. Some people may not like the idea that someone's always listening, but I appreciate she's got my back if I need her. Luckily, the scenario was fictional, and I was perfectly safe at my kitchen table.

For **Ben Carmen**, you probably didn't even know I "borrowed" that blood donor shirt from your closet to use as a reference for this book. I love that you couldn't wait to be old enough to donate. Your generosity convinces me I did a good job raising you.

Jonas Saul, editor and author extraordinaire, I'm always so grateful for your help and support in every way possible. I love bouncing ideas off you and then being able to deliver them in the finished manuscript.

To **Sergeant Joe Torok**, Broward Sheriff's Office, Crime Scene Unit, I'm sure you thought I was crazy when I asked if we could discuss blood splatter, DNA, and luminol! Luckily, I don't have any personal experience with a crime scene, but if you're looking to take someone on a ride along …

I'm grateful for **Lieutenant Steve Feeley**, Broward Sheriff's Office, who's always willing to jump in to answer questions about police procedure. I appreciate that he listens and then tells me if I can push it for fictional purposes or warns me I'm way out of the ballpark of reality. I still can't believe if someone pawns stolen merchandise, the victim has to buy it back. That's just not right!

For **Stacy Ostrau**, my inspiration for Jules. Don't you know Jules isn't supposed to go on a big adventure without Becky? Especially one that's not even in the same time zone! I would never write Jules moving away and breaking up the duo which is why fiction is sometimes better than reality. I'm just going to pretend you're still twenty minutes away. Denial is my new best friend.

For **Mark Summers** who understands my obsession when I'm in the middle of writing and editing, thank you for your patience. I love you!

This one came out fast and furious. For my advance readers including **Brittany Schroeder**, **Stacey Halpin**, and **Phyllis Jones Pisanelli**, I'm so appreciative of your time and feedback.

For those who allowed me to use their names in this book, thank you! If you found your name and didn't make it out alive, you might want to ask yourself why that might be. We authors need to express our discontent somehow, right?

ABOUT THE AUTHOR

Photo by Bill Ziady.

Liane Carmen is the author of *When Wings Flutter* and the Investigation Duo Series.

Whether she's writing about love that transcends death or a mystery that needs solving by two best friends, her goal is to deliver that unexpected twist for her readers. She enjoys writing about strong women and the relationships and issues that drive their lives. She's an avid reader, genealogy buff, and true crime enthusiast.

She lives in Florida with a houseful of pets and a college student who visits when he needs help with his laundry.

To subscribe to her newsletter, visit her website at https://lianecarmen.com.

For more information about her books and other ways to keep in touch:

https://linktr.ee/LianeCarmen

Made in United States
Orlando, FL
28 August 2023